GW01451393

# Plunge

## An Inglorious Series Novel

# KELSEY ELISE SPARROW

*Plunge*

Published by KES Imaginings LLC.

Cover Design by: Just. Write Creations
Cover Image by: Depositphotos
Editing by: Write on Time Editing
Formatting by: KES Imaginings, LLC

Published in the United States of America

To my biggest supporter

Laugh
As much as you breathe
And
Love
As long as you
Live
~ Author unknown

### *Also by Kelsey Elise Sparrow:*
**Inked to the Max**
Kentucky Running (*connected*), Paper Lipstick (Intro), Maximum Velocity
**The Norton Sisters**
Rayna's Peace, Zoie's Purpose, Nyema, A Secret for Christmas, Chyra, Lynnia, Wynter, Happy Holidays or Not
*Boardan High*
Singling Out Sable, Justice for Jenna, Mean Girls — *TBA*
**Whiskey Sweet Novels**
Whiskey's One True Wish (Intro), A Whiskey Sweet Promise, A Whiskey Sweet Treat, A Whiskey Sweet Revelation - *TBA*
**Stephanie Daniels Novels:**
An Author's Tale, An Author's Conclusion - *TBA*
**Properties of Magic**
A Witchling's Wicked Game, A Witch's Last Hope (Intro) - *TBA*
**Once Upon a Crime**
The Red I See — Coming Soon
*Mafia Romance*
Triple Check, Peace of Italy

To pitch or throw oneself headlong or violently forward, as a horse **does**.
· Label slang - To bet heavily and with seeming recklessness on a **race**

# INTRODUCTION
## *BROOKLYNN*

*Hampton, GA*                                    *One dark night* – Before

My throat feels dry. Dryer than I ever could've conceived. Cotton mouth has nothing on this. It is like the Sahara Desert has taken up permanent residence inside. My body feels as if producing any form of liquid is a forgotten function. I want to make it to the kitchen but that would defeat my current purpose.

*The door. An exit.*

Getting out of here is what needs to happen. I feel light-headed and weak but some part of me won't let go. I'm still fighting. It goes against my very nature to give up. So ... I'm fighting. I'm fighting to stay alive and dragging myself to what I hope is new air ... some form of freshness, newness ... life.

I'm flying blind. That's probably not the best phrasing. It would be if I were floating in the sky. The pain zipping through my body with every move I make is a reminder ... a constant torment screaming I'm not anywhere near the freeing winds that nearness brings. In fact, where I am is the exact opposite of my favorite place.

Straining even more to get the both of us to safety, my vision blurs further. The flames of the fire are chasing me, and my entire body seems like it quakes with fear it's going to touch her.

She can't ... I could perish in this thing as long as I knew ... she has to survive.

I don't know what I'll do if she doesn't. Somehow, I know I'm going to make it out of this. Reaching out, I grab hold of something that isn't the piece of furniture I thought it was. It turns out it is a person's hand. I want to cry. The feeling of relief that washes over me is short-lived as I turn and realize I no longer have the extra weight that told me she was with me.

Again, my body fails me. My inability to produce water frustrates me just as much as knowing I don't have the strength to lift myself up. I have to look like a flailing fish out of water. Yet, my loss of moisture doesn't matter to me as much as it probably should. My thoughts are elsewhere as I lose the battle to control my eyelids. They begin to close as heaviness surrounds me. Darkness begins to settle over me. As I slowly lose consciousness, one question moves through my mind.

*Where is my girl? Where is my daughter?*

The question repeats in varying versions as my vision clears just enough to see a doorway not far from where I am. So close and yet so far. I have no further energy if she is not with me.

*I lose.*

I just didn't know how much until it was too late. That's always the way, isn't it? Some part of my brain has accepted all of this and is ready to let go. That part of me knows there is nothing but pain on the other side of this. Pain, I don't believe I will be able to handle. I've always been the believer, the fighter, the overcomer. Not this time. This time, it's too much. The loss is too great. I can't do this.

I feel a lone tear seep from the corner of my eye as my vision blurs once again and I slip away. A loud crash happens just as my eyes permanently close.

# CHAPTER 1
## *JAXSON*

Savannah, *GA*

April 8 – Saturday

**One Year Later**

Noise. Noise. There's so much noise. More noise than a person would expect given the location of my damn house. In this house, I was promised peace and quiet. Solitude. That was one of the main reasons I wanted this palatial space. The little, ocean blue, two-story house has five bedrooms and three bathrooms. Everything about it screamed calm. Amid the chaos that my life has become, this house was everything I needed and more. It practically fell into my lap. It held up to the serenity and seclusion I required and relished for a nanosecond of a minute.

It's my own damn fault. I'm to blame for snatching my attempt at peace away. Had I not moved my family into houses that are practically a stone's throw away then I wouldn't have had this issue. Nope. Not me. I thought having them around would be good for my psyche. Who knew bringing them here would be one of the many mistakes I've made over the last six years? It took no time at all for them to make me regret bringing them to town and having them as close to me as they are.

Case in point. The precious, dulcet tones of one of the few women who has had the ability to worm their way into my heart.

The pitch of her voice is countering the throbbing bass of the drum that is pulsing its painful beat inside my skull.

*Another thing that's your fault.*

I ignore the insulting tone of the voice inside my brain. Instead, I pull a pillow over my head in a sad attempt to drown out the continuous conversation that's getting closer with every breath I breathe. The pillow does nothing but muffle the continuous chatter that is coming up the hallway.

"Here we go again. I swear it's starting to feel like moments of déjà vu."

Her words are closer than they were before. I groan knowing she's going to be in my room any moment now.

"He's been through a lot."

"I know." Her voice booms in the almost barren hallway. The voices stop and I breathe a sigh of relief until she clears her throat. I tense as she begins speaking again. "I understand that. We all have. He's not alone in this. That's the problem. It's like he thinks he's the only one who has had to adjust and reacclimate. He's not."

"Yep. You won't let anyone forget that." The male voice is recognizable as well. I should've known he'd be with her. "We should just let him sleep it off."

"Again? It's like that's your 'go to' solution. Just leave him to his own devises and hope for the best. Right? That's not what he needs. Somewhere inside of that non-confrontational head of yours, you know I'm right. He's not coming out of this without a swift kick in his ass."

She stops talking and it's quiet for another breath of a moment. Again, I'm hopeful and again, I'm disappointed. It's sounds like they're directly outside my door. He's apparently not finished with the subject because he's suddenly speaking again.

"Just so you know, I'm letting that smart ass comment slide. For now."

"It's not like I tried to whisper the words. I said them clear enough for you to hear. There's no reason for you to let anything 'slide'. Not when I'm purposely ..."

*That's it!*

I've heard enough and it's obvious she's not going to let go of her pursuit. Chucking the pillow which was previously over my head, I toss back the covers and my sheet before sliding out of the bed. Once I'm on my feet, a sudden breeze from the open balcony doors clues me in to my nakedness. I'm naked as a jay bird. I don't exactly know how that happened. Much of last night is a blur. I don't know what, if anything, went down while I was out. What I do know is I'm sick of the conversation that's happening on the other side of that door.

I don't bother to grab any of the clothes that are strewn about the floor, on the rack, or on the faux leather bench at the end of my bed. Kennedy is going to love this. The beautiful, former model is my current personal assistant and the wrangler of my wardrobe. She's the one who ensures whatever brand names make it to my closet are things I'm going to want to put on my body.

Kicking a pile of clothes out of the way, I then fling the doors open.

"Enough already! I can't listen to the two of you go back and forth any longer. Why are you here?"

I give them both an expectant look. The brown-eyed woman, Hope, gasps in shock at my state of undress. She turns her face away from me. Her dark brown hair with caramel highlights floats on the air as she tries to avert her gaze.

"Still quite impressive," Graham states.

The light brown skinned male's hazel eyes gleam with mirth as he smirks at me from behind Hope. He stands, looking over her shoulder then around me. He's dressed in his usual business wear sans his suit jacket which is hanging from his fingers.

"Jack. Ass. Why do I even ... I don't know which is worse. His constant disregard for any and everything or your blatant disrespect and disgusting comments."

"Both? Why does it have to be a choice? Impressive package, great rack, kissable lips, fuckable mouth. I can't help it if I'm able to appreciate all parts of the human body."

Those words might surprise others but not me. That's the type of shit I have to hear from this man. The first time he complimented me, I did ask him if he was trying to hit on me. It wasn't the compliment; it was how he worded it that had me wondering which team he batted for. He told me he wasn't going to confirm or deny anything but would say he appreciated the human body in all its forms. In the next breath, he stuck his tongue down our waitress' throat. That was the end of that conversation. I haven't questioned him since.

Graham is a man of action anyway. His actions scream louder than any words he will say. He's proven it time and time again both in and out of the pit. My pit crew chief is a lover of all things about a woman. He hasn't met a taco he'd turn down. Present him with a sausage and after he stopped laughing out loud, he'd leave that sausage where it stood.

His words not mine.

He winks at me. We share a knowing look before we each nod towards Hope. Graham stands a half foot taller than Hope's five-foot four frame. I've got him by a few inches. Mr. "Dark Ambition" flares his nostrils then widens his eyes before waggling his eyebrows. Leave it to Graham to be the comic relief in an awkward situation.

The "dark ambition" name is one that stems from his family. When he explains it, he says his brother gave him that nickname because he's the darkest of his siblings. I don't believe that's the real reason. Yes, he's darker than is sister and brother. I'm thinking someone discovered his proclivity to walking on the wild side or stepping into the dark side of bedroom antics.

[4]

# Plunge

Shaking my head, I slide through the space between the two of them then down the hall to the stairs that will take me to the main floor of the house. I hear movement behind me. As I reach the top landing,

"Ugh Jax! Why couldn't you put on some clothes before opening the doors?"

I chuckle as I keep moving towards my destination.

"Hope, you chose to use a key that was given to you solely for the purposes of emergency use. You know, things like the house is on fire or I'm locked out. Or ..."

"You're playing the role of dumbass, drunken Jax who can't recall important dates or family functions?"

Hope is the only person in the world who calls me Jax. She refuses to call me by the nickname everyone in the racing world calls me. It's as if she feels it's beneath her or something. I laugh at it, but it irritates others. Others like Graham.

I've made it to my destination, the kitchen, where preparations for breakfast are being made. Snagging a glass and some fresh-squeezed orange juice, I stand at the island then look back at Graham and Hope. It's then that I notice she's in a soft pink flowy dress with a floral design along the side of the skirt. She has on a single chain necklace with four hearts and the word love in the center. It's the one she wears daily. The other necklace is one that runs the length of her torso. She also has on heels.

Hope isn't the type to put on a heel just to show off the skill she has in wearing them. She's the one to put them on because the function demands it. If she's in heels, something important is happening. Her usual choice of clothing is a gray pullover, vest, and print leggings. Those have become her staples during the soccer season. It's the standard soccer mom uniform.

Graham is in a pastel blue suit with large, black buttons. Beneath the suit jacket is a crisp, white button-down shirt. He's left the top three buttons open. His sneakers match his suit perfectly.

Seeing the two of them standing in the doorway waiting for me to clue into their unspoken point doesn't help. It takes another beat for my alcohol-riddle brain to catch up.

"Fuck me!"

The words echo around the room as I really take it in. the kitchen is full of food. There's a hell of a lot more here than I'd ever be able to consume.

"Not interested," Graham announces.

"Neither am I," Hope agrees.

I rush by them and make it to the stairs just as my front door opens. Taking the steps two at a time, I am a hungover track star as I race to prevent my mother's birthday guests from seeing my bare ass. As I reach the doors to my bedroom, I hear my mother's voice.

"Please tell me I'm going senile in my old age or something. I'm hoping that wasn't my naked son I just saw running up those stairs."

"You're early. The team is still prepping things for everyone. We weren't expecting you to arrive for another hour," Hope says.

Her voice has gone up an octave as she tries to direct Mrs. Jeannine Shaw from her line of questioning.

"Nice try, My Darling Dear. Know that I know my son much better than most. I came early because I had a feeling it was going to take some extra encouragement to get that child of mine ready to celebrate me. I didn't want to leave anything to chance. Am I to assume he's up there showering and preparing to greet the guests for my party?"

"It shouldn't take him long, Mrs. Shaw," Graham offers.

"Graham, you know I love you like you're one of my own but I'm going to ask you to stop blowing smoke up my ass. If I know him, he probably just woke up. It's the reason I shifted the time of this event. I wanted to make sure to give him plenty of time to detox and make himself presentable."

Mother Dearest speaks a little louder. I know it's solely for my benefit. She wants to make sure I hear her. I'm quite sure anyone on the grounds heard. I should probably get the hell out of here. My balcony has a trellis. I could easily climb down it and escape all of this.

I might sound like the worst person alive, but most don't know what it means to be her son. Yes, I'm the one who set this surprise in motion. It doesn't mean I have to stick around for it. I shouldn't be held accountable for my big ideas when I'm under the influence. I tend to get a little ambitious and overly giving when I've been drinking. Those spirits take over and my own spirit shifts into overdrive.

I'm sure my mother would love nothing more than to tell the story of the time her lovely son promised her an amazing breakfast full of all her favorites but didn't decide to attend himself. She'd delight in telling everyone she knows how I ran away from a day of celebrating her just to fall into yet another bottle.

That would make her day.

"You changed the time? What time is it set to start?" Hope questions.

"Eleven. I made it a brunch instead of a breakfast. Kennedy made all the necessary phone calls for me. I guess she missed two."

"Mrs. Shaw, you do know this was meant to be a surprise, right?"

"Hope, I know what the intentions were, but I don't think I can take another one of his surprises. Besides, things have to happen the way they need. Let the chips fall where they may. I'm going to go settle on the deck. Guests should arrive in the next hour. Just signal me when things are settled."

I lean against the doors. Banging the back of my head once into them, I make my decision. Pushing off the large, wooden panels, I set things in motion. It takes me no time to get showered and dressed. Or so I think.

When I exit the bathroom, I notice all the clothes that had previously occupied any open floor space are gone. My sheets are as well. I'm guessing Patrick is here along with the guests. Patrick is the first male housekeeper I've ever heard of in my life. I'd mentally hired him on the spot for that alone. When his references came through, I immediately made him an offer. He's been one of the few employees who has been with me for the full six years I've called Savannah home.

*Home is where mother is.*

Having that thought fresh in my mind, I exit my bedroom for what my mind believes is the second time for the day. I'm ready and prepared to head back to the main floor to face the music. I walk down the stairs to complete silence. For a place that's supposed to host a "surprise" party for my mother's sixty-fifth birthday, it's awfully quiet. All the prep that was happening in the kitchen has ceased and not one soul is around.

Even Graham and Hope have disappeared. I walk through the rooms of the downstairs level wondering what happened to the party that I put in motion. Nothing. No one. Not one streamer. Not a balloon. Not a plate or a napkin are in sight. Not even the glass I'd used for my orange juice earlier.

I search for my phone. It takes me a minute to find it. It's in an obscure place. It's out on the deck on one of the sun chairs. I'm shocked to find I have missed calls and notifications. Hundreds of each. When I open the texts, I can't make any sense out of what I'm reading.

The messages are asking if I'm doing okay. Offers of getting someone to help with my "issues" are made. Messages from Graham and Hope are the most upsetting. They both want to know "why". They want explanations for my behavior at my mother's party. What they are saying makes no sense.

[8]

# *Plunge*

A couple messages have pictures to go along with them. I don't recognize anything from the photos. What throws me off the most is seeing the date on my phone. For a second, I think I've lost my mind. It's not until I check a few online calendars that I see I've lost two days.

*April 10* – Monday

*What the hell?*

How the hell did I lose two days? Forty-eight hours gone. Did I enter into some messed up vortex today? I stepped into the shower and took a swig of whatever was in the bottle in my bathroom. Fuck if I know what was in it. Whatever it was made me feel really good. Looking back on it, I probably shouldn't have had that last drink. I'm one thousand percent sure it hadn't been something I'd been drinking.

Given how I'm feeling, I can see why the two women I do remember being in my home suddenly weren't here any longer. There are pictures of me with the faces of two females from my scattered memory. Other photos and video show me showing my "natural ass" as Graham would say.

I am sitting at the island in my kitchen with my head in my hands when I hear footsteps. Even if I hadn't recognized the stride of his walk, I'd recognize the scent of his cologne. I know it because it was once one of my favorites before he stole my bottle as payment for making him wait an entire day for me to return home. That day, I'd apparently had meetings scheduled with some very important people who were supposed to be throwing a lot of money my way.

Graham covered my ass that day. It's been something he's had to do far more often than not. I don't know how he does it or why he's stuck by me all this time.

"This one was one for the record books. I never would've believed I'd see you do what you did the other day. You ready to get some clarity and stop fucking shit up?"

If I hadn't already seen the photos and videos, then I'd be confused. I'd also be ready to get into Graham's face. Since I've been painstakingly made aware of my own dumbassery, then I don't need a recap.

"If you came to tell me just how much I fucked up then you can save your breath. I don't need you to clue me in any further. I watched it all go down on my phone."

He grunts, nods, then takes a seat not too far from me.

"So, you know Doc's been here?"

Quickly lifting my head, I focus all my attention on the man who is more like a big brother to me than an employee. He shoots me a knowing grin before taking a sip of whatever is in his "to go" cup. Today, he's rocking a t-shirt, jeans, and sneakers.

"When was he here?"

He chuckles before he takes another sip.

"He's been here every day since the incident. Your mother said something about your eyes being off the one time you looked directly at her."

"What? How did I look?"

"Your mother said you looked like a crazed man. We all know there was only one other time when you've ever looked out of your mind. Doc came over, took some blood, and checked you out. He told us that you were either doing drugs or were drugged."

"I'm not doing fucking drugs. I haven't touched them in forever. That one time was one too many."

"Yeah, I know."

"Shit, I wasn't even the one who bought the drugs."

Graham nods his head before standing to walk around the counter to where I'm sitting. His big hands land on my shoulders then he squeezes. The pressure is just enough to get me feeling something other than the residual guilt from that incident a while back and the more recent one. The one I don't remember from a couple days ago.

"Yeah, I know. That incident was more than enough to get you scared straight."

"Not straight enough I'm guessing."

[10]

"You saw the recordings. You can judge that for yourself." He opens the fridge then pulls out a couple containers with fruit and nuts in them. "You had another visitor. Officer Kimball came by as well."

"Officer Kimball? Why was she here?"

"She was here to return your things. Some female was picked up and had them on her. The woman confessed to slipping something into the drinks y'all had that night. She said something about her friend, whose plan it was, ending up in the hospital. She didn't know what else to do."

I turn to face him, and he nods his head as if he knows what I'm thinking.

"What the fuck, man? How the hell is this my life? I didn't even know anything was missing."

"You mean in the time you were drugged, being a jackass to your family and friends, or when you were unconscious again from a drugging?"

I snort while running my hands over my hair. I've allowed it to grow longer than I normally would. It's helping me keep my anger and frustration in check right now.

"This is insane."

"Here comes the tough question. It's the one you don't really want to face. You don't have a choice anymore."

"What do you mean?"

"You have to come with me today. I think it's beyond time for you to deal with all of this before something really bad happens."

Standing up, I begin pacing the tiled kitchen floor.

"You mean like having my shit stolen or losing time? Bad things like that?"

"Yeah. You ready to finally do something about it?"

"It sounds like I don't have much of a choice in the matter. Not that I plan on fighting you or anyone else on it."

Twenty minutes later, I see I've been driven to a vanilla ... more French vanilla mansion with Italian Renaissance architecture. The gate in front opens to cemented steps. The towering glass doors to the right are made of mahogany wood. Tiled flooring on the porch leads to the massive door.

If I didn't know any better, then I'd believe we were going to someone's home. Having lived in Georgia my entire life, it's the norm to have a business run out of one of the many houses in the city. The nuance of such a thing isn't something new and would be lost on me. It's a regular thing here in Savannah.

Stepping out of Graham's silver Mercedes-Benz, I am met with a crowd of people. In past TV and radio interviews, I've been asked if I'm used to this kind of recognition. I'm not. I don't tell them as much. I usually respond with something like "It comes with the territory" or "It's an adjustment". They laugh then we move on to something else. No matter what I do or where I go, I tend to attract attention. How they found me here, I don't know. Turning to my left, I lean into Graham so he is the only one who can hear me.

"I'm thinking we need to talk to the security team. Someone has to be leaking my locations if all these people are here today."

Graham nods then lifts his phone to his ear. It's not his job to handle that type of thing. Usually, it's my manager, GiGi's, job to take care of things like this. She's not here so my pit crew chief and closest friend is making the call on my behalf. Serves him right for taking my damn phone. I direct my next statement to the crowd.

"Hey everyone. I'll sign whatever, just don't trample each other to get an autograph."

The women squeal and dance in place as I begin signing whatever they put in front of me. Being a race car driver can be exciting. The thrill, the rush of danger, the speed are all the things that made me want to do this. Having people scream my name, adoring fans, and fan clubs who support me are bonuses.

Didn't think my reentry into therapy would start like this.

# CHAPTER 2
## BROOKLYNN

I'm so not ready for today. Why is the beginning of the week the hardest one to start? Mondays are the worst. This day has to get better. I've had enough already. My day started off like crap. An ice-cold shower because the hot water heater decided to go out. Head out to my car to find that I have a flat tire. I didn't even have time to deal with it because I was running behind. I had things I wanted to get taken care of before going in to work. It's one of my co-workers' birthday so I was supposed to pick up balloons and a cake for her. The first Lyft I ordered was cancelled so I had to wait for the second one. That meant my day was even further behind. By the time I picked up my breakfast sandwich and coffee order, I had ten minutes to get to work. I barely made it in on time.

The last thing that happens to make this one of the worst Mondays ever occurs just as I arrive. As I am heading inside the building of the Hope Foundation House or HFH, I nearly trip because my sneaker string gets snagged on one of the corners of the last step.

"Brilliant! That's all I need."

As I right myself and fix my clothing, I'm met by the one person I don't need to see right now. I'm not in the mood for her energy.

"It is a brilliant day, and I am going to make the most of it."

Today she's wearing her reddish-brown hair with blonde highlights up in two partial puffs and some of the curls are falling out of them. They dance around her head as she bops. Yes, she's one of those who has "pep in her step" every, single morning, afternoon, and evening.

"J, I might actually lay hands on you today if you don't bring it down a notch."

My voice is a little lower than normal. My allergies have been going haywire. The sudden season change has me downing allergy medicine every morning. Something else I forgot today. The other thing I forgot was to put on deodorant. I'm trying to get inside and to my locker so I can remedy the situation as soon as possible.

Journee smiles as she pretends to lock up her mouth. I shouldn't take out my frustrations on her, but I haven't had my morning coffee. I'm one of those people who perpetuates those signs and t-shirts that say things like, "First coffee then I do all the things". I am not a nice person before I get caffeine in my system.

Once I've dropped off my packages and put away the cake, I grab my breakfast. As soon as I'm back in the reception area, Journee is making her way back around. If she did her normative route, then she's set to head up to the third floor to check on the patients up there. Those are our residential patients. Journee is the head nurse and a part-time scheduler here. She's also one of my closest friends.

The most energetic bunny and nurse to ever walk the face of the earth stops by the desk and gives me a look before she begins to circle the nurse's station. I take a drink of my coffee and close my eyes while allowing the blissful warmth to move through my body. A shiver runs down my spine. I have a full body reaction to it. I take another sip before I open my eyes.

When I do, I have three sets of eyes staring at me. One belongs to one of our regular doctors. The second belongs to one of the patients who happens to be new to the foundation. Of course, the third set belongs to Journee. All three sets look as if they are questioning what's just happened. Journee leans over the counter to stare at me. She suddenly rushes around the desk to squat down next to me. Making a show of unlocking her lips while she leans in closer as everyone else turns to pretend like they aren't listening to what we're saying, Journee begins to ask her question.

"Hey honey, did you just ... um ...?" She looks around to see if anyone is looking. I smile to myself because she doesn't see all of the periphery looks we're getting. "Orgasm from a cup ... nope a sip of coffee? If so, I need to know where the hell you get your coffee."

"Better yet, can we find a way to get this one laid."

Mrs. Sexton's words sound as if they echo around the main floor. If I were anyone else, I'd be beet red with embarrassment. I'm not so easily humiliated. This would be difficult to accept if it weren't a regular kind of thing coming from the fifty-five-year-old with electric blue hair.

"This is why I love you, Mrs. Sexton."

Journee laughs and those curls of hers bounce as she does. I smile to myself as I take another sip of the precious, liquid amazingness in my cup.

"She *is* one of our favorite people. Even if she tends to make inappropriate comments. Can't a woman enjoy a cup of coffee?"

"Um ... there's enjoying a cup of coffee then there's enjoying a cup of coffee," Mrs. Sexton teases.

Journee stands up then crosses her arms as she gives me side-eye. When she nods her agreement with the statement, I work not to come up with another response.

"Mrs. Sexton, did you need to make a pit stop before your session?" I ask the question in hopes it will get her off the topic that is turning my skin a shade of red I don't want it to be. "We'll be ready to begin our session in just a few minutes."

"Nice try, Girlie. I don't need to make a 'pit stop' or take a piss before our session today. I took care of that before I came here. I'm all set to go." The older woman signs in then pulls her handbag up higher on her shoulder. Once it's where she wants it, she continues. "If you don't want to discuss your sex life, then just say the word. I might question why that is. There's nothing to be afraid of. Men talk about their conquests all the time. Why can't women? Unless that's the real reason you don't want to talk about it. Is the garden not being tended?"

I swear Journee's skin is redder than mine. She is blushing worse than I am as we both try to figure out what to say in response to this woman's inquiries. My dark pink scrubs and Journee's burgundy ones seem to compliment this new flushed look we're both wearing.

"Mrs. Sexton, I'm going to plead the fifth, finish my coffee, then I'll see you on the stretch mat in five."

The older woman smiles before she winks at me.

"Your secret's safe with me, honey. See you inside."

She pats my arm as she makes her way to the first therapy room on the left. As soon as she closes the door, I turn to face Journee who's fighting back laughter.

"When I tell you that woman makes my day, every day, I so mean it." Journee snatches a piece of my croissant from the open container as she stands. I swat at her but miss. "Thanks for this. You know, she raised some good questions. Questions I'd love the answers to. Later."

Instead of responding to her, I grab the rest of my breakfast then head to the break room. Before I put my coffee and sandwich away, I take a quick bite then drink. A few deep cleansing breaths along with a couple affirmations and I am ready to start my workday. Hopefully, nothing else happens to make this an even more "manic Monday" than it already has been.

[16]

# Plunge

Three hours later and so far, nothing too farfetched has happened. Mrs. Sexton tried to set me up with her single grandson. I declined that setup. I don't know why but I feel like her grandson would be a little young for me. I'm a twenty-five-year-old, single … woman who has enough baggage to fill a passenger jet's cargo bay. I would probably send that poor boy home crying to his therapist. If he didn't have one, he would after spending time with me.

My second patient wasn't as chatty. Since I only see two or three patients a day during the three days of week I work, that part of my day goes by quickly. Now, I am at my current love/hate part of the day. The quiet time. As we sit in complete silence, Noelle and I work through charting last week's patient files. I'm proud of myself because I did follow one of the requests of my therapist's. I've limited my interactions with therapy patients.

Number three of the psychiatrist's suggestions was that I slowly return to work. I figured volunteering at the foundation would be better for me than trying to figure out my life at home. This made more sense. I've returned to duty part time and have been doing more administrative work than anything else. All the things most people are annoyed with or too busy to complete, I'm usually the one working on.

Noelle agreed with my choice. Noelle Embers is one of my other friends and my current psychiatrist. How she compartmentalizes the different aspects of our relationship as well as everything she deals with in her life is beyond me. The petite framed marathon runner is dressed in plum-colored scrubs today. Her white coat hangs on a coat rack near her office door. Her usually straight, jet-black hair is streaked with burgundy highlights and hanging loose around her shoulders today. Her soft peach tone skin catches the sunlight from the windows making her look like the goddess she is as she works. I can even see her freckles today.

My focus returns to the files sitting in my lap and beneath me. I've been sitting, staring out the window, lost in thoughts that dance across the late morning sky when muffled voices reach my ears. The commotion that grows louder on the other side of the door also catches Noelle's attention. Talk about disturbing the peace.

Dr. Embers' office is a warm beige with clear glass shelves on one side of the half wall of windows with the beige cover seat where I'm sitting. The other side is a wall of bookshelves. A taupe-colored couch with three white pillows and two red ones in the center sit under the shelves that house a variety of stone, glass, and clay items. Several silk tapestries hang in various parts of the office. Two hang over the dark wood bookcases. The one that hangs in the center of the wall above the couch matches the color of the walls perfectly. If it weren't for the dark wood item it's hanging on, I couldn't see that it was a piece of fabric and not a mural on the wall.

I've found most of the office and rooms in this building have a wall of bookshelves. Hers has strategically placed color-coordinated books, boxes, a framed fan, a clock, a sandglass, and other things that are lit by a background light on each shelf. She also has a blood red desk chair. Her office color scheme is black or dark brown and cream/beige with red accents. Her office is one of the places I love to visit because of the calm I feel. Plus, the décor speaks to me. Her Japanese heritage is prevalent in this room.

Giggles, rushed movement, and repeated shuffling has Dr. Embers up and out of her seat a few seconds later. She quickly crosses the distance of the large, dark chocolate Tatami rug that takes up most of the floor between her stark white rounded desk and the old wooden door of her office. It's then that I notice she's rocking her leopard print flats and not sneakers that match her scrubs.

Dr. Embers peeks out the doorway. After a few minutes, she closes it. She pulls her white coat from the rack then puts it on.

[18]

"Hey, what's with all the commotion out there?"

"I'm thinking somebody famous is here. That's usually the only time this much motion happens at once. That or a fi ... a drill."

She clears her throat then watches me for my reaction. I don't so much as flinch.

"I'm guessing that's my cue to head out the back. I probably should head home. That's not something I want to partake in today. I don't have any desire to meet the new celebutante with no real issue."

"O*ooh*, harsh. We'll have to get into that during our next session. I feel like there's something to unpack there, Missy." She takes a deep breath then fixes the collar of her coat. "Thank you again for putting together the party. It was a nice surprise. I'll see you tonight and I promise, I won't where the therapist hat."

"You're welcome. Anytime. I'm glad the doctor isn't coming tonight. I'd hate to have to uninvite you or worse kick you out for ruining the evening."

Noelle smiles then exits, turning the lock as she goes. I leave through the restroom which leads to the filing room. Her office is a converted bedroom which has a connecting bathroom to another converted bedroom. This room houses all our files in physical and digital form. There is a computer station here with two computers. We could work in here and most do. Noelle's office has a view of Forsyth Park. I love being in the Historic District. Sitting at the window seat is better than sitting in the rolling chairs found in the filing room any day.

I make a stop in the kitchen to snag a slice of cake. Cake is one of my weaknesses. I smile because it reminds me of a scene from the *Jumanji* movie; the new one with Dwayne Johnson and Kevin Hart. It's as I'm walking to the former dining room that is now a converted locker room that I catch a glimpse of someone familiar. The long, dark hair gives me pause. The person I knew wore his hair that way but the person he became as always kept his hair short and neatly trimmed. Besides, there's no way that's him. He lives on the west coast.

I do a doubletake but can't get another glimpse of him because there's a crowd around whoever it is. I dismiss the thought.

"There's no way that was Daire. Of course, he would cause that type of chaos, but no way could he be here." I'm muttering to myself as I enter the locker area. The ceiling fans are blowing and I'm loving the cool air as it washes over me. "Weird."

"What's weird?"

Journee's question startles me and instantly pulls me from my drifting thoughts. I welcome the reprieve because I definitely don't need to go down that road. It leads nowhere fast.

"Nothing. Nothing at all. Enjoy the rest of your shift and I'll see you at home."

"You sure? You seem a little off. I can cut my shift short if you need me to?"

"No. No. I'm good. I'll be fine. I have a meal to prep."

She watches me for a few seconds more before she nods then smiles.

"Okay, hun. Don't go trying to do everything. I said I wanted to learn, and I mean it."

I laugh because Journee is one of the worst cooks. She is amazing with her garden, loves all animals, but is horrendous in the kitchen. Still, she tries. She refuses to let this get the better of her. As long as she's willing to try then I'll be willing to show her. All the while making a backup dish or three just in case hers implodes in our faces. People laugh but it's happened several times in the past. Very messy.

"O-kay." I drag out the two syllables as I unlock my locker and grab my bag. "I'll save all the chopping for you."

She gasps then kicks my locker door.

"Hey! That's not all I'm good for."

"Never said that. You did. See ya."

[20]

# Plunge

I hear her groan as I slip out the back. Checking my watch, I note the time. The next shuttle is moments away. Speed walking to the stop, I arrive just in time. Taking the DOT is one of many things I like to do here. I rarely use my car. If I do, it's because I have errands I need to run before or directly after work. Journee and I usually come in to work together. Today, we didn't because we both had things we agreed to bring to celebrate Noelle at work. We had a small gathering at the foundation, but a larger shindig at home.

*Home.*

That word sparks memories from other places. My past. I beat them back. I don't want to deal with them. Seeing Daire has my thoughts trying to lead me down a road I don't have any intention of venturing. There's a good reason for it. The last time I strolled that way, I ended up in a very dark place. I'd like to steer clear of that nightmarish hell at all costs. Thank you very much.

The house I share with Journee is home and the only home I need to think of when I hear that word.

*Who are you trying to convince?*

I begin humming random melodies. They sound like children's tunes. It won't be until much later that I realize the significance of such a thing. For now, I multitask by making a list of what needs to be done when I get home while thinking of the first things that need to be handled.

Journee and I share a place here. It was Journee's at first. Now, it's ours. I've been back in Savannah for a little over a year now. I used to live here a few years ago. My mother lives here. She was born here and has always loved it. I was born in ... another part of Georgia. I lived here for two years before I moved away. She brought me back here after ... everything. We lasted one month before I couldn't take being under the same roof as her. Journee had posted a flyer for a roommate on one of the information boards at a center I visited once. The rest is history, as they say.

*As is everything in the past.*

I shake away the thoughts as I disembark the shuttle. Walking to our four-bedroom home while trying to focus my thoughts is an exercise in futility. I focus on naming the flowers and plants I pass on my way home. The Tuscan sun yellow, two-story house is a welcome sight. It's my signal to shift my thoughts.

Once inside, the real work begins. The hardest part of my day is keeping my mind from drifting. I can't allow it to venture into that territory of other. It's too much and I know I'm not ready for it. Setting the timer on my watch, I prepare for the uphill climb that is my mental fight against the past.

Music at an increased volume. Check. Random movie playing on surround sound speakers. Check. Three hours and fifty-six minutes and counting. Let the war begin.

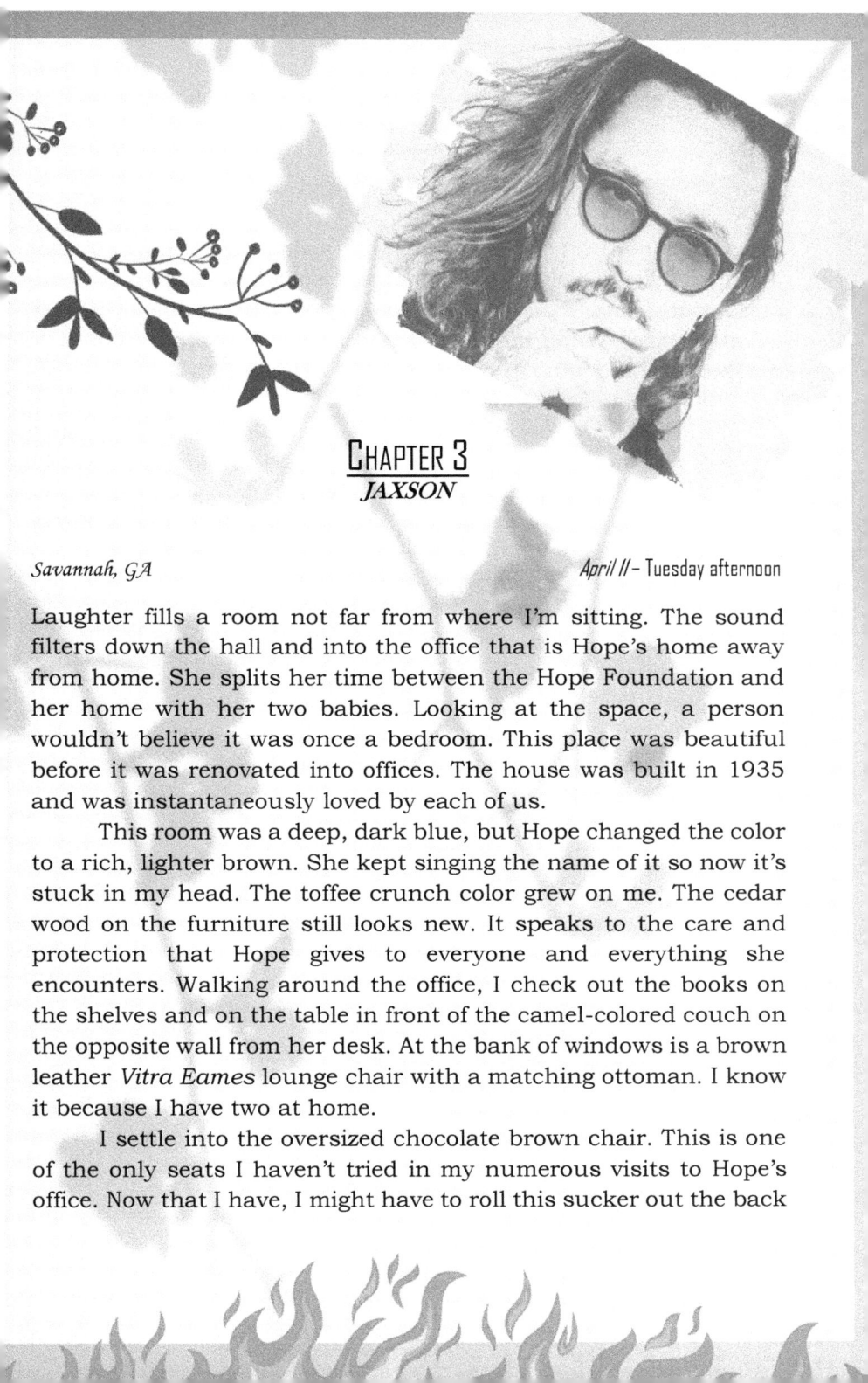

# CHAPTER 3
## *JAXSON*

Laughter fills a room not far from where I'm sitting. The sound filters down the hall and into the office that is Hope's home away from home. She splits her time between the Hope Foundation and her home with her two babies. Looking at the space, a person wouldn't believe it was once a bedroom. This place was beautiful before it was renovated into offices. The house was built in 1935 and was instantaneously loved by each of us.

This room was a deep, dark blue, but Hope changed the color to a rich, lighter brown. She kept singing the name of it so now it's stuck in my head. The toffee crunch color grew on me. The cedar wood on the furniture still looks new. It speaks to the care and protection that Hope gives to everyone and everything she encounters. Walking around the office, I check out the books on the shelves and on the table in front of the camel-colored couch on the opposite wall from her desk. At the bank of windows is a brown leather *Vitra Eames* lounge chair with a matching ottoman. I know it because I have two at home.

I settle into the oversized chocolate brown chair. This is one of the only seats I haven't tried in my numerous visits to Hope's office. Now that I have, I might have to roll this sucker out the back

door. My phone vibrates in my pocket and no part of me wants to even know who's calling me.

The door to the office opens and I catch her dark hair before anything else. She's in a pants suit and sneakers today. The jeans and t-shirt I tossed on make me look as if I plan to spend the day in my garage. Giving how the day started, it's a wonder I'm even dressed. Speaking to Dr. Embers didn't help. I actually feel worse.

It's the questions for me.

*"Did you come because you wanted to be here, or did you come because you thought it was what your family wanted?"*

*"I'm here. I said I wouldn't fight them on it."*

*"Yes, you're here but you've said nothing. It's the second day in a row you've done this."*

*"Maybe there's nothing for me to say?"*

*She writes something on the pad in her lap.*

*"Mr. Shaw, Daire, I've known you for how long?"*

*I shrug because I honestly can't recall how long I've known the good doctor. The Hope Foundation has been running now for about five years. I'm guessing that long. She's been around since pretty much its inception. It's the reason she's the Director of things. Fuck if I know her real title.*

*"Five years?"*

*"It's been … whatever. That's unimportant. What is important is I've known you long enough to know when you are the person driving a situation versus when you're allowing someone else to believe they are the one doing the driving."*

*"You're saying I'm not here because I want to be here."*

*"Are you posing a question or making a statement?"*

As I replayed the words on repeat, I questioned the truth of them. I don't know if my actions were to appease my family members or if I knew I needed to be here. Either way, I left my session with more questions than answers. The main question is …

"What the hell are you doing in my office?"

# Plunge

Leaning back slightly, I can see she's standing in her doorway looking rather peeved at the fact that I'm in her space. I don't bother getting up. I'm comfortable and I know that's going to piss her off more than anything else.

"How did you even get in here? You do remember you have an office space of your own right up the hall, right?"

With my head leaned back, I smile up at the one woman who is still willing to tolerate my face and my antics.

"Why would I go to the large, dusty, empty, lonely, dusty, lifeless space when yours is right here and full of so much of the opposite of all that?"

She rolls her eyes then closes her door. As she walks past where I'm seated, she pushes the back of my head while pressing the lever to disengage the reclining feature. Hope makes her way to the fridge hidden in one of the shelves and retrieves a drink. One sails through the air, headed towards me as she moves to the seat across from where I'm sitting.

"Your office could be all of those things if you would … what's that phrase again … use it."

I uncap the bottle of apple juice, take a drink, then cap it again.

"Thank you for the juice." I settle back in my seat, making a show of how comfortable I feel in it. I know it's going to annoy her as evidenced by the cap that hits me in the chest seconds later. "Hey. What was that for?"

"You know why. Now, toss it back."

"What would be the fun in being in that space if I'm just going to be in here with you most of the time anyway?" I toss her back her top. "Plus, you've got this place running just the way you like it. Me being here would do nothing but put a monkey wrench in your set up."

I hear her sigh and can practically see the disappointment in her face. My phone vibrates and I ignore it. I'm aiming to pretend it doesn't exist. It wouldn't be on me if Graham wouldn't have slammed it into my hand at the last minute as we were walking out the door this morning.

"Why are you avoiding her calls?" This question has me raising my head. I'm shocked to find her still sitting in the chair across from me. "She's going to keep calling and you know it. You might as well get over with. Quick and painless."

I chuckle because that's bullshit, and we both know it.

"Lies. You. Tell. You know full well my mother is not about to go easy on me after this last incident. One she came over to try to prevent from happening but ended up inadvertently causing to happen anyway."

Hope tilts her head as she sits forward.

"Huh? What are you talking about?"

"When I went to the bathroom to take my shower, I took a drink because I felt it was what I needed in order to deal with her. Didn't realize I was taking my sanity out of the equation when I took that dink."

"Seriously? That's wild. Still. You should stop avoiding her. Speaking of things you avoid. We should go over the list of people who have been hired or volunteer in the last year."

She stands then moves towards her desk. As she rummages through the files on her desk, I recall something that caused me to dream of a woman I've worked hard to push out of my dreams over the years.

"Speaking of that, I could've sworn I saw Bl ..."

*Knock, knock, knock.*

That couldn't have come at a more inopportune time.

"What time is it? Crap! I completely forgot why I came in here in the first place. As per usual, Jaxson you distracted me. I'll talk to you later. I should be at your place around 7:00 tonight."

She snatches a binder off her desk then rushes to my side.

"Love you."

"Love you too."

# Plunge

Hope kisses my lips then rushes out the door. I look around her office and wonder what I should do next. I have hours before my next session. This is one of the few places I can come that gets me out of my head enough that I don't want to lose myself in a bottle. I know I can't hide out here forever. Pulling my phone from my pocket, I ignore the missed calls and texts. Dialing a number I made myself memorize, I call for a car to take me home.

Home. The place with all the memories.

Yeah. That place. I can't run from everything forever. If I could, I wouldn't have returned to the one place that reminds me of the woman I've spent seven years trying to forget.

# CHAPTER 4
## *BROOKLYNN*

*The Past (April)* – The morning after
### One Year Earlier

*My lids feel like heavy weights. It's such a chore to get them open. When I finally squeak them open just a little bit, they feel dry and itchy. Great. Perfect. Is it allergy season again? Something beeps then there's a chime before a woman's voice comes over a speaker.*

*A speaker? Why would there be a speaker sounding in my house? That's crazy. I've lost my mind. Wait. I know these sounds. This sounds like a* Grey's Anatomy *episode. What the heck is going on?*

*I hear another voice but this one is closer than the speaker lady. Whoever this one is still sounds distant. He sounds slightly familiar too.*

*Suddenly, it all comes back to me. I spoke to him before. He was asking questions I didn't have the answer to, so I shut out most of his words. I figured he wouldn't answer me when I asked questions so why did I have to answer him.*

*What questions was I asking him? I don't recall what they were, but I know he wouldn't answer them. My head feels weird. Something feels off. I don't feel so good.*

"Well ... is there anyone we can call?" *I hear a male voice ask.*

# Plunge

I don't know how long I've been out. Hell, I don't even know what day it is. All I know is I'm sleepy … no groggy. My body feels like I've run some form of marathon or something. Everything hurts. I see that I'm ashy all over. Still, it doesn't stop me from trying to get the hell out of this bed.

I have someone. She's someone who needs me. I have a feeling I'm all she has left. It feels like the most depressing thing to say … or think. Unfortunately, it's the truth. It's a hard one I've had to come to terms with ever since I discovered my grandmother's secret.

She's never been one to hold on to anything. Granma Elle was always one to say, "I can't hold water. Telling me anything is like running liquid through a sieve." She'd smile then add. "Me trying to keep things is like a bird lookin' through a window. I'm just as transparent."

My lips crook up at the edges thinking of her. It's the oddest thing. Thinking of that force of nature not walking the earth, protecting me from everything. Even if it was myself.

"We are our own worst enemy, Moonbeam", she'd tell me.

Granma Elle's Cuban accent seemed like it was the thickest when she was expressing some truth about her feelings or spreading her wisdom to those she cared about the most.

A woman's heavy sigh brings me back to the present. Before she speaks, I feel her pity. It's not the first time someone sounded just like she does. I know this conversation is about me.

"No. No one." She takes a deep breath before something buzzes. "She's the last of the Emory line."

With that, she goes silent. I hear muffled words before the click of retreating steps seems to fill the room. A man with a kind face and dark eyes comes into the room. His skin is a pale tan. There is very little hair on his face. What's there looks like the result of too much time spent here and not enough time spent at home taking care of himself.

*He tries for a smile as he enters but that doesn't work. It doesn't reach his eyes. Instead, he plasters on a face I can read like it's a freshly written manuscript. The tears come unbidden as the woman's words begin to make perfect sense.*

*"The last of the line".*

*Those were her words. My heart ... the ache in it seeps into my soul. That precious little jewel ... my sunshine in everything, my ray of light is gone. I no longer have her smile to look forward to seeing. Her laughter is lost to me. Those perfect hugs that include my giggles from her soft curls tickling my nose, cheeks ... my ears. Her gentle kisses to my eyes or the Eskimo kisses or the three sniffs to my neck before she proclaimed, "You da best smelling mommy ever! You smell so good I da happiest gurl ever! Wanna see?"*

*She'd then perform some elaborate, happy dance that was sure to have us both smiling by the end of it.*

*All of it ... gone. Lost because of yet another slow burn. The slow burn of my grandmother's brain cells. Ironic that being my choice of words even in my thoughts. I think of the last memory of the three of us and it's too much. I can't do it.*

*My body expels a sound. It's a sound I never thought would come from me. It emits a tone I didn't know I could produce. I've come so far from where I was. Yet, there it is. The depth of it is clear. At the root of this powerful bellow is something so real. It's a tangible being in the room.*

*What has broken free this day, I will either deal with and conquer or it will forever be my burden. This thing that fills the room, the one I will wear like it is a suit of armor, is what will keep me from all that should ... this is sorrow.*

*I can't shake it. I don't know if I even want to move away from it.*

*How does one get over a loss as great as this? Honestly. No one truly knows, but it doesn't stop them from trying to offer up their opinion on the subject.*

# Plunge

So much lost that day and nowhere near enough gained. Some part of me knows this won't be the last thing I will lose. As the cloud forms, I feel a sense of calm settle despite my obvious devastation.

Welcome oblivion comes next.

I don't know how much later or earlier it is when I wake, but everything hurts. It hurts to even flutter my lashes. I listen but no sound. I open my mouth to speak, but nothing releases.

Did I lose my voice?

The question flits away as easily as it came as I work to make out my surroundings. The tell-tale beeps and tones of monitors lets me know I'm in the hospital. I can't make out much of anything. I instinctively move to reach for the thing that feels like it's choking me. Even that motion hurts.

How did I get here? What's happening to me? What's going on? Why can't I move? Why does everything hurt, including my heart? What's going on that I can't move?

I'm locked into a bed, cuffed, and unable to move. Tears continuously stream down my face as I scream.

Savannah, GA                                                April 11 – Tuesday
### Present Day

I hate that dream.

*Wrong.*

Exactly. For once, I agree with my inner voice. I hate that nightmare. It's the worst thing ever. It's like I'm Dorothy and I've clicked my heels several times but can't wake up. It plays out until it reaches its end. I wake up feeling like I've been clawing at myself. Everything in it feels so real but I still can't place it. I can't make it connect to anything else. It's the most frustrating thing.

I've relayed most of the pieces of the dream to the people who are supposed to be skilled at making sense of it all. I'm waiting for someone to shed some light on it. Make it not feel like I've no hope of figuring it all out. I want to know what it all means. Each one of these people has made it seem as if it is me. I'm the problem, the reason why I don't know how it fits into my world. I keep going to these meetings with a renewed hope that this time I'll get my breakthrough. Every time, I find I leave more disappointed than when I arrived.

Silently, I sit looking out the windows. In my hand is a bouquet of flowers. I watch as people live their lives. They are happy and I am not. I haven't been in a very long time. My normally long, brown hair is reddish orange. Today it is sprinkled with blonde and has springy curls due to my mixed heritage that I've put up in a wild bun. I'm dressed in burgundy scrub pants and a pink, off the shoulder shirt. I'd forgotten about this session, so I was in the middle of dressing for my weekly workout session when I rushed here to make it just in time.

Returning my focus to the windows, I watch people as they go about their lives. They are walking towards their intended destinations while I remain in this stagnant space.

*One false move and rotted wood gives way. I slam into the ground. When I land, I crash onto my hand because I'm holding my baby girl closely. I don't want any part of this touching her.*

I knew I didn't. I fought hard for her.

"Yes, you did, Ms. Emory," the psychologist tells me.

I have to blink. For a moment, I was back there. In the dream ... the nightmare. I could feel the heat of the flames around me, smell the smoke that billows and surrounds me, and see the fear. It is ... was like it was an extra body in the room. All of it feels fresh. As I think about what happens after, a wave of nausea and pain simultaneously wash over me.

I hear the doc's voice again and know that what's happening is real. It's not part of the waking nightmare that is my life. I don't hear this one's words any more than I've heard the words of the previous five psychologists before her. They all say the same thing and I know none of them can help me. They don't know what I've had to endure. They have no real clue what it takes for me to wake up every morning and attempt to have a semblance of an existence.

If it weren't for the people whose livelihoods depend upon me showing up and doing my job, I don't know where I would be today.

*Thirteen months.* Thirteen months, technically eight doctors, and a bevy of men to lose myself in and under have allowed me to

[32]

continue to be the great pretender I have become. Her words reach my ears. The words that give me the strength to pull myself together.

Standing on wobbly legs, I make my way to the sink to rinse out my mouth then wash my hands. Leaning on the counter, I straighten first my hair then my clothes. I nod to my reflection as I give myself one last once over. Turning, I walk out of her private restroom then to the chair next to the one where I'd been sitting. Gathering my things, I ignore her as she speaks. Her words are white noise in the background to my exit.

This one says something about the session just beginning. I chuckle as I walk to the door.

"Our sessions have permanently concluded. You cannot help me. As much as you think you can, you can't. It's sad because you came highly recommended. You can clear your things out of this office. Another will replace you shortly. My assistant will see to your payment." I open the door then turn to face the shocked woman. "I've made no progress. None at all. Oh, and my title is Dr. not Ms. Emory. Have a nice life."

Just like that, I'm moving on to doctor number nine.

I've lived through several travesties. None as heartbreaking as the one I can't seem to face. Every "doctor" who I've crossed paths with has said they can help me. Each has subsequently failed. I'm tired. I probably need to take the edge off before heading to my therapy session, but I don't have time to get to the range or the club.

*You did this on purpose. You scheduled the appointments like this so you wouldn't have time to go there.*

I have a secret. It's nothing like the one my gran once kept from me. In fact, mine is the total opposite of hers. It's all about how I get my men. I can't even think about it, or I won't go where I need to go. It's the one good thing I have going in my life. I should say the one thing I'm proud of accomplishing. Everything else is an act but this isn't.

I make up my mind. To work I must go. It's solidified when my phone rings five minutes later. I answer on the third ring.

Noelle Embers calm voice screams louder than any other person's silence could. We've been working together since we were twenty-three. She's one of three people who know my entire story. She knows everything. Since she's not only my colleague but one of my best friends, nothing is sacred. Which means, she's calling me to reem me a new one about firing yet another one of her friends. If it's not about that then she's calling to remind me about my other appointment and the meeting I have after it.

"Emory."

One word and I know I'm on her shit list. She's not interested in my explanation because she's getting tired of this inane process. Noelle doesn't have to speak the words for me to know just how pissed she is right now.

"Embers. Tell me Dr. Violet Brown was not just given her walking papers after six sessions with you?"

"Dr. Brown wasn't given her walking papers after six sessions. She was given them after five. The last one can't be counted as a session. I've told you, many times before, no one else has been as helpful with my issue as you have. We should continue our 'girl chats' and see where they take us."

I'm being a bitch, a needy bitch, and I know it. I'm an only child who is spoiled by her grandmother. A grandmother who is probably pissed at her for not calling to check on her. It's been forever. Part of me is afraid of how she will respond to my phone call. I wonder if she's still pissed at me.

A sudden searing pain hits me before a flash of some image then I'm back in the present.

"Embers, I can't keep doing this with you. As I've told you before, I can't be your psychiatrist and your psychologist. I can treat you by giving you the medication you need but you need to see someone willing to treat your mental block. There are things you need to deal with, and you know it. I swear you're fighting me on this on purpose."

"I am not. I would do no such thing."

"You can put on your posh voice all you want. I know what you're doing. It's easier for you to settle into this life and this world because it's better than facing the hard truth you have locked away in that head of yours. You're hiding. The problem with hiding …"

"Eventually you will be found. Yeah, I know. What if what's hidden is worse than what I have going right now?"

[34]

"What if it's not? What if it's better than anything you could ever imagine?" She's quiet for a beat then she's speaking again. "Um, did you ever figure out what those letters from that caller meant?"

I cross River Street heading towards E. Bay Street. I'm in the mood for a walk. I figure it might help me clear out some of the darker parts of my mind. That is until she brings up yet another confusing clue in my world.

"No. I have no clue what it means. Why do you ask?"

The next sound she makes is even more confusing. She sounds upset. That's out of character for her.

"No reason. Dr. Brown stated you mentioned an assistant and having *her* take care of paying the doctor. I was wondering if that was connected to that in any way or if you were just trying to be funny."

I hadn't even realized I'd said that.

"I don't know why I said it. I guess I was taking my posh personality to another level. I'll be there shortly. I'm thinking of stopping in at Leopold's, did you want anything?"

"Nah. I'm good. I'll see you soon. We can talk about setting you up with another psycholo ..."

"Sorry. You're breaking up." I smile as I increase the volume so I'm louder than Noelle. "If you can hear me, I'll talk to you later. I'm going to hang up now."

"Cute. Very cute. You're so funny. I'll see you soon and Ms. Shaw, we will talk. Bye for now, Ms. Hilarious."

Laughing, I end the call and continue towards my destination. As I'm walking up E. Congress Lane, a flash of pressure hits. My head feels like it's ready to explode. A memory of two women. The women don't seem happy. I recognize them. The two are arguing. It's my mother and my grandmother. Whatever they are upset about bothers me. I don't feel so good.

My heart aches as I think of the pain of it. They gesture to where a younger version of me sits. I see the reflection of the pain

I'm feeling in the window. Tears prick my eyes as I clearly see that little girl's hurt and recall how bad that day was.

Just as quickly as the memory comes is as quickly as it fades away. My breathing increases and my heart rate accelerates. I lean against the closest thing I can find. It's a streetlight. I count down from five. Visualizing the chart I was made to memorize, I begin to walk myself through the steps.

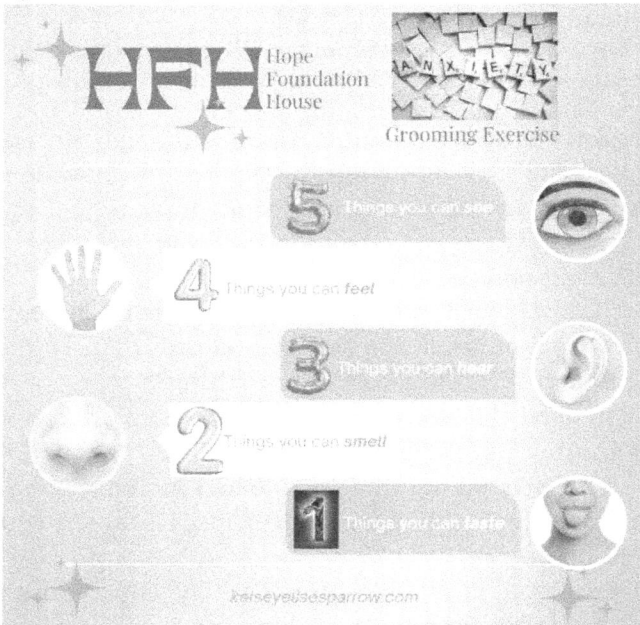

Five things I see. Five things: a streetlight, people, bikes, shoes, and cars. Four things I can feel. Um, I can feel metal, gravity, wind, and tears. Three things I can … hear. I can hear construction, cars honking, and shoes on the ground. Um … two. Two things I can smell are something sweet and bacon. What was the last thing? See, feel, hear, smell, and … taste. One thing I can taste is the mint from the gum I put in my mouth after I left the park earlier.

# Plunge

I take a deep breath and wait for my heart to stop trying to jump out of my chest. Now I must decide if I want to go straight to HFH or contact my family to find out what's pieces I'm missing. Again, another puzzle piece has dropped into my lap, and it looks nothing like the picture I've already put together.

# CHAPTER 5
## *JAXSON*

A fan once asked me what's my favorite color. At the time, it was a hard question to answer. I never really had one growing up. At one time, I favored blue because it was the main color purchased for me. I thought it was suitable for my taste. The darker the blue, the better. It seemed to fit my personality. I've always had a darker, more dangerous side. It's the side that caused my parents and siblings to worry about me.

Throughout high school things changed. Mainly my color preference. I had subtle incorporations of a light gray. The gray would be in the stripes of my plaid or the lining of my jacket. It would be in the underside of my baseball caps or the outer design of the bag I carried. Nothing was sacred. My damn boxers were even gray.

It took me years to realize I'd unwittingly incorporated the color into everything I could see. Why? Why else. It matched the eye color of the woman who owned my heart at the time. Once I understood why the color was included in everything I owned, I purposefully changed the color of my wardrobe back to blue. We were no longer together, and I didn't want a reminder. Anything from my time with her, I immediately tossed into a room where I keep a bunch of shit I don't want.

Seeing them was a constant reminder of something I didn't have. I'm not one who willingly accepts that I can't have something. In this case, I had no other choice. She chose for me.

"Have you given any thought to what we talked about yesterday?"

Quickly turning, I see that Dr. Embers has an expectant look on her face. A slow smile spreads on her lips. It's there because she knows I wasn't paying attention. She's caught me.

"Right."

I dig my wallet out of my back pocket. Pulling out a ten, I put a ten into the donation jar on one of the black barrel style tables in front of me. Normally, it's five dollars. I double it because I know I'm prone to do get lost in my thoughts again. This is a given. Paying a cost for wasting any of our time is supposed to deter me from doing it again. So far, it's not working. Believing I saw *her* isn't helping. As a matter of fact, it's making it worse.

I clear my throat and sit forward on the couch. It's an ongoing joke between us. I don't have to sit on the couch. I'm only here because Dr. Embers was asked to check on me. She's over a few groups we have here at Hope House. We also went on a date a long time ago. It was fun but we quickly understood there was nothing between the two of us. We've been frequent associates and maintained a friendly attachment because of HFH.

"Run it by me again. Please."

She quirks a dark eyebrow. The hint of red eyeshadow gives the look a bit more of an edge. I smirk because the intimidation look suits her. It works in her favor.

"Mr. Shaw, why did you come see me today?"

I glance her way before standing and walking to one of the windows. She turns in the chair at the table where she sits when any of her patients visit her office. It's gives her the freedom she needs to observe them and how they respond to freely explore the space. They get to determine what's comfortable for them. There are several choices in the room. One is directly across from her at the bean-shaped table. There is another convertible table that seats four in a more traditional style seating area.

I've sat at that table once. Just to have the experience. We had tea. Some of the best tea I've ever tasted. Where they sit tells her a little something about them. She refuses to tell me what each seat means.

"Dr. Embers, I don't know if I'm ready for group sessions. I've barely gotten used to individual meetings."

"Good to know you know you are willing to answer a question. Even if it isn't the one I'm presently asking." She writes something on the notepad she pulls closer to her. I may not currently be her patient, but she notates everything. "Still not the one I asked, but a response was given. Progress."

I chuckle because it's one of the things I'm always being given shit about. I don't answer a direct question and I do things in my own damn time. I'm never on anyone else timetable. That's the controlling asshole side of me. I make no apologies for it.

"Salty, Doc?"

Dr. Embers glances up from her notepad to glare at me. If I were smarter then I'd tread lightly but I'm not. I smirk as I move to the cabinet that houses two side by side miniature coolers. One houses her lunch and the other beverages. She purchases variety packs of drinks and stores them in her closet. I appreciate not knowing what drink I'm going to find. I pull out a can and see it's Dr. Pepper. It's been a while since I had one of these. Shrugging, I retrieve the rest of it.

When I turn around, she's standing directly in front of me.

"This is yours if you can answer my next two questions without one of your quips." I'm already prepped to respond when she adds on to this challenge. "I dare you."

*Fuck!*

I have to bite back what I want to say. I literally bite my lip. Opening and closing my hands, I look the doctor in her deep, brown eyes.

"Hit me." That perfectly arched brow wings up again. It's her turn to fight the urge to respond with a smartass remark. "You know what I mean."

She chuckles before returning to her seat and setting the drink down on a glass coaster.

"I do. First question, do you think it's time for you to get back to work ... at your company?"

I wait a beat for her to deliver the second question. When she doesn't, I groan. I return my seat on the couch. My mind and body won't allow me to sit anywhere else. I've come to see the therapist, so I need to sit on a couch. It feels weird to sit elsewhere. I've tried it.

"The second question?" A smile begins to spread on her face, and I quickly amend my response. I add a big sigh before I do. "I hadn't thought much about it, but I could start going back to 'the office'. It shouldn't be a problem."

The question does make me wonder why I hadn't come back before now. I guess it was easier. I can't exactly wallow and drink when I'm here with people who are trying to put their lives back together.

*Ding. Ding. Ding. There you have it.*

Yeah, sometimes it happens like that. I unwittingly answer the real question asked.

"Sounds good. I'll pass the information on. Unless you'd prefer to do it? No, that was not my second question. That's coming in a moment."

*Fuck!*

I groan again then prepare myself for the next question.

"My second question is why are you here?"

I smile before standing and tapping the table in front of her.

"I came by because I needed to check on my favorite doctor." Lifting the sunglasses, I place them on my face. I had them hanging from the pocket of my t-shirt. "Thanks Doc. You can have that, if you want it. Oh, and dare completed."

I stroll out her office door. whistling a tune, I make my way to the main floor of the building. I have a therapy session. it's one I'm more than amped for now that I've won a dare.

"Bring it on!" I mutter as I practically skip down the wide staircase.

Usually, I prefer to take the elevator. It's one of the older features of the house I enjoy. Today, I want to work my legs a little before my session. I cut off the follow up thought before it can ruin my good mood.

*April 12* – Wednesday, an hour and a half later

Shock and awe are what I feel as I stand inside my office. Hope was right. It's been a very long time since I've been here. I spoke to her after my physical therapy session. she looked relieved when I said I was coming back to work. That was surprising. I expected her to put up more of a fuss. I went for a short walk then grabbed take out from *The Collins Quarter*. I had a hankering for chicken and waffles. Kennedy called ahead and had my order waiting for me. I told her I'd need her at the office soon. First, I needed to assess the damage.

I slipped in through the back entrance. My hope was I'd avoid the crowds and the possible chance of being accosted coming this way. This afternoon was going to be spent handling juggling business and personal calls. During my talk with Dr. Embers earlier, I realized I didn't want to sit looking at the four wall of my home office today. I could sit in my other office and reviewing financials for this company amongst other things.

Walking into the room with the faux vaulted ceilings and windows taking up two of the four walls has me wondering how it's possible I don't spend more time here. Several pieces of furniture are covered. It's been almost a year since I've worked out of this office. I'm guessing Hope had Cassandra cover all the furniture. Cassandra Tyler is our shared assistant here at Hope House. I'm sure she's going to be happy I'm back.

*Probably not.*

Of the two of us, I'm the one who calls on her more. Hope is pretty self-sufficient and more willing to handle things on her own. I take in the room using just the natural lighting. All but one piece of furniture in the room is being protected from dust, webbing and all the other shit that piles up from non-use.

On the leather couch I personally purchased is a sleeping form. Occupied.

Squatting down in front of the form, I almost fall on my ass as take in the familiar features. Her long, dark hair is not the same color. That's different. The full lips, perfectly arched eyebrows, and the dimples that cut deep when she smiles are all still there. All the curves are as well. Even in her sleeping state with scrubs on, it's clearly still there.

I'm momentarily stunned. I sit staring at her for a few seconds longer before I come to the realization that I must look creepy as hell sitting here.

*Get the hell up, Daire.*

[42]

*Plunge*

She's right there. An arm's length away and I can't touch her. I have to get out of here.

*Did Hope set this up?*

This seems like something she would do.

Making myself walk back out the door, I head down the hall to Hope's office. Too many thoughts and questions form in my head to focus on one at a time. All I know is I need to get to Hope and try to make sense of what I just saw. She has to know who that is and who she is to me.

*Who is she to you?*

She's … she was … I don't know. I can't put it into words. All I know is what I'm feeling right now is not good. It can't be good. This rush of emotion that makes me want to turn back around, go back into that office, and kiss her until neither one of us has control of our breathing isn't a good thing.

For starters, I'd probably feel the sting of her ringless hand.

*Really? You took time to take stock of the state of her hand.*

Hell yeah. Some part of me wanted to know that she didn't belong to anyone else.

*As if that could be possible. You know whose she is.*

Damn right. She's mine. Always has been and forever will be. That's how it will forever stand. She should know that.

*What if they're the type who doesn't wear rings?*

Who, the fuck, would let that beautiful gem walk the face of the earth and not lay claim to her? Not one man in his right man. If he's been given rights to her heart, the smart thing to do would be to let everyone in the world know who is giving it to her on the regular. No way in fuck would she walk around ringless.

*Like you did, Asshole?*

If I'm not hallucinating or having some messed up mental moment, then I'm getting a second chance. If that's the case, I'm not about to fuck this up again.

Slipping into Hope's office, I take a seat on the other side of her desk. She looks over from her computer screen to give me a quizzical look.

"Hey."

"Hey to you too."

"You're here. Why?"

[43]

Her question isn't one I was expecting so it takes me a moment to come up with a response.

"Why am I here in your office? Why am I here in the building? Or why am I in existence? I have an answer for the first. I might have an answer for the second. The third one, possibly, isn't a question for me. I could take a crack at it, but do you really want me to do that?"

Hope laughs then shakes her head.

"Why are you in my office, Jaxson?"

"Funny you should ask that." I adjust myself in my seat before I continue. "I was just in ..."

Her computer chimes then bell goes off on her phone. She turns then quickly stands.

"Shit. Sorry. I need to go. I have a meeting." She kisses the top of my knee as she passes. "We'll talk later. I'm so happy you're back. I'll be glad to have some of these meetings off my plate. Right now, we're putting together the anniversary event and we still haven't come up with a theme. See you, Jax."

"Right."

I'll have to ask her about that later. I pace Hope's office, trying to work out what I want to say. I should know since I've thought about her and this moment plenty of times over the years.

I make my way back to my office. Only to find she's no longer there.

*Did I dream she was here? It could've been someone else.*

I guess I'll find out from Hope later. Or I could just leave it alone. It's not like this was something she arranged. I'm not pushing myself on her. Her choice was to leave.

Decision ... not so much made but accepted, I turn my focus to the task of getting reacquainted with my office. It's the safest thing for me to do.

# CHAPTER 6
## BROOKLYNN

*Savannah, GA*                                                    *April 13* – Thursday

I've loved exactly three men in my life. Twenty-five years of life and no more than that number has captivated me in the way any of them ever have. The first is my father, Stanford Jamieson Hensley. He was the second Stanford in our family. My mother and I lost him when I was seventeen. The second male was my grandfather, Stanford Jamieson Hensley. He was the first man to have my absolute full attention as well as the first male named Stanford in the Hensley family.

The last. I once believed he would be the very last man, I'd ever give my heart. Sixteen-year-old me never would've believed our future to be otherwise. There are days when I wonder how we got so far away from the two over-the-moon, lovesick teenagers we once were.

Thinking back, the seven of us never would've believed we could've ever gone our separate ways. If a person asked any one of us, each member would've responded "never going to happen. Even going as far as stating how inseparable we were, and nothing would ever tear us apart. We were Daire, Blaze, Ryder, Cynt, Nee, Tuck, and Coma. The Magnificent Seven of Fillmore High School. Before that, we were the Midas Crew of Dalton Junior High.

That seems like a lifetime ago. I have different friends and a whole new life now. Instead of trying to find someone to share my

life and my bed, I spend time with men who get paid to be with women.

I feel like I tried dating at one time, and it didn't feel right. I look at the process now and there's too many opening for complications. Questions are asked and expectations need to be managed. It's more than I'm willing to deal with at this time in my life. Instead, I hang out with guys who have no expectations. They have a goal of having fun and moving on.

I lucked up one night and stumbled across a bar where a nice group of guys told me they regularly hang out. Long nights of "entertaining" some wealthy women with no "finish" makes the guys open for my type of fun.

I don't do it often. I'm not a regular. Just when I need to take the edge off. Considering most of them don't do much for me than help me to have the occasional "happy ending", I don't go around that often.

That's my secret. I'm fine with it. Not everyone is, but I don't care. For now, it's what I need and how I deal.

Why was I even thinking about that?

Oh, right. Journee asked me last night if I'd ever been in love. I told her I had. I also told her I wasn't able to talk about it with her yet. That's a lot to unpack and she didn't have the time for it last night. She'd been getting ready for a date.

Me? I remained at home, watching *Hulu* until I fell asleep. Of course, I dreamed of the past and times with the M.S.O.F. and my "other half" all night. To the point I went rummaging through my things trying to find any of the t-shirts we had made or even the jacket. I couldn't find any of it.

"Crap. I'm going to have to call her."

I haven't really spoken to my mother. We don't have the best relationship. My mother isn't and hasn't ever been the typical mother. I think she got pregnant for the sake of pleasing her husband. It had nothing to do with love or wanting to pass on a piece of herself. She did it because she didn't want him to toss her aside like an old newspaper. My mother enjoyed decorating my room and dressing me up more than ever did spending time with me.

"A lesson I learned the hard way," I mutter the words to myself as I turn on some music.

I don't know what I'm going to do with a day of nothing to do. I'm dancing around in my watermelon print pajamas. Movement out of the corner of my eye causes me to jump back knocking my lamp onto my bed. I notice it's Journee as I move to put the thing back on my nightstand.

"You scared the shit out of me. what are you doing home?"

I turn the music down to a much lower level so I can hear her.

"I was trying to get some sleep before my late shift, but my roommate and friend has decided she needs to have a dance ... party," she informs me with an added yawn at the end. "What the heck are you doing up ...? what time is it? I'm too tired to open my eyes enough to see your clock."

"It's 8:52."

"Right. You're usually up at this hour. don't have a list or something quieter to do?"

I snort as I look at her satin and lace floral print.

"Don't you have company to entertain?"

I waggle my eyebrows, but it's lost on her since she's looking at me through slitted eyes. Her messy hair falls into her face as tilts her head.

"I'd come up with some snide comment but that would take too much energy. Company or Steven wore me out last night and this morning. I have an hour to actually sleep. I love you but I will seriously hurt you if you wake me up again." She slowly turns to walk out of my room. "Just an FYI, he's somewhere in the house. I think he said something about finding his clothes so he can go to work. I can see your nipples."

"No, you can't," I call after her exiting form.

"The rainbow nipple rings are cute," she calls from her down the hall.

I immediately close the door and wait to hear the front door shut. When the alarm announces that it's closed, I grab my phone from the nightstand and arm the alarm. I wait for a few minutes to see if I hear anything. When I don't, I'm tempted to turn the music back up. If I didn't know Journee as both the lovely, perky sweetheart at Hope House and the crazed killer Barbie I know at home, I'd try my luck. Since I do, I'm not even going there.

Once upon a time, I was just as dangerous. The M.S.O.F. weren't known for being the kindest people. We weren't purposely mean or rude, but we also weren't the ones to pick a fight with either. We had each other's backs and took care of the family that we'd created.

A family that is no longer linked. I miss them. I miss that time. I miss who we were to one another. I miss what we dreamed we'd become.

*"He doesn't know?"*

The memory flits in then out again. At least, I think it's a memory. I don't know the voice. It goes by too quickly. I can't tell who the person is referring to when they speak. I'm lost. That's the most frustrating part of it.

This is why the last therapist was fired. If I'm being honest, it's the reason they all were. None of them could help me connect the dots. I feel like I'm one link away but it's just out of my reach. My phone rings.

**M.R.C.**?

Yet another thing I've been trying to figure out. What does M.R.C. stand for? I've answered the call before and a person starts spewing information at me. Before I could even respond, the call either ended or they begin speaking to someone else. Seeing as I feel that's one of the rudest things a person can do, I ended the call.

Now, I've taken to ignoring the calls. Internet searches have come up with things that confuse me further, so I've left it alone.

Until today.

"Hello?"

"Dr. Emory? Oh, wow. Okay. I've been ... I'm so sorry to bother you. It's just that some gentlemen are here. They said they had a meeting set with you. I didn't gain access to your calendar until a few hours ago so I couldn't call you to remind you that this was coming. I've handled most of the other events and paperwork I was asked to handle. You have some clients that are expecting you today. Their charts need to be updated and you're needed to sign off on continuation of their treatments. I spoke with a Dr.

Godfrey. He said you were cleared to return to light duties over a month ago. We haven't seen you in office. When I've previously phoned you, our calls kept getting disconnected."

Whoever this person is must have me confused with someone else. I mean, yes, I've been cleared for light duty. Yes, I've been able to return to work. No, I have no idea who this person is or why they're calling me.

"Wait a second. I think you have me confused with someone else."

"No ma'am. I don't. Your mother had me set up a secondary office here. The other location is being run by Penelope Netters. All her references checked out and she came highly recommended. She used to work for a company out of Los Angeles called Corporate Cares. A woman by the name of Rylee Donavan gave her a glowing recommendation. If you could be in office ... soon, that would be great. The men will be back at 10:30."

"I'm sorry. Where's here? And who are you?"

The woman on the other end of the line laughs mirthlessly.

"She wasn't lying. She was actually telling the truth. My name is Paislynn Waters. I've worked for Moonbeam Rehab Center 4 almost two years no. I am your executive assistant here at the Savannah office. I'll send you the address the office. I can't believe your mother was telling the truth."

"Huh, that's a lot of information. I'm going to have to call my mother ever value story. if everything checks out then I guess I'll be there shortly."

"Thank you. thank you very much. I'll be glad to see you again Dr. Emory."

I guess I'm calling my mother a lot soon than I believed I would.

*"Hey there, Moonbeam."*

That memory I know well. It's what my grandmother used to call me. I should probably make her my next phone call. She's probably still pissed at me for leaving things the way I did, but I should reach out.

First, I my mother. Taking a deep breath, I dial the one number I don't purposely dial often.

"Hello, Coleman residence," a male voice says after the phone rings twice on my side of the call.

"Hello, is Mrs. Coleman available?"

"Yes ma'am. who may I ask is calling?"

"Will you let her know Brooklyn is on the phone, please Sir?"

"Yes ma'am. Will do."

"Angel cakes, it's so nice to hear from you. To what do I owe the pleasure of this phone call?"

"Mom, I think you have some explaining to do."

"What do you think I did now? I happened minding my own business. I've also been trying to do everything I could to do right by you. You sound upset, like I've done something wrong."

"I guess you can say that I'm upset. I just got off the phone with someone by the name of Paislynn Waters who says that she is my executive assistant. She also says you gave her instructions to open up an office here in Savannah on my behalf. Could you tell me what that's about?" She's quiet for few minutes which lets me know she knows exactly what I'm talking about. "You know all about Moonbeam Rehab Center, don't you?"

"Yes, I do. I promised I'd make sure it was taken care of and ready for you. Ms, Waters has been doing a great job handling things while you've been away."

"You promised who? Who told you to keep it going on my behalf?"

"You. I promised you I take care of your business for you. The doctors said you needed time to recover."

I remember the doctors telling me it was going to take some time to recover. Moving towards the bathroom, I think about what isn't seen. Pulling up my pajama shirt, I look at my tattoos. Last month, I got tired of seeing the damaged skin on my neck,

[50]

shoulders, and back. I decided to have it changed to something I could stand to look at when I'm in front of a mirror.

I have a gilded mirror with a reddish orange fox that has a forest background in it. The fox is a cunning and sly animal. It can also mean to baffle or deceive. I think I chose it because it looked good. Seeing it now, I see it's a fitting choice. I've done my share of deceiving. I had to be cunning and sly in the past. If I weren't, he never would've believed me. He wouldn't be who he is.

I shake myself to veer from the path that train of thought would take me down. I got the animal figuring it would cover up the harsh red my skin had been. Again, I have to do a mental shift.

*Focus.*

Instead of seeing what was there before, I see what's there now. From my lower left clavicle around to my left shoulder there's a bouquet of my favorite flowers, pink hydrangeas. My grandmother had these all around her yard when I was younger. I'd later learn that we share a favorite flower.

"Brooklynn! Brooklynn Emory, are you listening to me? Did she end the call?"

My mother's voice snaps me out of my thoughts. For once, I'm grateful to hear her voice.

*That's a new one.*

The snide thought makes me smile.

"What were you saying? I was … never mind."

"I'm not going to repeat all of what I just said. I will say that I tried to honor what I was tasked with. It's been quite a daunting endeavor and I'd appreciate it if you would acknowledge that. I've had to …"

There it is! The reason I have to limit my interactions with my mother. Everything is about her. All she does is for her sole benefit. Even when she's supposedly doing something nice, there's some angle in it for her, some way to lift her up. I'm so over the martyr act.

"Good. Night!" I pinch the bridge of my nose as I look at my reflection. The woman before me looks like she's tired and is over all of this. "Thank you so much for EVERY LITTLE THING you've done!"

"Little things? Little? You just don't know what all I've done. Changes that have happened. I've not been able to travel as I've wanted."

"Ma? Mom? Mother!"

"What? Why do you insist on interrupting me?"

"The main reason is because I was told I have a meeting that's supposed to happen in forty-seven minutes and I'm nowhere near dressed or prepared for it. I don't even know what the meeting's about."

"Oh. Well, okay. That's fair enough. Your meeting is about the finalization of procuring the final two floors of the building. The first two floors are yours. The previous tenants finally moved to their new space so you can do the additions you wanted."

I want to ask more questions, but I don't I'm not in the mood for another tangent and I don't want to run the risk of being late for this expansion meeting.

"Thank you again, Mom. I need to go." A thought pops in my head just as I'm getting ready to end the call. "Oh, have you seen my t-shirts and jacket with the letters M.S.O.F. on them?"

"Yes, they're here. Hanging in the closet in your room. I needed to switch out the furniture in your room for ..."

"Nope. Sorry. I don't have time to listen to whatever you were going to say next. Thank you. Will you ... have someone put that stuff into a box or suitcase and I'll pick it up later?"

"Are you sure? You want to come by the house?"

Her question makes me stop what I'm doing to look at the phone. Why does she sound suddenly nervous? I don't understand. At the same time, I don't have the time to dissect that either.

"I'll see you later."

"All right. If you're sure, I'll see you then."

# *Plunge*

Looking at my reflection as I end the call, again I wonder what that was about. I shake out my much shorter hair. I had so much of it cut off recently. I'd wanted to shake things up. I needed to be in control of something since the damn mental puzzle was besting me. Major inches were cut. The length of my hair went from almost touching my ass to barely touching my shoulders. The changes didn't stop there. I had my hair colored to match the fox's fur in my tattoo.

If the teenage me could look forward see the woman I became, maybe she wouldn't have been so afraid of the future. Setting a timer, I start the process of getting ready. I set up my own challenge round with certain tasks. If I hit my timed goal and complete the items on the list, I create in the morning then I'm able to treat myself to something. I also put my chosen treat on the list. I start my list.

Nineteen minutes later, I see I beat my timer.

"YES!" I do a low cheer and give myself a high five.

My hair is straightened. I have a button down, large collar shirt with my sleeves folded over to the elbows. I decided on a flowy, copper toned, ankle-length skirt with black, closed-toe heels. The heels have a cute, sunburst like design from the toe to the thin strap that wraps around my ankle.

"Looking good. Are you trying to seduce the new therapist?" Journee asks as she settles in on one of the stools at the kitchen counter.

I don't expect to see her downstairs when I come down, so I'm startled when she begins to speak. It's a rare occasion to find her inside. She usually sits in the sunroom which is right off the kitchen. Considering I wasn't expecting her to be home, I shouldn't be surprised she's in a different place.

The sky is starting to darken as the clouds shift. That probably has something to do with her change of location.

[53]

"Um, I don't have a therapy appointment today. I'm on my way to the office."

"The office? Is that what we're calling Hope House now? Wait, is there an event I've forgotten about? I was planning on wearing my *SpongeBob* scrubs today because we have kiddos coming in today."

I hear the panic in her voice and rush to calm her

"I'm going to the office I didn't know I had until two phone calls that changed the trajectory of my morning happened. We have so much to talk about, but I have to go. Evidently, my offices are expanding, and I have papers to sign. How did this become my life?"

I leave my friend, speechless, in our kitchen, as I snag a breakfast bar and rush out the door to the meeting.

Two hours later, I'm leaving a conference room and being led to my office. Upon entering, there's no doubt in my mind this is my office.

"I made sure it was a replica of your other office. We didn't think you'd want anything to change. Creature of habit that you are. Um, I'll leave you to get reacquainted with your space. please let me know if you need anything from me."

The kind young woman with dark blonde waves that dance around her shoulders as she speaks nods, taps her ever-present clipboard, then steps out of the door. She closes it behind her.

Taking in my office, I notice a miniature *Squishmallow* toy on the black glass tabletop of my desk. I have a collection of these at home. The *Renne Coffee* is sitting on the corner of the couch in my office. I saw *Paislynn Pumpkin Spice Latte* in the corner of Paislynn's bookshelf. If ever I wondered if this was my office that along with the black, white and pink design would tell me.

Everything outside of this space has the yellow Moonbeam logo color accenting it. The black, white, and wood is carried throughout. Pops of color in the various therapy rooms give off a different vibe as a person enters. I love the artistic way the lobby area bleads into the wall-less store that offers sandwiches and beverages for next to nothing. Paislynn said the display cases that are in the waiting area and strategically placed around the building were a genius idea. Apparently, that was mine. It drives the patients to stop in the store before they leave.

It's more than I could've ever imagined. I remember wanting to do this. I had notes and drawings about what a space like this would look like. Seeing it live and in living color is mind blowing. I spin around in my chair as I look at all that is mine. Three of my walls are half wall, half windows so I have a panoramic view of Savannah.

How did I get so fortunate to have this? Today, I added the second and third floors of the building to my offices. My mother was in on conference call. Paislynn had me sign some papers that had my mother's signature on them. I have a copy of those papers and other files to review at my leisure. Still, I have questions.

I truly want to know how all of this happened. Nothing is clicking together. That puts a huge damper on the feeling of joy I just had. I need to go somewhere familiar. Home.

When I arrive home a little later, I'm all alone. I release a breath I didn't realize I was holding. This feels good. I know this place. Taking a seat at the kitchen table, I see a note on top of one of the folders Paislynn handed me.

I have a decision to make. It's my office. I'm the owner but I haven't been there. I need to decide if I'm ready to take back the reigns or hand them over. The top name on the list is the one name I shouldn't have been surprised to see.

My mother's. Do I want to go to a place where I know no one but it's everything I've ever wanted? a place that might lead to some of the answers I've been claiming to want. Or do I want to remain in the comfort of the place I know and remember well? Remaining in blissful ignorance of the time I've lost, never recalling what caused the physical and emotional scars.

[55]

Decisions. Decisions.

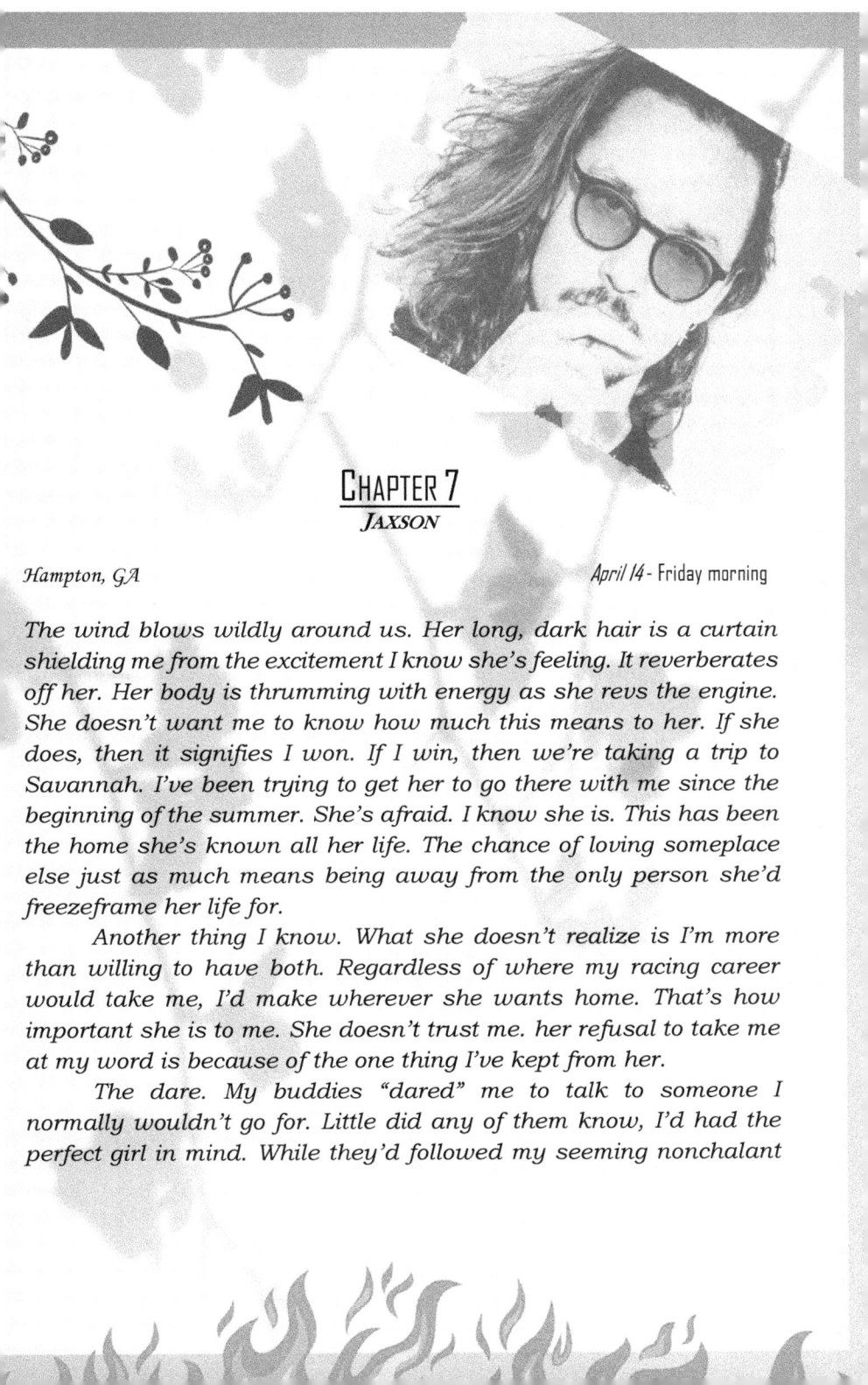

# CHAPTER 7
## JAXSON

*The wind blows wildly around us. Her long, dark hair is a curtain shielding me from the excitement I know she's feeling. It reverberates off her. Her body is thrumming with energy as she revs the engine. She doesn't want me to know how much this means to her. If she does, then it signifies I won. If I win, then we're taking a trip to Savannah. I've been trying to get her to go there with me since the beginning of the summer. She's afraid. I know she is. This has been the home she's known all her life. The chance of loving someplace else just as much means being away from the only person she'd freezeframe her life for.*

*Another thing I know. What she doesn't realize is I'm more than willing to have both. Regardless of where my racing career would take me, I'd make wherever she wants home. That's how important she is to me. She doesn't trust me. her refusal to take me at my word is because of the one thing I've kept from her.*

*The dare. My buddies "dared" me to talk to someone I normally wouldn't go for. Little did any of them know, I'd had the perfect girl in mind. While they'd followed my seeming nonchalant* walk towards my car trying to seek out the "perfect" girl, I'd secretly led them right to her.

I'd been watching her for a while. She was always with the same group that include two other girls. They sat in the same area near one of the big oak trees on campus for lunch. It was usually because she would lead them there. She always had a book with her or a motorcycle magazine. If they followed her, she'd hide the magazine inside the book. The first time I caught her hiding it, I couldn't stop the chuckle that came out.

The guys thought I was laughing at them. They didn't know I'd noticed someone outside of our group. Correction. The other guys didn't notice me noticing her. Graham, overly observant bastard that he is, saw me watching her the next day.

When I led them to where she was sitting, I noticed the knowing smile on Graham's grease-smudged face. He'd been spending more time in his parents' garage. His parents were arguing too. The difference was his parents had decided to divorce. Mine argued like it was their daily sport.

Once the guys spotted the group of females, the debate began. I let them go back and forth, weighing the different aspects they thought I liked about each of the girls. Truth be told, each of them would've been perfect candidates. It wasn't like I had a preference or anything. A female is a female. I count it a privilege any of them are interested in me. The rumor mill had circulated stories that I have a preference and I like variety because they haven't seen me with one girl for long. I'll never tell them they're dead ass wrong.

Ryder and Graham are the only ones who know I haven't stuck with one because I have issues. Life at home doesn't offer a grand example of "happy life". Mom and Dad deal with each other because they have three kids together. If they love each other, they don't really show it.

I was about to open my mouth to point out something the other guys might not notice when Graham speaks up.

"*The one with the long, dark hair and colored glasses is all wrong. She's not his type at all. Did you see what looks like her dad's or big brother's shirt draped around her waist? She's totally wrong for him.*"

If Graham and I hadn't been two of the closest buds at Filmore High, we would've been instantly. Ryder turned to look at Graham then looked at me. I tried to school my features, but he squinted his eyes at me. He looked like he was trying to see through me. A beat later, he turned to the last two members of our group and let them know she'd be the one.

That's the truth of the "dare".

I did ask her to go for a ride with me that day too. She laughed like I was joking. She looked from her friends to me to exactly where my car was parked. That was all I needed to know. I saw the "no" well before she spoke the word. Digging around in my backpack, I pull out the next issue of the magazine I knew she was hiding. I wrote my number down on the top of the inside page with a note to take a look at page thirty-three.

I walked over to my car. The guys followed me, giving me crap about her turning me down. When I looked out my window, I noticed her looking at me while her friends were talking to her. She was confused but I could see the interest.

The next day I rode my bike to school and parked it where I usually parked my car. I got to school early. The night before, I realized I had no clue when or how she got to school. I waited for what felt like forever. Standing leaned against one of the columns, I watched her get out of the car. An older gentleman was in the driver's seat. As soon as she stepped out of the car, she looked around. I saw the instant she saw it.

A smile played at my lips as I watched her wave to the driver then make her way to where my bike was parked. She pulled out the magazine and looked at the bike in the photo then mine. They guys and I each built versions of bikes we'd seen in that magazine.

*My dad happened to know the photographer and wanted to show off our accomplishment. One of the best moments of my life.*

*My phone buzzed in my pocket. An unknown number was calling me. Somehow, I knew it was her. Answering on the second buzz, I found out I was right. I hadn't even noticed her pull out her phone. We ended up talking the entire time we went our separate ways to our classes.*

*Thus, how we started.*

*She eventually admitted I won the bet, and I took her to Savannah. We ended up at a bench in Forsythe Park, sharing fries and a Leopold's banana split. She made me laugh out loud and I told her I loved her. Right there on that park bench, I told a woman who wasn't a member of my family I loved her.*

*Three years and four months later, she ripped my heart out and left me broken.*

I don't know why I'm thinking about her. She's in my past. I need to leave her ass there. She's living her live.

*In the same city and state where you are. That can't be a coincidence.*

It doesn't matter. I'm not chasing her. Plus, I need to focus on fixing my shit. I get off my ass, close up my home office, get dressed, and take said ass to work.

*Where she works too.*

I groan as the car pulls up to the building. I'm not thinking when I climb out of Graham's car, so I don't immediately notice the crowd out front.

"Perfect," I mutter as I plaster on a smile. "I really need to get my car back."

*Savannah, GA*                                        *April 14* - Friday morning

The small crowd of women follows me through the front door and to the makeshift reception area. The head nurse comes from around the corner and gives the women their marching orders. Another woman, Amanda, I think, tells Graham that something needs to be done about this continuous entourage of mostly women.

I'm glad to see the crowd is dwindling. I was hoping coming through the front entrance would be safe by now since I've been here every day. I guess I was wrong.

I turn to Graham and spout the words of our usual joke.

"They just can't get enough of me."

His usual response is "Nope. Not until they have enough to clone you."

If he says the second part, I don't know. My focus goes to the woman. Tingles and heat dance over my skin as I try to get a look at her face. There's a woman at the desk who is trying her best to keep from looking my way. The short, red hair looks familiar, but I don't know why. It's been a long couple of days. Hope, Graham, and I have been busy working on getting me up to speed on a few pressing items I didn't know were happening. We've also been working on event planning for the anniversary of Hope House. My other task has been working double time not to cross paths with my mother.

Having all of that roaming around up there while fighting the urge to drink and gamble has my brain working overtime to figure out where I know the hair from. The frame is slightly hidden beneath the larger scrubs. They don't look like they belong to her.

Then she speaks and I know exactly who it is.

"All these years and he's still exactly the same," she mutters. "Arrogant, cocky, and egotistical."

I probably wouldn't have realized it was her had I not heard her voice. It is. It's her. Brooklynn Emory. The "one who got away". The one who still makes my heart skip a fucking beat and my pants tighten around a burgeoning bulge. She's the only woman in the world who has ever had this effect on me. If only she knew what she does to me.

"Did you say something? I'm sorry. I didn't catch it."

I did. I heard every word but I'm not going to admit it. My goal is to get her to do what she obviously doesn't want to do. She needs to face me. All that fiery red hair and the colorful shoulder tattoo peeking out from the oversized shirt she's wearing threw me for a moment. I don't know why but she reminds me of something. I just can't put my finger on it. I'll have to get used to it. She's always had a dark fall of hair. Hair that she's always worn straight. Seeing curls in her hair, even loose ones, is different as well.

She turns to face me.

*Fucking success.*

Success I instantly regret. Her gray eyes focus on me. Those eyes are the things that have haunted my thoughts for far too long. Their color instantly reels me in. I can spend hours staring into those pools of gray, like a misty sky on a storm-calling night. They are beautiful. The color shifts depending on how pissed off or happy she is.

Given the look of them right now, she's plenty irritated with me. I can guess she has plenty to say to me. Her previous words are like little jabs. She is just getting started. I can tell.

"You want to know what I said?" she poses it like it's a question, but any idiot can tell she's not asking me anything. Still, I begin to answer her with a nod that she cuts off. "I said I'm not surprised with your actions. You haven't changed one bit. Not that I expected much. Still the same old Jaxson Shaw. Oh wait. That's not who you are anymore. You're Daire Deville, right? Famous racecar driver and regular panty dropper. Always has been. Always will be."

She's wrong, but she doesn't need to know that right now. It's been a long time. Brooklynn would be surprised to know just how different I am from the kid who left Hampton, Georgia and never looked back. I'm not going to tell her any of that. It's not the right time and she's obviously still angry with me.

Despite her apparent irritation with me, I give her my famous Jaxson Shaw smile. When she throws her arms up in frustration

[62]

then begins to give me her back, I slide over to her. The fans were all but forgotten the instant I saw her. Now, their groans and mutterings of displeasure reach my ears. I hold up my finger, indicating to give me just a minute.

"Oh, I've changed. I've changed in ways that would shock a smalltown girl who only wants a smalltown life."

I don't know what motivates me to say those words other than they've been the ones on repeat in my head all this time. Words I loathed hearing right before I left for California all those years ago. The instant the words are out I can practically fill the atmosphere around us shift.

She steps forward then immediately takes a step back.

"No. Nope. I'm not doing this with you. I have many, many things I could be doing. That's what I'm going to do. Just an FYI, this is a place where people come for assistance and guidance. It is not the place for you to meet your next groupie, race whore, or whatever you want to call them."

She unleashes the full power of those eyes as she gives me a once over. Her gaze is full of contempt and disgust just before she walks away from me. As I'm watching her leave again, Hope picks that moment to step into my line of sight.

Not. What. Or who I want to see.

Hope's expression is one I know almost as well as I know the shades of Brooklynn's peepers. Not what I want to deal with right now. My mind is still reeling from having truly seen Brooklynn Emory.

"Bring it down a notch."

"What? Wait … why? I don't know what you're talking about."

"Yeah, okay. Know that just as you've changed over the years so has she. Don't let the snarky comeback fool you. The woman you just spoke with has a lot going on. You may have been here in Savannah these last few years, but you haven't been around to know what's going on around you. Before you ask, I'm not privy to sharing anyone else's story. I don't know what the history is between you and Dr. Emory, but I know she's not ready for what you seem prepared to unleash on her. Hell, you're not exactly ready to truly release anything yourself. All I'll say is tread lightly. That cargo is marked 'Fragile' for a reason."

I'm standing there trying to make sense of her words. If I'm being honest, I'm wondering what the hell I've missed being couped up in my own little corner of Savannah. Having fame and money means a lot of things come to you. Evidently, a lot of the world has come to Brooklynn as well, given the look in her eyes and the way she carried herself.

I've been a damn good reader of the "Book of Brook". I can she's got some weight on her shoulders. The outside changes seem to be masking some deep-rooted issues. The depth of it is unknown. I want to make it my personal mission to get to the bottom of it. Even if it means learning I'm at the root of the darkness.

*That's probably not the best course of action.*

She has some pre-conceived notions about who she believes I am. She also has some decided beliefs about how I live my life. As much as I want to correct ... Dr. Emory, Hope is right. That woman isn't the woman I used to know.

I turn to say as much to Hope.

"You're not there anymore," I say to the space where Hope had been standing.

That's when I notice the fans are still patiently awaiting my return. Apologizing, I take the time to sign all the things they thrust my way then make my way to the second-floor offices. I have some work to do before today's therapy session. The books and furnishings of my office have collected dust long enough.

A small smile plays at my lips because I know it's going to come as a shock to both of those women to find me in that space.

# Chapter 8
## *Brooklynn*

*Savannah, GA*                                    *April 14* - Friday afternoon

*Of course, he's here. I mean, why not?*

Six years apart and there he was. He was standing right in front of me. I knew the moment he walked in the room. I felt it. That familiar warmth that only the nearness of him could elicit. I wanted to crash into him. My body hummed with nervous energy. Other parts of me heated and wanted to climb him like a tree.

It felt like no time had passed. Yet, it had. We weren't the eighteen- and nineteen-year-old any longer. Those two were madly in love, had made plans, and then undid those plans with one decision. One choice changed the course of their lives. When I told him "Goodbye", I thought that was the last time I was going to see him.

Never in my wildest dreams did I ever believe he'd not only return to Georgia but end up at the same place I was. This is the place I come to find comfort. It's my safe space. no one, except Noelle, knows about him. I mean she knows everything about him. What is he even doing here? I'm sure he has the money and resources to seek treatment elsewhere.

Hold on. Is he a patient? Please tell me he's not one of the patients who receives physical therapy here.

"That would so suck right about now. That's all I need is to have to be the person handling his therapy sessions."

It makes me wonder if Hope knows. How does Hope know him? What if he comes here because he's with Hope?

*Why are you asking that question?*

Right. It's none of my business. It doesn't matter. He's not important. My reason for being here has everything to do with the patients. I need to see Noelle anyway.

*Noelle!*

Does Noelle know him? Of course, she does. She's over the entire therapy department. Has she connected the dots of Daire and Jaxson?

*You're drifting into dangerous territory here, Chick.*

I'm supposed to be heading to Noelle. After that, I have another patient to see. Or is it the other way around? Maybe I need to take a break.

I have to look like a crazy person. I've gone in three different directions in the last five minutes. When I head back towards the stairs again, I run into Journee.

"Are you alright? You've gone towards the elevator then towards the front staircase then towards the back stairs then towards the break room. what's going on with you?"

"So much."

"What's going on with your clothes? Why does it look like you're wearing someone else's scrubs?"

"I am. I had to snag whatever extra set we had in the closet. The ones I wore in I had to toss in the wash."

My mind drifts to the one person I shouldn't be thinking about right now.

*He doesn't know.*

The words float through my mind as the night Daire headed of to become Daire Deville pops into my head.

"Is that really all you're going to tell me?" Journee slaps her hands onto my shoulders as she turns me so I'm facing her. "What happened? Why did you need to change your scrubs?"

I'm momentarily confused by question.

"Oh. I took the Trolley from the park this morning. I decided to go for a run. Someone decided my lap was the perfect place for their lunch and their morning iced coffee would be a perfect complement to my coffee print scrubs. That hot and cold was a great wake up call for the person who wasn't able to stop off to grab her usual morning pick me up. Huh?"

Journee's light brown eyes look heavenward as she stands waiting for me to explain why I just made that sound.

"I'm about to walk away from you and leave you standing right where you are. There are other things I could be doing than waiting for you to share your thoughts."

I smile before I put her inquisitive mind out of its misery.

"I might've taken my hangry out on someone who probably didn't deserve it. You know how I am when I don't get my morning coffee."

She nods. Sadly, she has firsthand knowledge of how horrible I am when I don't get my morning fix.

"It also explains why you can't figure out which way to go. Aren't you supposed to be in with Mrs. Hamilton?"

I snap my fingers and rush towards the back rooms.

"Thanks, hun."

"You're welcome!"

Forty-five minutes later, I'm done with Mrs. Hamilton, and I am ready for my much-needed break. I'll see Noelle after. She usually takes a late lunch on Fridays anyway. I head up to my favorite quiet place. This room has one of the best couches I've ever slept on in it. When I reach the usually dark office, the light is on. That gives me pause.

No one ever uses this room. I don't even know who it belongs to, but I know it hasn't been occupied in the last five months. I look around to see if the signage has been updated. Hope and the other people who have offices on this floor and the third floor all have their names on a wooden plaque on the side of the door. there still isn't a name on this one. The inside is fully furnished but I've never seen anyone inside.

That damn feeling moves over my body, and I make a split-second decision. I figure going inside is probably my safest bet. As I slip inside, I feel around for the light switch. I move away from the door because it has a plexiglass center to the wood frame. My shadow could be seen if I stood against it. He has no reason to come in here. It's the last thought I have before another door opens and the lights come back on.

I turn around to find him coming from the restroom that's connected to this office.

*Great choice, genius.*

"Twice in one day. More than I've seen of you in, what's it been? Six years?"

He tosses the napkin or paper towel he was wiping his hands with into a trash bin I didn't know was in this room. The room looks different.

*Yeah, the light is on. You tend to pull the shades and keep it a lot darker.*

That could be it.

His words play back in my head, and I'm irritated. Did he just ask me to tell him how long it's been since the last time we saw each other?

"Hit your head that many times that you can't count? Sometimes, it's okay for you to be on top."

*What? What the hell am I saying? I don't need to think about that.*

# Plunge

"Six years and my sex life is the first thing you mention? Why are you so interested in it? Does it bother you to hear that I've been with a lot of women since we were together?"

*Say no. change the subject. leave.*

There is no reason for the two of us to be in the same room. You don't need to know why he's here. You have no claim on him or his life, or his... manhood. You can leave. Aren't you supposed to be on break anyway? Turn around, walk to the door, open it, and leave. You have two feet. This is one of the reasons they were created. Make your exit. It's been done before. You know this. So, go.

No matter what my mind is screaming at me, I don't move. Nope. I remain right where I'm standing. instead of turning towards the door, I turn to face him. Folding my arms, I look directly at him then immediately wish I would've followed my mental directions.

His sea green eyes look at me, throw me, and I swear I'm that's stupid lovesick teenager again. I'm frozen in place, wishing my life would have taken a different path.

*This is why you should have left but no you had to be the stubbornness.*

When my thoughts are right, they're absolutely, one hundred percent accurate.

# CHAPTER 9
## *JAXSON*

When Brooklyn and I parted ways earlier today, I didn't expect to see her again this soon. Actually, I expected we'd have some awkward passings in the hallway. I should have known she'd end up back here since this was where I saw her the first time. I didn't know this was a regular thing for her. At the time, I thought it was a fluke.

Imagine my surprise when I exit the restroom and find her standing, looking at my office door.

"I'm not. I don't ... your love life or whatever is your business and none of mine. It hasn't been for a long time now."

Her words do nothing but piss me off. Some fucked up part of me wants her to be bothered. I want her to have some type of reaction to the perceived persona that comes with the Daire Deville name.

"Exactly. You made sure that was the case, didn't you?"

Brooklyn reacts like she's been physically slapped. Part of me wants to take away the hurt even though I'm the one who caused it. The other side of that coin, the darker side, wants her to bleed pain so she can know just what the hell I went through.

I make the mistake of looking into her eyes. What I see, I don't like. Tears are forming. She blinks several times. I can tell she's trying not to cry. No matter what I'm feeling, I don't move.

"Looks like everything worked out in your favor. Good for you. If you'll excuse me, I have patients who need my attention."

She turns on her heel then walks out the door. The action is familiar. Too familiar. It's like I'm reliving that moment all those years ago. This isn't what I wanted.

"Jax? Hey Jaxson! Are you alright?"

Hope snaps her fingers in front of my face to gain my attention. I shake myself as I turn to face her. I didn't even hear her come in.

"What? What's up?"

"What's up should be my question. What was that?" She tosses a file folder on my desk then puts her hands on her hips. "Oh no. Please tell me you haven't fucked this up already. I can't ... I can't have shit start here, Jaxson. I can't. This place is too important. Did something happen I need to deal with or is it too far gone and there's no coming back from it?"

Tilting my head, I fold my arms over my chest and watch Hope. Taking a beat, I wait to see if she's done with her accusation.

"First off, I need you to calm the hell down. You need to do a yoga pose or something. You went way left on that." She opens her mouth to speak but I cut her off with a raised hand. "*I* didn't do a damn thing. Notice where we are. If I'm here, that means she came into the space we set aside for me. She was here and words were spoken. That's all. Now she's gone."

"What?" she practically screams.

"I could've sworn I requested you calm down. I'd like the ability to hear once you leave."

"Just tell me if this is going to be a problem. Let me know right here, right now."

"Things will be fine. You'll see we'll be one big happy family in no time."

Hope sighs and I can see she doesn't believe a word I'm saying. She's probably right to think that. It's not exactly like I

[71]

believe what I just said myself. This situation is probably a recipe for disaster. I don't know how things are going to work with the two of us being here with the connection we have. What I can do is my best to make sure I'm not adding to the list of problems Hope has to deal with daily.

My goal for today is to keep my distance. With that thought in mind, I send Hope on her way, and I get back to work on the financials. I also have an acquisition report I need to review.

*Savannah, GA*                                                    *April 15* - Saturday morning

It's happening again.

*Heart is pumping faster than it should. The breathing is increasing. I'm panicking. We are on the road. This was just a drive. It's something we've done plenty of times. We've even been on this road before. All we're doing is going for a drive. It's been too long since we've done it. I had a moment where I was happy and filled with calm. The joy of knowing someone is proud of me suddenly fades into the background.*

*Ahead of us, a child is in the middle of the street. He appears to be happy he caught something. That's short-lived as fear is reflected on his face.*

*The sudden jerk jolts my heart. The sound of skidding tires ramps up the adrenaline in my veins. Screaming. I don't know what's being said. I can't make it out. The impact of the car. A tree that's coming closer than it should. The glass flying.*

*I hear sirens. Someone mentions a pole. A loud sound. It's like a chainsaw then crunching. The sound echoes then ebbs and flows like waves around me. There is pressure then a pulling. Pain. Excruciating, unbearable pain.*

*FUUUCCCCCKKK!*

I wake up yelling at the top of my lungs. I hear rushing footsteps from one of the other rooms. The hem of my shirt is in my hands then I pull it over my head. I use it to wipe the sweat that's pouring off me.

"Sir? Oh. Let me get you some water," Kennedy says.

I hear her retreat from the room I'm in.

"Fucking hell! I'm so tired of this," I tell no one.

I'm alone in the room. This is one of the reasons I was drinking. Not that it kept the dreams away. They still came. I was just numb to whatever I was feeling. I'm in the theatre room. I came in here to watch some of the footage from some recent races. Graham procured them for me.

Normally, we all sit down as a team to watch them, but I didn't want to wait until this evening to start. Yesterday evening, was a free one for me, so I stayed home. I got tired and was too lazy to go upstairs to my room. The location wouldn't have changed the outcome. I probably still would've had the dream.

I walk over and pick my shirt up off the floor. Instead of waiting for Kennedy to bring me the bottle or glass of water, I walk out to meet her in the hallway. I need to work some of this excess energy off. Rounding the corner, I almost run into her, startling her. She just about drops the tray she has in her hands.

"Shit. Sorry. Didn't expect you to be there."

"No, Sir. It's my fault." She gives me a strange look as she tries to figure out which way I'm headed. "Did you want breakfast? I know it's a little earlier than normal."

I look down at my watch and see it's a little after six in the morning. That's a hell of a lot earlier than my normal time. Over the last few months, I haven't risen before nine.

"Have you eaten yet?"

She looks surprised. What kind of asshole have I been over the last few months if that surprises her?

Kennedy shakes her head. Her usually loose, curly, hair floats around her shoulders as she responds.

"No. Not yet. I was going to eat after I brought this to you." She tries to hand me the tray again. I tap it then point to her. "Oh, thank you for letting me work today instead of Monday."

I smirk as I move passed the tall, lean, marathon runner. She's wearing jeans and one of the JDJ t-shirts we just had designed.

"You know you could've just taken the day off and been paid for it. You didn't have to come over and work today. I think we need to get you an office over at HFH. The two of us work together a lot more than people know we do. Plus, I think you have a handle on my moods. Better than most. Please go enjoy breakfast. I'm going to work out. Thank you."

Her golden-brown skin catches the sunlight from the windows making her look like the goddess she is. She's a lifesaver and one of the best assistants I could've ever asked for. Cassandra will probably be a lot happier having Kennedy join us at the office. Kennedy already knows all about my temperaments and demands. Plus, Kennedy has seen me at my best and worst.

She's been more than amazing with all the changes that hit over the last year. Kennedy and Patrick have seen the absolute ugly side of me. Being two who have spent the most time alone in this house with me, next to Graham and Hope, it was unavoidable. I've been an absolute bastard. They've been paid handsomely as well as sent numerous apology gifts. The team doesn't know I know she has dreams to be the next Gemma Gordan.

My mom once said she didn't understand how I still had people willing to spend any time with me considering how awful I have been to them. When Beck, Chance Devereaux's crew chief, recommended GiGi as manager and suggested Graham for my pit crew chief, I didn't hesitate. I made the phone calls to make it happen. It was one of the best decisions I've ever made. I haven't looked back. I've busted my ass to make sure all the members of my team were taken care of before I saw a dime.

Seeing me through one of the most difficult losses of my life has been something each of them has said they didn't mind doing. If the situation were to arise anew, they'd even told me they'd be willing to do it again. Me trying to piece myself back together is the least I can do after all I've put everyone through. The guilt is what tends to send me to the bottle. Today, I'm taking it to the gym.

The first thing I do is stretch. As I do, I take in the man looking back at me in the mirror. When I was in my late teens and early twenties, this hair was neatly trimmed. I used to have a beard. It wasn't too thick. Just enough to say I had facial hair. The guy peering back at me has shoulder-length hair, a trim mustache, a soul patch, and some hair on his chin. My arms are tatted, and I've gained some extra padding from not spending time in this specially designed gym. Looking down my body, I see the scarring on my leg that will be a forever reminder of that day. I have other reminders, but I won't dwell on those.

Clapping my hands together, I nod at my reflection.

"Let's go to work, Shaw."

The words echo off the walls of the empty room. I pop in my earbuds, and they instantly connect to my workout playlist. I move through some of the new exercises I was recently shown. As I start the movements I know by rote, I'm immediately lost in thoughts of the past.

Driving has been something I've always wanted to do. It shouldn't have surprised anyone when I chose this for a career. We used to race each other in our toy cars when we were kids. Learning to ride bikes gave us another thing to race. All of us. The whole crew would be on our bikes, tearing through the neighborhood.

As we got older, we progressed from dirt bikes to motor bikes. I still remember the feel of that first test drive. No one could've told me that wasn't going to be what I would do with the rest of my life. It's what I felt I'd do. I loved racing down and around our makeshift course we'd created in an abandoned lot. It was a feeling none of us could describe. We just loved it.

The progression to motorcycles was easy enough. We pretty much built our first bikes. We then built the first motorcycle I ever rode. That building helped us prepare for all the work we've put in over the years on the different motorcycles each of us has owned. The first time I drove a buddy's 1970 Chevy Cheville, I knew things would never be the same.

The music shifts in my ears and my voice fills them.

"I started drag racing when I was fourteen. My mom is going to kill me for sharing that. Sorry mom." There's a pause then laughter can be heard. "It was the most intense feeling. Nothing felt as amazing as it did the first time I won. That was it. I was bit by the bug. I was reminded what I wanted to do with my life. *NASCAR* was all I could see in my future."

Slowing the treadmill, I pull out the earbuds. Standing in the doorway are Graham and GiGi.

"Whatever you are working on, I'm not interested in it. I'm watching for entertainment purposes only. I'm not ready to be that person again. If that's what this is going to be about then you might as well turn back around and head back out the door."

GiGi turns to look at Graham. Her pink outfit looks like she came to kick back and chill verses work. If that's the case than I'm all for it. I'd prefer it. Graham is one of the only men I know who could make a cream sweater, navy chinos, and polished leather boots look like office wear.

"We are here for a chill Saturday afternoon hangout session," Graham tells me.

Even he doesn't sound like he believes what he's saying.

"I'm hitting the showers." As I walk by him, I lean in to tell him. "Not one word of that is believable when you arrive with your work bag."

He looks down at his hand like he forgot the thing was there. I hear GiGi's laughter as I continue up the hall towards the stairway to my room.

The only time I've ever seen Graham completely dressed down is when he's in his garage. He's just as much of a grease head as I am. No one would know that if they looked at him.

Plunge

"We have two things to discuss. Little things. One won't even take long."

I chuckle because that's probably one of the first lies he's spoken in years.

"You know he doesn't believe you," GiGi tells him.

I hear them following me up the hall.

"We've gotta talk about it because he got the ball rolling. He's not going to be happy if it falls through because he didn't want to talk about it."

"Your funeral. I told you we could set something else up."

That gets my attention. I look back at the two of them.

"Just tell me. What did I say I'd do that I've forgotten about?"

"The first one's yours," Graham tells GiGi.

"Jerk," she says with a roll of her eyes. "The dinner with Logan Alexander."

"No. Hard fucking pass. I love Hope and you know I do but I'm not having dinner with her dickhead of a brother. A dinner that is really an interview. That fucker can kiss my ass. No way in hell did I agree to meet with him. Considering how he handled things the last time, I'm surprised he has the balls to ask. Let him report on the taste of fucking soggy kitty litter."

The two of them look at one another then mouth, "Damn". I see Kennedy's reflection in the glass door of the theatre room. She's in the kitchen listening to every word.

"What's the second thing that won't take long?"

Folding my arms, I wait for Graham to let me in on the other thing.

"It's the JDJ auction. Are we giving the money to the same organization or a different one this year? Also, did you want to have that organization's logo on Heart Breaker?"

Heart Breaker is the name I gave my car. They all think it's because I was nicknamed that after my "reputation" with women went public. They should know me better than that. I'd never name the thing I drive after something so trivial. It's named after the woman who was so aptly given that name after she decided the future didn't include the two of us.

"Yes, and I don't care. I'm going to shower. I'll be back down in a few."

Now I need to figure out what I am going to do to keep my mind from dwelling on the one woman I don't need to think about since I'm trying to stay on the right side of sober.

Why can't life be as simple as a racetrack? A start and a finish. Everyone trudging forward, heading for their target goal. It would make things a hell of a lot easier. Maybe just maybe I'd be happier.

# CHAPTER 10
## *BROOKLYNN*

I'm at the Hope House on my usual day. Ready for my usual workload but it feels wrong to be here. At the same time, it feels right. It's like there's something drawing me here. At this time and in this space. This is where I need to remain. It's my break time so I venture out to the solarium. In between individual therapy sessions, group sessions, and seeing clients for their physical therapy appointments, I take a much-needed break.

It feels weird being here now that I know there's somewhere else that is my own. Discovering there is a piece of Savannah that's mine is it pretty heady feeling. That's the upside. The downside is me trying to let yet another puzzle piece enter my brain. The puzzle is still in disarray, but I have some corner sections all put together. Those corner pieces are all one color. Now there is not only a new piece, but it has its own distinctive coloring that doesn't match anything I have already on the board.

Releasing a heavy sigh, I take in my surroundings.

It's peaceful, quiet and allows me a moment to be alone. This area isn't used often. Every once in a while, classes are taught here, and every inch of the space is used. When it's not in use, most of the employees come out and sit. They'll read or listen to music.

Most know it isn't a place for menial conversation or a social hour. If a person comes out to the solarium, then they are looking for a moment's peace away from it all.

When I come out here, I have my wireless earbuds and my ears and I'm either reading or playing the game on my phone. Since I left my earbuds in my locker, I don't have those to add this extra barrier to keep people from talking to me. Pulling up one of the three games that I keep on my phone, I begin to play the next level of *Harry Potter Puzzles and Spells*. If it isn't this game, then it's one- or two-word games that I play. I used to play those simulation games like *Chapters* and *FarmVille* but got bored with them.

I'm working my way through the last obstacles of the level when I see movement reflected in my screen. The muscles in my stomach clench and a shiver runs down my spine. I know this feeling. It's one I thought was a fluke. I thought it manifested because of young love and not because of the boy behind it.

I was wrong. Dead wrong as the warmth of his breath as it causes heat to rush over my body.

"Wouldn't have taken you as one to play this sort of game."

"What? You've got to be kidding me right now."

"Nope. I'm not kidding."

"I wasn't talking to you. Not that it would matter."

"What does that mean?"

"Nothing. You can't be out here."

"Who says?"

"It's … there are rules. This is an employee only area."

He takes a seat across from me. He's making himself comfortable, acting as if I haven't said a word.

"Right."

"How did you even get back here? Only those who work here have a pass."

"True. You're right about this area being restricted."

I know my brows are furrowed because I'm confused as to why he's still out here. I'm even more puzzled as to how he got past the doorway.

"You still need to explain what you're doing here. Did someone let you back here or something?"

"Or something."

"You're doing this to irritate me, aren't you?"

He chuckles and I feel like that deep, rumble jumps from his side of the solarium to right where I'm sitting. It practically pulses through every fiber of my being. He should not have this effect on me. How is it possible this man impacts me like this when no man who has come after him could make me perk up the way he does? All he did was chuckle. What they heck is wrong with me?

When I look up from my phone, the phone I haven't been paying attention to, he's giving me that knowing look. I hate that look. It's the look that says he knows where my mind drifted. Yet another thing that shouldn't happen. He shouldn't know what I'm thinking. It's literally been years.

"I haven't done a thing. I'm simply sitting here, minding my own business, soaking up some good ole vitamin D while enjoying the afternoon breeze."

"Really? That's all you're doing. None of this has anything to do with slowly driving me insane or invading my personal space."

He begins to play with something, but I can't make out what it is because I'm too focused on his face. He has the look. Daire has a number of looks that put me instantly on high alert. This one is one that has the hairs on my arms standing on end. It makes me nervous and uncomfortable. He's thinking of something. Whatever it is, I know I'm not going to like it.

Daire's up and out of his seat then inches away from me. I feel the heat of his body as he hovers over me. He slowly leans down until his face is right above mine. He's staring at me. Our gazes are locked with one another's. His breaths become my own and vice versa. Leaning closer, he keeps his gaze connected to mine until the last instant. His lips graze my ear before the heat of his breath tickles my lobe. When he speaks, the rumble of his voice vibrates against my neck.

Try as I may, I can't stop the shuttering response my body has to his words.

"This is me being in your personal space. Being five feet away from you is the exact opposite."

"Um, am I interrupting something?"

Daire slowly rises then takes a step back. I don't know exactly what he's seeing but whatever it is, he's enjoying it.

*That's great. That's just what I need.*

"I've always been a better show-er than a tell-er. No ma'am. You're not interrupting anything, Ms. Forrester. I was just helping Ms. Emory with understanding the meaning of 'personal space'." He places his hand in his pocket then pulls something out. He flips it a few times in his hand before he taps the back of his neck with it. "Enjoy the rest of your workday, ladies."

"You too, Mr. Shaw," Journee says as she moves to the seat Daire just vacated. "Oh, my goodness! How do you know Mr. Shaw and why did you call him Daire?"

Her words don't immediately register because my stupid brain is stuck on how good his ass looked in his jeans as he walked away. After giving myself a mental slap, I hear what she said.

"Why are you calling him Mr. Shaw? Is he a patient here or something?"

I finally focus on Journee. It's then that I notice she isn't paying attention to me. Her eyes were on the same thing mine were. Shaking herself, she then takes a drink of whatever is in her cup. I feel a twinge of unexpected jealousy.

*Let's reign that in. That's not an option. Reroute that energy to something else.*

Exactly. So, I do.

Plunge

I think about Journee instead. Her hair is curly and free today. She's rocking her midnight blue scrubs with moons on them, which means that's probably coffee in her cup. We are so night and day it isn't even funny. I'm wearing my sky-blue scrubs with suns and rainbows. Her brows furrow as she looks at me.

"You don't know who that is. Do you?" she asks me.

"Do you?" I instantly reply. "I feel like I'm missing something. Was that a HFH badge he had in his hand?"

"Yes. I answered one of yours. You answer one of mine."

"That was Daire Deville. Famous racecar driver?"

"Really? He races cars? That's interesting and news to me. I just know him as Bossman Shaw. The man who is co-owner of HFH."

"Co-owner? What? Since when?"

Journee chuckles then. When she realizes I'm serious, she stops. Abruptly.

"Oh. Right. You seriously don't know. He has been with HFH since its inception. He's the reason it's called the Hope Foundation House."

I start to tap my nail on the screen of my phone. The rate of the tapping increases as does the feeling of nervousness that courses through me.

"How is it possible that I didn't know that? Why haven't I seen him around? Why is he around now?"

I have a sudden horrifying question. I'm unable to speak it aloud because the possibility of it being the truth would be too much for me to handle. What if I'm the reason he's coming around?

"I'd have to say I don't know the answer to any of those questions. I'm guessing you haven't seen him because you haven't been here when he was around. Anyway, he's here now and so are you." She tilts her head as she looks over her cup. "Is there something I should know? Did something happen between the two of you?"

[83]

"No. Nothing you need to be concerned about or anything. I think I have my answer."

"Answer?"

"Yeah. About my next move."

"Your next move? Are you moving? What are you talking about?"

I walk over to her and kiss her cheek.

"Thank you for your help." I turn to rush to the door. "No, I'm not moving out, but this makes things so much easier."

"What things?"

I don't acknowledge anything further. For the first time in a long time, I have a clear, defined, decision that I am sure of. Everything in my life recently has been a jumble of unknowns that cause me to be more confused than anything else. I'm practically floating as I leave the solarium to meet my first of three patients I'm seeing today. It's going to be odd not coming here, but it's for the best. I realize now being here at HFH was just a steppingstone. I have a feeling I need to make this next move in order to move in the right direction. I'm tired of the unsure version of myself.

Who knows, maybe just maybe this will lead me to the answers I've been searching for. At minimum, I'll have to spend less time in the presence of Daire Deville. That's a win in all categories.

# CHAPTER 11
## *JAXSON*

My office has been newly decorated. It reflects the new me. The one I'm trying to project. I've been asked numerous times when I'm going to focus on something productive. HFH was supposed to be the thing I needed to ground me. It was. For a time.

Things happened and I veered left for a while. Drinking, sex, and gambling became my fixations. They were the things that got me through my day to day.

*Bang up job those things did.*

I was getting nowhere fast. Seeing Brooklynn, the one who lit up my night, was the shock to my system to give me a new guide. The fresh needle on the new record. The new shine on a leather seat. No, I wasn't ready to get back behind the wheel yet. What I was ready for surprised the hell out of Hope. I was ready to take back the reigns of my co-chair seat. Hence the makeover.

A faux rock design of black and white stones served as the background to the mahogany wood bookshelves of one wall. The wood is the same tone in the ceiling, the end tables, and my desk. I purchased a new leather black and light gray couch with large back pillows. It butts up against the bottom of the bookshelf. A table, large ottoman, and two large chairs make up the sitting area. The gray and black theme is in each of the pieces. The two chairs'

backs rest up against my desk. The large executive chair is comfortable and sturdy.

I lean back in it as I review notes from an upcoming project while finalizing the numbers for our anniversary event. I look over at my black and white framed photos of Chance Devereaux Donavan, Zander Donavan, and one of me. The three photos are on the wall of champions. When I was in the hospital in Los Angeles, Graham and GiGi set it up so the two stopped by my recovery room to talk to me. While they were there, they signed some things. It was one of the best days of my life. At a time when I didn't know if I'd ever get behind the wheel again, it was a great experience. I'll cherish those items for the rest of my life.

The gray wall where those photos hang is mocking me right now. I'm frustrated because I'm biding my time. I'm waiting to hear back on some details of a project Graham, and I have in the works. I don't do well with waiting. Graham went to speak to one of our biggest sponsors. Monty, Anderson Montgomery, prefers to speak directly to me. I've been unavailable since I'm in rehabilitation mode.

It's been a time of me in a state of avoidance. I've been avoiding things that cause me stress. If I'm stressed, I drink. When I drink, I do dumb ass shit. I figure de-stress and I don't drink in excess. Don't overdo the drink and don't end up with my ass literally out shocking my mother's closest friend into an almost heart attack.

Fucking true story. How the hell they caught video of it isn't something I want to dwell on. I don't know if I'm forgiven for that one or my most recent idiotic antic.

I still haven't spoken to my mother. I've been working the phone tag angle by purposely calling or texting her when I know she's busy with all the things she does for JDJ Incorporated. I run Jaxson Daire Jr. Inc. and HDH from this office. My mother oversees the fan club, event planning, and charity auctions that happen under that umbrella. I had to do something to keep that woman busy and away from the racetrack. She worries, which is understandable. I haven't had the best track record.

Jeanine Shaw and Hope work closely on the charity aspect. Hope stepped up while I was on … hiatus. Since I'm back, she's slowly stepping back to focus on things here.

I need a distraction. As if on cue, the door to my office swings open. Hope stands at the door in a red pants suit. She stops short to take in my office before frantically shaking her head and her hands. She blows a stray bunch of hair out of her face as she holds the door open.

"What did you do?"

"I'm thinking you're going to need to narrow that question down for me."

I sit forward in my chair then point to the open doorway with my stylus. She rolls her eyes as she allows the door to close. Striding towards me, she points her finger in my direction.

"Oh, I'm not in the mood for your charm or any of those cute quips you come up with when you're trying to be funny."

She's in a mood.

"It's a gift. I don't even have to try anymore. They just come to me."

Hope stands with her arms folded, glaring at me.

"How long have you been back? Two, three weeks maybe. My goodness. I thought, 'this seems okay'. He's back to work. He's on the right track. He's been warned about the right people. The man is even going to all the meetings and therapies. I should've known better. What the hell is wrong with me?"

I literally have six different responses to that question. She must see into my soul or something. At that very moment, she slams her hand down on my desk.

I clear my throat.

"Hope, while I can appreciate your need to rail at me while you're in this current state of anger, I can't say that I like being accused of whatever you think I've done. What grievance am I charged with today?"

Hearing how calm I am speaking to her takes some of the wind out of her sails. She's used to me giving as much as I'm given.

Her eyes widening is an added bonus. She walks to stand between the two chairs so she can get a closer look at me.

"Are you feeling all right? Normally, you yell back at me if I come in hot the way I just did."

"I'm not feelin' the whole loud convo moment. Plus, you looked like you had some things to get off your chest. Feel better?"

Standing, I move to the bookshelf in the corner and pull one of the shelves to reveal the hidden compartment that houses a refrigerator. From the fridge, I snag one of the bottles of water from the door and pull one of the *bai* drinks from the lower shelf. Handing the *bai* drink to Hope, I move to the sitting area and take a seat on the couch. She sits on the ottoman.

"Yes. I do. I still want to know what happened, but I feel a hell of a lot better. I guess therapy is doing good things for you."

"It is. This time. What happened and why do you think I'm the reason for it?"

"Dr. Emory left. She said something about returning to her clinic and it was time."

I settle back in my seat with one calf resting on my other knee. I'm wondering what the issue is. I'm sure Brooklynn was a damn good doctor and was wonderful with the patients, but it sounds like it was time for her to go back to her paying job. I hadn't noticed she wasn't around because I keep running into her around town. I've seen her about as often as I would've had she been in the building.

"I must be missing what the problem is. Why does her leaving make it seem as if your world imploded? Wasn't she a volunteer?"

Hope's face shifts to some weird expression I don't recognize. This one is new for me. I don't know how to interpret it.

"She was."

"Do we not have the staff to cover the time she met with patients?"

"We do."

"Wasn't she working with an assistant who was covering for her while she was out?"

"How did you know …?"

"I might've been running around half-cocked for a minute, but my brain isn't so baked I forgot how to read past paperwork and files. I've been spending a lot of time going over the financial reports. Before you go diving off into some fit of rage, I was checking to see if we needed anymore funds allocated to the budget. Despite my being away from the helm of JDJ, we still had a good year. The result was we had some extra money. I wanted to see if HFH needed it first before I split it the way I normally do."

I'm off the couch and moving to return to my desk chair when she responds.

"Wow. Okay. You really seem fine with all of this."

That has me stopping in my tracks and turning to face her.

"What do you mean?"

The look on her face says she's said something she didn't mean to say. Guilt is written all over it.

"Shit! I wasn't supposed to let you know I knew."

"Knew what, Hope?"

"About your history with Brooklynn Emory."

"Huh?" I tap my empty water bottle against the desk as I slide my tongue along the inside of my cheek. "Which one broke?"

She's confused for a minute before she catches my meaning.

"Your mother."

"Of course, she did. Doesn't matter. Things change. I thought I'd pursue her but decided against it. If she wanted a relationship … she's gone. Again. It's fine."

"Right. Are you still wearing the ring?"

My head snaps up. Hope begins to move towards the door. I move around the chair.

"My mother couldn't have told you about that since she doesn't know anything about it. How do you know about the ring, Hope?"

She opens the door and on the other side of it is Graham. Hope looks from me to Graham then back again. I have to bite my tongue because I know exactly how she knows about the ring. If I know Graham, it didn't take much for him to tell her.

"I'll see you later. Good luck," she tells Graham as she slips by him.

"What was that about?" he asks.

I see he's out of his business attire and in jeans today. I'd love nothing more than to ream him a new asshole right about now but GiGi's with him. The beautiful Samoan woman is wearing a red and yellow printed dress with one of those fabric things thrown over her shoulders. Her dark hair is up in one of those buns women master in their youth.  She's rocking heels that match the colors. When she looks at me, her expressive, brown eyes are full of joy. By the look of her, she's ready to celebrate.

"Nothing. I'll deal with it later. I take it the meeting went well."

"Better than we could've imagined.  We're going out to dinner to celebrate," Graham informs me.

"We are?" I ask.

"Yes, Kennedy already made the reservations. We're heading to *The Olde Pink House*. Gemma is really looking forward to it."

Gemma, GiGi, shoots Graham a death glare.

"Mr. Shaw, may I put in the request now that I never have to travel alone with this man again?"

"That's not a feasible request to make. Besides, it's not my fault you walked in on me at that moment."

"I knocked. I even called out your name. How was I supposed to know you would be changing?"

"Me telling you I'm going to use the room to change clothes wasn't warning enough?"

I laugh because one thing I learned the hard way about Graham Tucker is he goes commando. Every. Day. Of. His. Life. Since the moment he discovered "free balling", he took it and ran with it. He told all our friends he saves a fortune not having to buy boxers. GiGi's glare cuts to me before returning her hateful stare to him.

"Let me hit send on this email and we can head out."

GiGi mutters something that makes Graham smirk. I lock up my laptop then grab my jacket off the coat rack. The other two follow behind me.

"You could've covered yourself when you saw I was in the room," GiGi mumbles.

"You could've turned away instead of fixating those brown eyes on a certain appendage."

I snort as we make our way to Graham's car. It doesn't take us long to get to the restaurant. As soon as we arrive, I feel a familiar tingle as the hairs on my arm stand up.

"Fuck me," I mumble.

Graham turns to look at me. Confusion is written all over his face.

"What?"

I turn and lock gazes with stormy, gray eyes. Reading her lips, I see she has the same reaction to me as I do to knowing she's here.

This evening just took a definite turn. Unexpected is not enough of a word to describe it.

# CHAPTER 12
## *BROOKLYNN*

*Savannah, GA*                                      *April 24* - Monday evening

Excitement pulses through my veins as I enjoy a drink called "Water of Life" with my friends. We decided to have dinner together to celebrate me returning to my actual job and Journee taking a day off. Our goal tonight is to get her as drunk as possible. She needs to be so drunk she won't change her mind and go in to work tomorrow. Noelle is also saying this is her late birthday present to herself. She's been wanting to go out with girlfriends for quite some time now.

Noelle wanted to go somewhere that didn't serve food she could create in her kitchen. *The Olde Pink House* has been on her list of places to come with her friends for a while now. Mine too. The dining room here is elegant. The rich colors of the walls, chandeliers, and drapery look as if they were snatched out of the past. The white tablecloths make me nervous. I worry every time I lift my glass. I just know I'm going to spill something.

My hand begins to tremble as that damn feeling rushes over me again.

"Do you know what you want?" Noelle asks as she continues to peruse the menu.

# Plunge

My eyes are on everything but the menu. He's in the building. I know it. He's within touching distance of me. It's just a matter of where. Why do I keep seeing him everywhere? I decided to go for a walk, decided to stop in a local shop, flippin' heated skin happens. Turn around and there he is with some woman. He looks up, like he knows I'm there too, and tosses a wave my way. A wave. I head over to Tybee Island to clear my head for a day. I'm walking along the beach and who do I see well before I feel his presence.

*I'm enjoying the feel of the wind blowing around me. My hair is loose and catching every wind. It reminds me of the time I was here before. I love the peace and calm of the salty air that comes with standing on the beach. I recall standing here before, listening to the sounds of the birds as they enjoyed the morning sky as much as I did. Then, the darkhaired girl I wasn't alone. She had the love of a boy. A boy who had big dreams.*

*Those dreams she once supported, even pushed him to pursue them. He nuzzled her neck and whispered words of love and affection.*

*I wiped away a stray tear as I thought back to that time. When I looked down beach, there he was. He must not have noticed I was on the beach yet. I thought of rushing off, back towards my car. The pearl-gray Hyundai Elantra doesn't see the open road often. I felt like taking a drive. I'm not ready to go back to my life.*

*I square my shoulders and meet my fate. The instant I decide, he sees me.*

The time on the beach was mostly pleasant. It was until I insulted him. Again. I think the most infuriating part is it doesn't seem to faze him. I'm used to the man who fired back at me. No verbal warning shot or anything. Just guns blazing. It hurts like hell, but you know he responded. There's a deadly reaction. This version of him freaks me out. He doesn't act as if it bothers him at all. Some part of me must take it as a challenge.

My eyes meet his and I feel it. I'm locked and loaded. I'm ready for whatever he has for me. I watch as his mouth forms the same word mine does as his green eyes darken. The host nods then leads them into the dining room. They are walked right by our table. He nods to us then keeps walking.

My entire body deflates.

"I'll catch up," I hear a familiar voice state.

"I'm not waiting for him. We're ordering whether or not he's at the table," the woman with them tells Daire.

If he responds, I can't hear it because Graham "Tuck" Tucker is greeting me. He squats down between my chair and Noelle's, so he's eye-level with me.

"Hey Tuck, how're you doing?"

I lean into him to give him a hug. He is nervous but happy to see me. I can feel it coming off him in waves.

"I can't believe it's you. When Daire said you were working at Hope House, I was shocked. I had no clue you were even in town. How long have you been here?"

I try to keep my eyes on Tuck's handsome face. Epic Fail. My focus keeps shifting to where the waiter is taking Daire and the woman. It isn't until Tuck asks me his last question that I return my eyes to his hazel browns. Graham's eyes are Noelle before he looks back at me.

"I'm surprised you're here. I thought you were a lifer."

"Things changed. I work with Daire. I have been for a while now." His expression changes and I wonder what's wrong. "I heard …"

He's quiet for so long that I wonder what cause him to stop speaking. When I focus on his face, I see he's looking at Noelle again. they are having some silent conversation I've missed. When I look at Journee, she's too busy asking the waiter about an item on the menu to notice what's happening.

"Did you want to sit in my seat? It looks like you two have more to say to each other."

[94]

Both laugh but it's off. Tuck leans his broad frame over to give me another hug.

"I should get back to my group. It was nice to see you again, Blaze."

I close my eyes because I know I'm going to field questions. Journee is practically salivating as she waits for Tuck to leave.

"Oh Tuck, what were you going to say?" he gives me a questioning look. His eyes flick to my right to Noelle again before he responds. "I was just going to say I heard something about you leaving. Now I know where that was." He pulls his phone out of his pocket then makes a show of pointing to it. "Gotta take this. It's probably Daire. Nice to see you."

He turns and I notice Daire is standing in the doorway signing autographs for two or three people. Tuck joins him, returning his phone to his pocket.

"That was weird. I wonder what that was about," I state as I look at Noelle.

She acts as if she didn't hear what I said. Before I can call her on it, Journee is calling my name. The other name.

"Blaze? That's new. Where did that one come from and how do you know the chocolate god?" she asks.

She waggles her eyebrows. The lights catch on some of the glitter powder makeup she put on for tonight.

"It's a nickname. My high school friends gave it to me. That's where I know *Tuck* from."

"It sounds like that name has more of a story behind it."

I watch Daire finish signing. He looks my way and Tuck looks too. Tuck blocks my view as he falls in line behind his friend. Tuck waves as he follows Daire to their table.

"I'm going over there," I announce.

"Why would you go over there? What's the point? Besides, it's girls' night."

Journee and I share a look. Noelle is acting weird. I feel like I'm missing something and I'm guessing Journee is wondering what the hell is going on given her look.

"Are you okay?" Journee asks. "I've never seen you initiate contact before."

Noelle and I look down at her hand, noticing she's holding my wrist. I hadn't even realized that was happening.

"Nothing. Nothing is wrong with me. I'm fine. I just don't think you need to open that can of worms. You've said it yourself. They were your friends from high school. I think we all know a lot can happen when a lot of time has passed."

I watch Noelle and notice she's taking little breaths in between her statements. Whatever it is has her working overtime to calm herself. The waitstaff brings food to the table. When a plate is placed in front of me, Journee smiles.

"I didn't realize I said what I wanted out loud."

"You did. Now, I want to eat so it can soak up some of the liquor I plan on consuming tonight."

We all laugh as we dig into our respective plates.

I don't think about the Noelle/Tuck situation until I'm walking back out to our porch to grab the box left on our doorstep. The return address is my mother's. I'd forgotten I was supposed to go over to her place that day.

After I check on Journee, making sure she has everything to tend to her hangover needs, I make my way back down to the living room. When I open the box, a letter sits on top of the items I asked my mother to put inside.

*[handwritten letter, partially legible]*

> My Darling Girl
>    I don't know what happened to you stopping by the house the other day I figured you weren't able to follow through with your plan I can't say that I understand it or fully comprehend what's going on with you Still I try to be what you need me to be during this time Here are the items you asked me to gather up for you
>    Whenever you are ready feel free to reach out to me I know I wasn't there for you when you were younger I'm trying to make up for that with ___ you're not ready for that conversation
>
>    I look forward to the day when you are I'd like to say congratulations on returning to your company My hope is this is leading you back to the life you had before
>    Good luck Bon Chance!
>
>                 Love you dearly
>                 Your mother ___

Very little about my mother's letter made sense to me. yes, I'd forgotten to stop by her house, but there wasn't any major thing behind it. It simply slipped my mind. Something is going on. I know it. My mother knows it and I'm thinking Noelle does too. Whatever it is has to be big if they are working this hard not to slip up.

I feel like it has something to do with my memory and that missing piece. The closer I get to piecing it all together, the more I feel like everyone I know is in on keeping this from me.

The guilt I have from carrying my own secret around tries to rise to the service. I beat it back with the key I've been holding onto this whole time. It's the key I will guard with my life.

That thought makes me wonder if that's what Noelle and my mother are doing with theirs. I take that line of thinking to bed with me and chew on it until I finally drift off into a fitful sleep. My dreams shift between trying to puzzle out what's going on in my life and trying to understand what's happening with Daire. Neither lead me to any real rest.

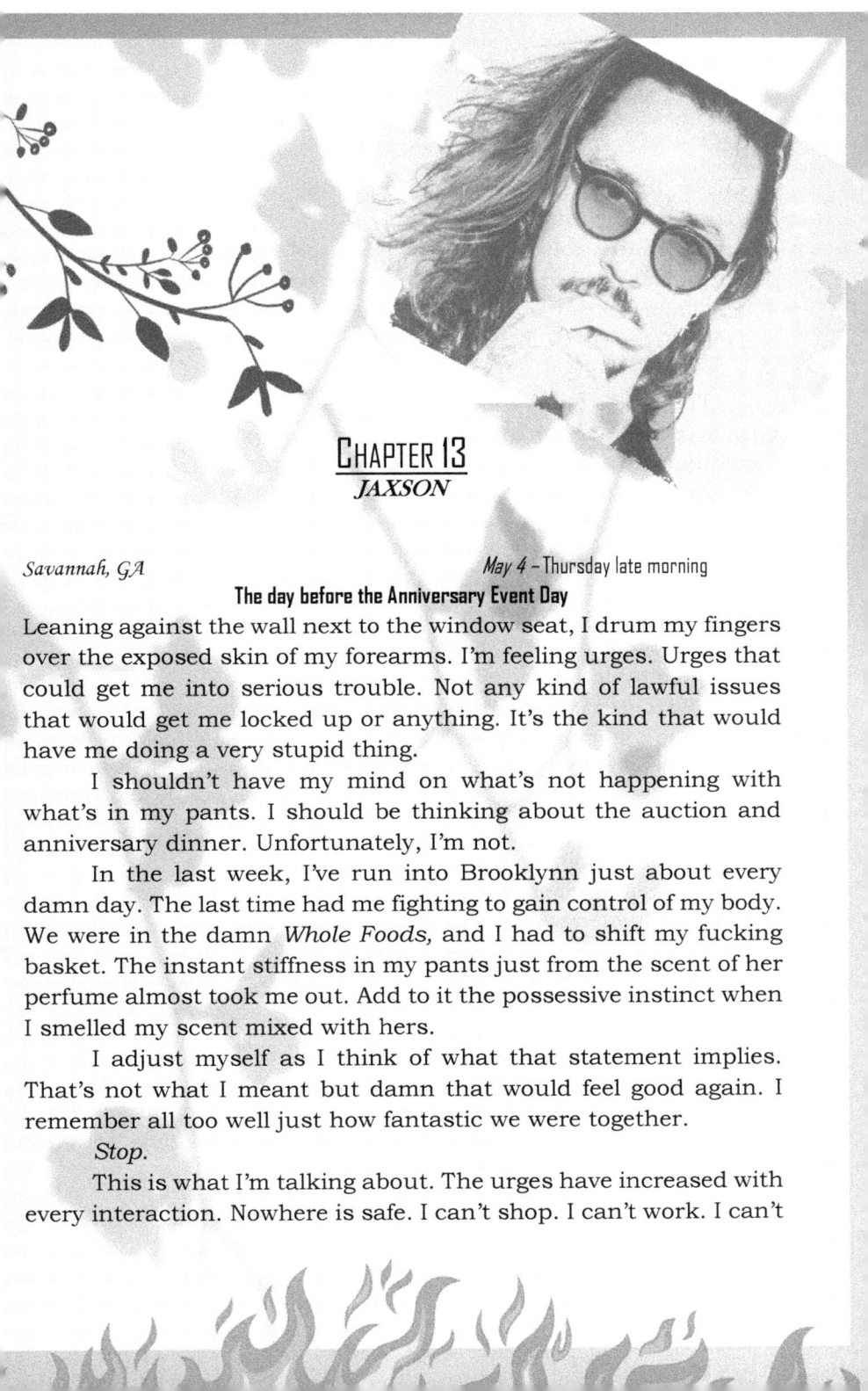

# CHAPTER 13
## *JAXSON*

### The day before the Anniversary Event Day

Leaning against the wall next to the window seat, I drum my fingers over the exposed skin of my forearms. I'm feeling urges. Urges that could get me into serious trouble. Not any kind of lawful issues that would get me locked up or anything. It's the kind that would have me doing a very stupid thing.

I shouldn't have my mind on what's not happening with what's in my pants. I should be thinking about the auction and anniversary dinner. Unfortunately, I'm not.

In the last week, I've run into Brooklynn just about every damn day. The last time had me fighting to gain control of my body. We were in the damn *Whole Foods,* and I had to shift my fucking basket. The instant stiffness in my pants just from the scent of her perfume almost took me out. Add to it the possessive instinct when I smelled my scent mixed with hers.

I adjust myself as I think of what that statement implies. That's not what I meant but damn that would feel good again. I remember all too well just how fantastic we were together.

*Stop.*

This is what I'm talking about. The urges have increased with every interaction. Nowhere is safe. I can't shop. I can't work. I can't go out to dinner without having some type of contact. Not the type my body is screaming for.

My mind wanders and I see the two of us together. Our bodies giving in to the need that is so obvious when we are in the same space. I ache to feel and taste her. I try to hold on to the anger that comes when I think of the reason we aren't together. It's all her. She made a choice. Still, her breasts fit right in my hands.

The anger fades quickly. The main reason is I'm horny. It's been weeks since I had any of my female visitors. I tried to set something up, but it didn't work out. The instant she had me in her mouth and I felt the slickness of her tongue, I slipped into thoughts of Blaze. Turns out women don't like you referring to other women when that have their lips wrapped around you.

The instant her name slipped out of mouth, I got out of the danger zone. It's come down to self-care. That's why I'm having problems being near the woman. She's the one starring in all my thoughts and dreams.

*She walks into the room at the back of the garage. I look up at her and something's different about the way she's looking at me. Her gray eyes flare as she stares at me. I've just come from the main house. I'd been out here working all day and needed a shower. This is the time she usually stops by to see me, so I didn't want to be smelly and dirty when she came by.*

*Problem was, I left my clothes out here. My parents don't like any of out "gang related" t-shirts, so I keep them out here. No one but me every really spends any time in here so they're safe.*

*She's early. All I've had a chance to put on are a pair of jeans. Blaze steps forward, directly into my personal space. Her hands are on me in the next breath. I've been encouraging her to get acquainted with my body because it's as much mine as it is hers. All we've done up to now is some heavy petting. She's heard some horror stories from some of the girls she knows about their first time so she's worried.*

# Plunge

I've been able to get my hand down her pants and brought her to climax by playing with her clit. That was as close as we came until two days ago. She spread her legs for me. and I got my first taste of her. It wasn't enough. I shredded her cute, pink panties then drove my tongue deep. I've only been with two or three girls, but they showed me a thing or two about pleasuring a girl.

When Blaze screamed my name, I thought I was going to shoot my load in my pants. I couldn't do that. I made her climax again before I let her rest. She shocked the shit out of me by climbing onto my lap, unzipping my pants and sliding her wet slit over my length. I got so excited I instantly started to orgasm.

I was so lost in the thought of that moment I didn't notice Blaze had dropped to her knees in front of me. She didn't even bother with the button or zipper of my jeans. She pulled my pants away from my skin, slid her hand inside, then held on as she tugged. Once she had the access she wanted, she ran her tongue over the tip.

Right there, against the door to the back room, I got my first blow job from her.

She had to have been given pointers or something because she did a damn good job. Her hands and mouth worked in tandem with each other. She bobbed off and on the length of my me. What her mouth couldn't hold, her hands worked. She even licked up the underside and played with my balls.

I was gifted a second time when I told her I was about to come. She strolled over to the bed and parted her legs. The sight of the little strip of hair between her legs had me squeezing the tip of my cock to keep from losing it.

"Be gentle. Remember."

The sweet reminder had me taking her swollen lips and kissing her deeply. I slid the head over her clit and slid down her until I reached her opening.

"So wet. All for me."

"Only for you."

*She unzipped her jacket as she kissed me. Seeing yet another part of her bared for my eyes only had me growling low in my throat as I kissed her again. I slowly made my way down her body. Kissing and sucking on her breasts before continuing down her body. I licked around her clit before flicking my tongue over it.*

*"Daire, I'm wet enough. I'm ready. I'm so fucking ready. Please."*

*I stood up immediately and did what she asked. Lining up, I slowly began to glide into her slick heat.*

*"Tight. Baby, you're so tight."*

*"Mmm, hmm."*

*A tear slipped from her eye, and I kissed it away. I stopped moving. Instead, I waited. she took a few deep breaths. When she realized I wasn't moving, she opened her eyes. Those stormy grays looked at me with so much heat I slowly moved my hips just to show her I could make that look shift.*

*She smiled then ran her nails up and down my back. I kissed her as she lifted her legs. I slipped in a little bit further and she moaned. It would take a little more push, pull, and squeeze before I bottomed out. When I did, we both moaned.*

*"Now, the real work begins."*

*She laughed for all of ten seconds then it turned into a deep, pleasurable moan.*

Her moans are one of the things I used to look forward to hearing. My weekly goal would be to find a new place and a new way to hear her moan.

"I think we need to talk," I hear her voice, but it takes me a second to realize it's her real voice. "Did you hear me?"

"I did."

When I don't say anything else, she looks annoyed.

"Are you going to continue to do this?"

I settle into the seat of the window with my arms still folded. I'm sitting because I'm trying to ensure she doesn't see how hard I am. I don't want her to get the wrong impression.

"You're going to have to clue me in to what you think I'm doing."

"Really?"

"Yes," I snort while spreading my legs slightly.

This isn't the most comfortable state to be in when have a conversation. Argument? Discussion? Whatever the hell this is.

"Look, I know this is an awkward situation to be in. We didn't expect to live in the same city again. At the same time, I don't think it's right to act as if you have the right to not speak or acknowledge my presence when we are in the same room."

Well, there goes my hard on. I'm fighting a different urge now. The audacity of this female. She begins to look down at the ground and not at me. That just won't do.

"Eyes up, Blaze." She immediately complies with the request. I can see she's irritated with herself for doing it. "This situation is what it is because of one person and one person alone."

"You're right. You. You are the reason that we are where we are. I thought we could have a civil conversation and act like adults."

"That's hilarious. Coming from the woman who walked in here going on about how I wouldn't speak to her. Did I hurt your feelings?"

"Oh no, you did that a long time ago. When you left that was the last time, I ever trusted you to do right by me and my feelings."

She drops her eyes again then moves towards the door as if she's going to leave. I want to scream but I don't. I do the opposite. With all the calm I can muster, I say one word.

"Interesting."

Her head snaps up as she puts her attention back on me. With her nose turned up in the air, she speaks one word.

"What?"

I smirk at the confusion, disgust, and annoyance she projects in one word.

"Your parting statement is telling me you can't trust me."

I clear my throat, fighting the laugh that wants to choose that moment to come out. Nothing about this is funny. This is the woman who has owned my heart despite ripping it out of my chest and showing it to me all those years ago.

"That's right. Is ... that amusing to you?"

Of course, she caught that. She has no problem reading that emotion but can't seem to see the pain I'm currently in and have been in since that day.

"Slightly. You seem to be under the impression that the hurt road belongs solely to you. You have identified it as your own and act as if you're the only one who has travelled it." Her expression is one I'm used to seeing. Many a woman have shown me a version of this appalled look, but I press on this time. "Yes. Shocking, right? A man telling a 'wronged' woman she's not the only one who was scared by a certain event. How dare he? Well, it's my name, sweetheart. It should be expected."

"You are the most arrogant, self-righteous ..."

Stepping into her personal space, I cover her mouth without covering it.

"Let me stop you there because I'm not finished. Plus, I figure you need to save up the insults, so you don't have to repeat yourself later." I'm close enough that I can feel her gasp on my hand. I continue. "You seem to remember our relationship ending with you being left behind. Let's paint the full picture. Me, sitting with you, telling you how I felt about you, letting you know the first piece of the puzzle of my lifelong dream has been dropped into my lap. In response, you rain on my parade. You tell me you couldn't take a risk with me. I am then told the life I dreamed of having wasn't one I could share with the one person who meant ... *everything* to me."

She looks up at me upon hearing the crack in my voice. Tears fill her eyes and I have to look away. Those eyes have haunted me long enough.

"Jaxson ..."

"You were the only one I told what I wanted to do with my life. You were the one who told me that it was possible to even achieve it. *You* ... you were the one who encouraged me to go for it. When I had it within my grasp, you told me it wasn't your life, and I would have to go it alone." Out of my periphery, I see a tear run down her cheek. I want to tell her I've shed plenty of my own. I don't. I blink, step towards the door then lean towards her. In a whispered voice, I say, "You sure you're the one who should have the trust issues?"

I don't wait for her to respond. Opening my office door, I walk out of it, leaving her with those parting words. As I walk down the hall to the back door, I begin to mutter.

"Now call me whatever the fuck you want to because I'm not going to be around to hear it."

When the door slams shut behind me, I have every intention of that being exactly what I do. I'm taking this as a sign of me putting all that shit in the past and leaving it there.

Intentions don't always lead us where we want, but fuck all if we don't try to still get there.

# CHAPTER 14
## *BROOKLYNN*

*Savannah, GA*                                   *May 4* – Thursday afternoon
### The day before the Anniversary Event Day

I'm growing increasingly irritated with every minute that passes. It's starting to show in my actions. Every garment of clothing on the rack is yanked with a little more force than the previous one. When I look up, I notice the crease in the salesclerk's forehead as she watches me. As soon as she sees that I'm aware of her observing me melt down, one of her eyebrows raise. The question is clear. She wants to know if I'm done with my little tantrum. Offering her an apologetic smile, I lift one of the shirts from the rack then move on to one closer to where Journee is standing.

She shifts from side to side as she studies an orange, floral dress. Journee looks up from the dress to my reflection behind her.

"You're quiet and no longer snatching things. Does that mean you're ready to talk or is the woman behind the counter going to have to say words to you about the handling of the clothes?"

I hand her a red, short-sleeved chiffon that matches perfectly with the details in the orange dress. She immediately perks up as she pulls it off the hanger to add to her chosen purchases.

"I'm fine. There's nothing wrong with me."

"Really? Sounds good. Glad to hear it. I mean, I'd be irritated to discover the man I've secretly compared others to, wondered how he was doing, and even quietly pined after was living a happy life without me." She pauses then adds another item to her "to purchase" pile. "I'd want answers and demand explanations. Why is she worthy of the life the two of you were supposed to lead?"

I'm nodding my head as she speaks a lot of the things I've wondered about over the last week or two. He and Hope seem like they would be a happy couple. Journee has determined they are together from what she's claimed she's seen. I think she's enjoying the thought of being seen as a spy. I'm thinking they are close friends. Might have the whole FWB (friends with benefits) thing going.

I just can't believe I've worked with the Hope Foundation for as long as I have and never knew Hope was connected to the Shaw family. I've always known her as Hope Alexander so it's an easy miss. Plus, it's not like I had other things to think about or anything. I've been doing my own form of therapy.

It's why I was bothered by him not speaking to me. He shouldn't give me the cold shoulder if he's found what he needed in his better half. When he went off on me, I found I was even more confused. I'd gone in there with the intention of closing out one crazy aspect of my life, not making it that much crazier.

Regardless, I have no right to wonder any of those things. We went our separate ways. The main reason we did so was because he made the choice to leave. I'm not bitter about that. Why would I be?

"Like I said, 'I'm fine'."

"Great. That's great to hear. I'm so glad to hear that." She turns to face me then smiles. Journee walks around to stand in front of me. "Help me out here, honey. What exactly happened between the two of you? What I know, I've assumed and pieced together from bits of information. It isn't because you clued me in on anything."

"Okay. You pay for your stuff, and I'll stop by the store. We'll meet back home in half an hour, and I'll share. I don't want to bare my soul while doing retail therapy."

She nods her head then grabs her pile. I leave her in the store then head out to complete my tasks. I'm leaving the bakery when I feel that familiar feeling. I search the area and see him hugging the woman I saw him at the restaurant with last week. He looks up then turns like he's looking for something. I'm so glad he doesn't see me. After this morning, I can do without running into him for a while.

When I see him head in a different direction than the way I'm heading, I send up a prayer of thanks. I feel like a spy as I duck behind things trying to make sure I'm free and clear of seeing him. I don't claim success on this mission until I'm safely inside my home.

I'm glad Journee isn't there when I arrive. It gives me the time I need to get settled and calm myself. By the time she does get home, I've had time to get showered and changed into my comfy, *Minnie Mouse* pajamas. When she sees what I'm wearing, she drops her bags at the door and darts upstairs.

An hour after our agreement to come home to talk, Journee and I are sitting down on our favorite couch facing each other. We're both comfortable and surrounded by snacks.

"All right. Tell me about you and Mr. Shaw. I don't mind dirty details. If you have some, do share."

We tap spoons and dig into our ice cream of choice.

"First off, Mr. Shaw is and always will be Daire to me. Jaxson Daire Shaw has never met a dare that he didn't accept. It's one of the things I have forever dislike about him. It's the reason we met. I should probably be grateful for the daring side of him."

Handing me a glass of wine, Journee grabs a pillow from the floor.

"Okay. I'm going to need a little bit more of an explanation of the whole dare thing being the reason you two met."

*Plunge*

"Right. Sometimes I forget you haven't always been around. It feels like you've been here the entire time. It's weird knowing we've only known each other a year. I had this whole other life ... Daire and I went to high school together." I huff out a breath before continuing the story. "The story goes, he had been interested in me for a few months but hadn't gotten up the courage to let me know. He says, he used this situation to his advantage. Tuck and Rye tell it a little different. They say they knew he was into me and gave him the nudge he needed by offering up the dare. Evidently, his older brother let it slip to his friends that he hated being dared to do anything. He felt this weird obligation to complete the task. Not that it was put that way when it was shared with me, but whatever. They dared him to introduce himself to me. That same day, he did. Two days later we went on an official date. That was it. We were inseparable afterwards, until we weren't."

I scoop out some of the ice cream, rocky road, my favorite, then eat it and another spoonful. Journee eats and drink. Patiently and silently waiting for me to continue my story. When I don't, she gently prompts me. first with her tickling me under my thigh then her words.

"Enough with the suspense building. You explained the dare thing and told me how you met. You've yet to tell me what happened to end things. Spill. I can tell you want to tell me."

Taking a large sip of liquid courage, I open myself up to the memory of that day.

"Right. It started off as the best day. It was beautiful. I was excited about an annual event. I kept going on about it being one of the many firsts I was looking forward to having." My hand itches to move to the belly from my memory. It was huge because I only had weeks to go. "We were all excited because it was the first time in a long while that everyone from the Magnificent Seven Crew was going to be together. Someone was either out of town or grounded.

We were all going, and we did. It was one of our last full group photos. It was the perfect day until it wasn't."

Tears begin to form in my eyes as I recall the events that followed.

"Oh Sweetie, I'm sorry. I didn't know it would make you cry."

I shake my head. For what reason, I don't know. I'm sitting there with my friend. I'm not back in that moment with the big belly. It's not happening but my heart feels like it is.

"It's weird. When I told my therapist the story, I didn't react this way. With you, I'm a big ole baby."

"Well then, let me hold the baby."

She holds out her arms and I snorfle (snort and sniffle) before snuggling into the warmth of her hug.

"That day quickly shifted. Daire gets a phone call that takes him from the fun. That darkens the light of the day. It's like he's the thread that gets pulled to ruin the sweater. The group slowly goes their separate ways. I was left with my best friends at the time. Cynt, Cynthia Matthews, Nee, Sabrina Renee, and Nee's guy who also happened to be Daire's best friend, Ryder Dean. They went with me to the hospital. All remained with me after as well."

"It sounds like you had a good group with you. The way you say their names, it's full of love."

"They were the best. I loved being with them. They were my safe place. Life at home with … it was different. Anyway. I got really bad news at the worst time in my life. It was a very lonely time for me. By the time Daire made it to the hospital I wasn't receptive to his news. What started out as me sharing a piece of the hell I'd gone through while he was gone became so much larger."

Journee shifts so she can see my face.

"What happened? What did you do?"

I can't look at her. I've been carrying this around with me for years and not many know what I'm about to share with her.

"I gave him what he wanted. By not telling him everything, he was able to do exactly what he needed to do."

[110]

"What?"

"He wanted to go off and be the famous race car driver like his idol Chance Devereaux."

"There was more that happened to you that day. Things you didn't tell him because you knew he wouldn't go."

"Oh, he was going regardless. Nothing I said would've changed that."

Journee shifts again so she can stand. She grabs her ice cream then takes it to the kitchen. When she returns, she has her thinking face on.

"How do you know he wouldn't have changed his course of action if you never gave him the option or all the information?"

"Believe me, I know. His choice was made well before that moment. That was something he'd been dreaming of for years. It was … his way out."

My voice is small by the end. That time was so much more. I have a feeling Journee knows it. Just like I knew it then.

"Have you talk to him about any of this? BTW, I was totally wrong on the Hope front. I have a feeling this isn't over between you and Mr. Shaw."

"You'd be wrong there. He's super pissed at me right now. As much as I love you, I don't think any of your enthusiasm is going to change that."

"Why does it seem like there is more to the story that I don't know?"

"That's because there is. I might've gone to his office today to confront him only to accuse him of leaving me. To which, he responded by clearly advising me that I'm to blame for our breakup. That it rests solely on my shoulders. I feel like that's being a little excessive."

Journee makes a face that says she agrees with his assessment of the situation.

"Hey! You're supposed to be my friend."

"I am. I'm one of your biggest fans. Since I am your friend, I'm more than willing to point out when you're wrong."

Grabbing my chest, I fall back into the couch.

"You're kidding me, right?"

She shakes her head back and forth.

"Let me ask you a question. You have to answer honestly."

I nod my head.

"Okay. What's the question?"

"If you had the chance to do it over again, would you do the same thing? Would you make the exact same choices you made before?"

Well, that just takes the cake. Why'd she have to put it that way? That will go down in my history book as one of my greatest regrets.

Journee leans to the side to look at me.

"You have your answer. I can see you do. If that is the case, why are you holding on to this stubborn stance of a choice you no longer support?"

"I … I don't know." I stab my spoon into my ice cream. "How did you do that? Are all thirty-year-olds this smart and wise? If so, I want to be thirty."

"Nope. I'm a special type of thirty. They don't make them like me anymore." I toss a pillow at her as she sits down with her popcorn. "BTW, you need to talk to him. When you do, you need to apologize. Isn't that what you will want from him if the shoe was on the other foot?"

Sometimes I really don't like having friends who are much smarter and kinder than I am.

*She's right.*

Yes, I know she's right. Doesn't mean I have to like it. We settle in for the night and I mentally make a list of ways I can try to talk to Daire tomorrow at the Hope House anniversary event. At the back of my mind, I know there's another piece of our story I didn't share. It's a critical piece.

# Plunge

That night, I sleep without nightmares or thoughts of a bunch of puzzle pieces chasing me.

# CHAPTER 15
## *JAXSON*

### The morning of the Anniversary Event

*Tap tap tap. Tap tap tap.*

*Knock knock knock knock knock knock knock.*

The rhythmic knock isn't the one I expect. That knock belongs to one person and one person only. It can't be him because he told me his ass was out of the country for the next week. Him and his main squeeze are supposed to be off enjoying an island or some shit. Not that I could imagine his big ass on a beach.

Snatching the door open, I see I was right about the owner of the knock. The big bear of a man has half a foot on my six-foot four height. He's so tall, Graham's five ten height is well hidden. It isn't until I pull the larger man into a huge hug that I see my other friend.

"Look who I found wandering around Savannah trying to find something to do with himself," Graham says as I hug my other friend.

It's been a while since we've all been in the same room. I'd forgotten just how tall this asshole was.

"It's about time you brought around someone I actually wanted to see."

Graham's face falls as Trent, Ryder's half-brother, enters. Both men file in as soon as I step back. When I turn to grab my drink, I see it's been commandeered by yet another friend. He pulls the glass back from his lips then glares at it as if it offended him. He was obviously expecting something other than the sweet tea I was drinking.

"Are you trying to kill me? What the hell is in that drink? Pure sugar cane? My god, I think I lost a tooth and formed a cavity with one swig of that shit."

"Nobody told your pretty-boy self to put your lips on my glass. Hell, I should be the one worried about illnesses. Who the hell knows where your lips have been, Rye."

"Only fucking place they will forever be." Ryder straightens to his full height before looking back at me. "Between the finest legs ever created and don't you forget it."

"I can't even argue with you on that." I have to ignore the twinge of irritation I feel not being able to reply how I once would. It's a painful reminder of the conversation I had with Brooklynn yesterday. "Not that I'm not happy to see both of you, but what brings you to Savannah?"

"One, we were invited. Two, I didn't realize we had to have a reason to visit a friend. Three, we came down to celebrate this great thing old Daire Bear did."

Graham laughs and I join him. I'd forgotten all about that name. It's been a very long time since I've heard it.

"That's great! where are you staying?"

Trent and Ryder both look at each other then look at me. at almost the exact same time they both say ...

"With you."

"At your place."

I look at Graham who shrugs his shoulders. The brothers laugh then slap my shoulder.

"We're kidding. we're staying at the hotel where the whole shindig is happening."

"Convenient," I tell them.

"It makes it easier for Trent to get some ass and move on."

Again, I laugh, but this time I don't really feel it, given the current state of my affairs, I might be in the same boat as Trent. I don't know why I'm saying might when there is no way Brooklynn and I could have a future.

I shake myself trying to get rid of thoughts about Brooklyn. I have a great event happening tonight and that is going to get most of my attention. My friends from Hampton are going to get the other part.

"We have a couple hours to kill, what do you guys want to do?"

Just as I'm asking that question, there's a knock at my door. I don't get a chance to answer the knock before the door is being opened by Ryder."

Hugs abound and go around for a few minutes. When they break apart, everyone is all smiles. It's a great feeling.

"Looks like the Midol crew is back together."

Each of us groans. We've hated that old joke since our parents overused it in our teens.

"Same old Hope. Still corny and dorky as ever," Ryder says.

We all laugh. Hope doesn't, which makes us laugh that much harder.

"Very funny. I just came by to make sure you were ready to give your speech tonight, Jackson."

"Yes, I'm ready. Unless you wanna do it?"

She laughs, one that is without humor. I know she hates speaking in front of people. It's one of the reasons I volunteered to do it.

"Nopers. That's all you."

She leans in then kisses my cheek.

"See you in a few hours. I'm going to head out early. I'm going to hang out with these two idiots before the event."

"Are you trying to woo them into living in Savannah?"

"I'm already sold. Nee and I have a place here. We've been in Hampton for a couple weeks in the summer to help out with some projects her father wanted to complete. We're trying to ..."

"Convince me to move here. Runt misses his big bro. Not that he'd ever admit it," Trent finishes for Ryder.

I try to ignore the pang of hurt hearing that causes me. I'm not fast enough. Turning, I pretend to look for something to mask the burn I feel as my eyes water.

Graham, good friend that he is, claps his hands, drawing attention to him.

"Let's get out of here and start doing a 'hard sale' of the greatness of Savannah."

By the end of his spiel, I've regained control of myself. I'm able to follow them out without incident.

"Thanks, Man."

"Anytime, Bro. I've got your back."

We exit Hope House. Me in hopes of getting my mind off the past. My friends, in hopes of convincing another to join us in Savannah.

*Savannah, GA*                                    *May 5*- Friday evening

### The Anniversary Event

The guys and I have spent the day... afternoon visiting old haunts. We've gone to some of the touristy places as well as visited a couple shops Trent took interest in. I discovered Trent next things with bugs on them as well as items that have mythical creatures designed into them. The biggest 1 has to do with Dragons.

I'm left to my own thoughts and devices for a little too long. they went to go raid the bar and I've been left alone. My thoughts immediately go turn Brooklynn. Not today get to venture too far away from her. Lately she's been at the forefront, especially after yesterday's conversation. I speak to a couple people including Brooklynn's friend.

"Good evening, Mr. Shaw."

"Good evening, Nurse Forrester." Graham is suddenly back at my side. he hands me one of the glasses in his hand. "Enjoy the party."

The two acknowledge each other before he speaks to me. I notice that she's alone. I don't see Brooklynn with her.

"Don't worry, it's non-alcoholic." He takes a good look at me then groans. "Alright man, you said what you said now get out of your head."

"It's rhyme time now?"

"No, it's time to have a good time."

"What are we talking about? Why does it look like you're brooding over here in the corner?"

"If you two brilliant men notice, we're not in 'the corner'. We're standing at a table, on a rooftop, at a party."

The two of them chuckle as Trent rejoins our group.

"Is he still pouting?" Trent asks as soon as he takes a seat

"What the hell is going on? Is that what you guys think I'm doing?"

"That's what we know you're doing," Ryder tells me. "Who is this about anyway?"

I look at Graham and silently threaten him to keep quiet. He raises an eyebrow, gives me a questioning look, smirks, then turns to face the other guys.

"Get this. It's the same one man from high school."

The guys start snickering and all I can do is shake my damn head.

"Blaze? After all this time, it's still blaze?" Ryder questions.

He looks different without his cut on. if I didn't know any better, I swear he was wanted a businessman who came to make a donation via the auction. He smiles then pats my shoulder. The guy is still happy handed. Always has been probably always will.

"Can we talk about something else?"

"Nope. you open the floor to this so let's get into it," Graham announces. "Have you seen her?"

[118]

# Plunge

At first, I think he's talking to me, but I quickly realized Graham is speaking to Ryder. I was prepared to give him shit about not paying attention when I'm bearing my soul. Now, I have to change my reaction.

"No. How's she doing? you know, after everything?"

"How is it that you haven't seen her, and you live here? I see her everywhere."

Ryder shrugs his shoulders.

"I guess it's because we run in different circles. I ran into our once and we hugged. We did a quick check-in with each other because she was headed to a meeting or something. That was like three or four months ago. I haven't seen her since. That was the one and only time I ran into her."

"Doesn't have that homing beacon that you too seemed to have," Trent adds.

"Homing beacon?" I ask.

Graham snorts then puts his best to his mouth.

"You mean that six sense the two of them have with each other. that shit used to freak me out."

"Oh yeah. Right. it was like you guys or really one another like magnets. It was weird. Does that still happen?"

Graham is nodding his head well before I can offer up an answer.

"Yeah. Man. yeah it still does." shake my head then remember what Ryder initially asked. "What did you mean earlier when you asked about how she was doing? What everything?"

Ryder looks like Graham with confusion written all over his face. When he looks at me, there's a question written there.

"What are you talking about, Man? You know about what happened to the Hampton house right?"

Graham is shaking his head and trying to get Ryder's attention.

"No. what ... what happened to the Hampton house?"

"The house is gone. There was a fire there about a year ago. No, it's been about a year and a half now. The house burned to the ground. Blaze was inside. Chad is really gnarly scar on her back and part of our arm. I hooked her up with this sick tattoo artist up in Atlanta and she got it covered."

"Whoa. I had no idea."

I look at Graham and he pushed his hands in the air in mock surrender.

"Don't look at me like that, man. I couldn't tell you anything about that when I learned about it. You've been going through your own shit. Remember?"

He's right. I have been. Now I feel guilty about not being there for her when she was going through what had to be a hard time and a big loss for her.

A piano signals for everyone's attention so that effectively ends the conversation. Hope as a spotlight on her and says words that I don't hear. My mind is still with Brooklyn and a loss she suffered. I don't know yet if anyone was hurt but I know what that house meant to her. She loved growing up there.

Any further reactions need to wait because I hear my name being called.

"That's my cue. It's showtime."

It doesn't take me long to speak to what the foundation means to me and my family. I share an anecdote or two about how it came about, mentioning my niece and the surgery that started it all.

Macey, Hope's daughter, is the reason we came up with the idea for Hope House. We wanted to create an all-in-one resource and healthcare facility. Those who come to Hope House are usually at their wit's end and need some guidance. Or they don't have the time or know-how to get the care their family member needs. We provide all of it. When Macey was diagnosed with diabetes, none of knew. By the time we received it, she was seriously hurt. It led to her needing to have a portion of her arm amputated. The research and after care was the worst of it. All of us spent so much wasted time looking up anything from the best treatments to mental health concerns to quality foods. It was a stressful time. After having a conversation about it all, Hope House came was born.

I exit the area that is the center of the dedicated auction site. Hope kisses my cheek and I whisper congratulations to her. What most don't know about Hope is she's a licensed psychologist with big ideas. She also has a business degree. I listen as people commend us for a great event. Some even mention looking forward to winning some of the prizes.

A reporter steps forward and tries to snap a few photos. I purposely avert my attention elsewhere. The usual question is asked of Hope, and she expertly avoids it. The follow up question comes, and it causes a smile to play at my lips. I move away from the group and to an actual corner, a quiet corner. I snag a drink from a passing tray and have a seat as I ponder the answers to those questions.

The first question is always about the nature of our relationship. It's our business, not that of the public's. The next question is about the name. They ask if having such a facility named after one person feels like a lot of pressure. Hope and I always laugh when she's asked that question or something similar to it. It isn't named after Hope. That being her name was just a coincidence. Very few in her close family call her "Hope".

Like my family, they call her by her middle name and that one only. The name of our facility is called Hope because that's what we want to offer people. It's also a nod to Brooklynn. I used to call her "my hope". I don't think anyone else knows that.

As if she knows I'm thinking of her, I feel that familiar tingle.

I watch her as she makes her way to the outer area which is almost as breathtaking as she is. I'm seated in one of the more obscure corners of the rooftop but is a perfect spot for observation. *Bar Julian* is and was one of my favorite places to visit when I was younger. Ryder and I used to come to Savannah just because we could. Having family in the city made it convenient.

Our uncle used to spend a lot of time at this hotel when he just wanted to get away from it all. He'd said it was our late aunt's favorite view. When I missed her and needed to clear my head, this is where I'd come. The view of the city, with its hustle and bustle on one side and the Savannah River on the other, gave me plenty to get lost in.

All of it pales in comparison to her. Tonight, she's wearing a bronze color dress that skims her ankles at the back. It has long sleeves with a belt. The dress buttons in the front but not many of the top buttons are closed. She moves to face her friend, Journee, who is wearing a matching red version of her dress. That's when I notice her entire leg is on display. Her gorgeous leg looks like it goes on for days. I don't know if it's the light that's hitting it or some issue with my vision, but it appears to glimmer in the glow from the bulbs.

"Now, I'm fucking uncomfortable," I murmur to myself as I finish the last of my drink, thankful to find it doesn't have any alcohol in it.

That must be Hope's doing. Her way of continuing to take care of me without physically doing it. I watch her and wonder if she remembers this rooftop.

The waiter I hadn't noticed turns toward me to ask if I need a refill. His bent body effectively blocks me from taking in the vision that is Brooklynn. Quickly fishing out a bill, I hand it to the male while trying to move him out of my line of sight. He acknowledges whatever I hand him with a grateful reply then says something about returning as fast as he can. When I look back in the same area, I have my answer to my question.

Given the expression on her face, she remembers exactly what happened the last time we were both here. Yeah, she knows exactly where we are. This location was a coincidence even in its

# Plunge

significance. I hadn't expected the two of us to be on this rooftop again.

# CHAPTER 16
## *BROOKLYNN*

### The morning of the Anniversary Event

Hope Foundation has become the place I escape to when I need to get away from everything. For the first time ever, it's also the place I've come to find answers and get clarity.

"Never thought I'd ever think that about this place."

"Hmm? Did you say something Brook?" Journee asks me.

Today, she's rocking twists in her hair and her fun print scrubs. That means we will have children in the building. As much as I love kids, I don't think I can handle them today. My mind is too wrapped up in the past to focus on being the playful person I become when I'm around little ones.

"Nothing. Do you know where Mrs. Hope is?"

Journee gives me one of her patented looks that causes me to plaster on a smile. I don't want her to worry.

"She was upstairs in the conference room. Today is the anniversary thing and they have interviews all morning. I thought you were going to be at MRC today."

"I'm going over there after ... I'll see you later."

# Plunge

I head to the stairs. I was going through the items of the old box my mom sent me. inside were some things I expected. It also had a few things I hadn't. One was a journal I'd kept that was dated from a year ago. Inside was a list I'd created.

1  Write down or type up some of the things I've been feeling (Dr Alexander ~~suggests blogging or even vlogging~~)

2  Talk to family members

3  Return to work. On a part time basis. Have assistant help with routine (~~if details can't be recalled~~)

4  Face the pain I'm hiding

*"Dr. Alexander? Who is that?"*

It suddenly hit me like a two-ton brick. I got dressed and rushed over. I stopped by the conference room, but no one was there.

"They must've finished early," I mutter under my breath.

Someone clears their throat and I turn to find Cassandra pointing to the corner office, Hope's office.

I walk in that direction but slow when I hear voices. Instead, I take a seat in the waiting area that looks as if it was once part of a library. When I look up, I notice the placard.

Hope Alexander, PsyD

*How had I missed that?*

I stand when I hear movement close to the door. I don't recognize the woman Hope is speaking with, so I patiently wait.

"He's such a beloved person."

"Yes, he is. The fans love him. So do so many others," Hope responds.

Hope watches the woman go then turns to face me.

"Dr. Emory, come in. I have a few minutes to myself before the next interview. It's good to see you."

I smile and follow her inside her office.

"It's good to see you too."

I close the door behind us. So many questions float through my mind. I don't know where to start.

"Is everything ... are you alright?" she asks.

"You're Dr. Alexander?"

"Are you asking me or lobbing an accusation?"

She runs a wooden rake over sand as she listens to me.

*"I understand if you want to see someone else. It's not a problem. I hope you'll continue group therapy.*

"You were my first therapists. You were the one who got me making lists."

She sits back and waits for me to finish. I wait for her to deny it or something, but she doesn't.

"It's true. I was the first person you came to see. You made some breakthroughs, but something happened. Afterward, you asked about other treatment options. I suggested Dr. Embers. You've been working with her ever since."

"Wow. Do you know what happened?"

"Sorry. No. I just know you were ... 'piecing the puzzle together' and you thought you had the final piece, but something happened."

"That sounds like me. Do you have any clues?"

She shakes her head. Her long, blond hair moving with the motion.

"I don't think so." She taps the miniature rake on the pad with the sand. "You were supposed to visit your mother that day."

"Hmm." I take a seat. "I wonder if those things are connected."

[126]

"What things?"

I pull my hands through my hair as I try to figure things out. I'm opening my mouth to speak when Hope puts up a finger. I notice the ring on her ring on her finger and think about some of the things Journee said.

"Yes. Good to hear. That means I can eat something. Please. You're a Godsend. Thanks Cassandra." She types something on her computer then looks over at me. "

I glance at the magazine cover and shake my head. Seeing the picture with him surrounded by women bothers me. It shouldn't because he isn't mine. He isn't anything to me.

*Yes, he is.*

That time has passed. The ship has sailed.

I'm finding I need to continuously repeat those words. If not, I hope for other things. Things that aren't an option because I set fire to our relationship.

*Finally!*

Yep, I'm taking ownership of my part in the way our lives turned out.

"Daire Deville, 'the panty melter'. They reference that name with every story they write about him."

I look at the magazine then back up at her.

"Right. The ladies love him. He loves them right back. I don't see how you do it."

Hope stops what she's doing then turns to face me.

"You're right. He does love his fans. All of them. He's more than willing to put aside whatever he's doing to make sure they know how much he appreciates them." She stands then shifts some papers then suddenly looks over at me again. "Wait ... what did you mean? How do I do what?"

"Be the woman in his life when all these other women are fawning over him or throwing themselves at him."

Hope gives me an incredulous look before doubling over laughing. I giggle as well for a moment. Until it hits me that I don't know why we're laughing. This causes her to laugh even harder.

"You believe Jaxson and I are ... a couple?" She's in hysterics all over again and I'm growing increasingly pissed off by the nanosecond. "I'm not even going to apologize. I can't because I needed that laugh. That was priceless. You didn't know. I thought everyone who is close to Jaxson knew this about him."

"Knew what?" The words are spoken between clenched teeth. This is what Journee or even Noelle feels like when people take forever to get to the point. "What is it that I don't know?"

"Jaxson hasn't 'dated' anyone in quite some time. All those females who throw themselves at him are stopped at the gates or doors."

Now, I'm even more confused because I was just staring at her wedding ring and band. I noticed it was similar to the one Daire wears on his hand. Well, Journee helped me notice they were similar. I lift my left hand then tap my ring finger with my thumb.

"Okay. Clarification needed. What about your wedding bands?"

She looks down at her hand as if she forgot all about the heart shaped diamond and ruby encrusted ring shimmering in the rays of sunlight that bounce right off it. I guess having that stunner resting on your hand perfectly securing your relationship status wouldn't cause me to worry either.

*Jealous much?*

I refuse to acknowledge those words.

"Oh. Right?" Hope drops into a large, red chair that sits in the corner of her office. It's the perfect reading nook with the bookshelf on one side and a little table beneath the one-panel window. "I'm so used to having this on that I don't realize it's there most of the time. My husband ... my late husband picked this out for me. It represents … represented us perfectly. I should probably stop wearing this."

The last of her explanation is mumbled. Her words are practically whispered as she begins to play with it. She dabs at her eyes with a tissue I didn't see her grab before placing a kiss on the ring.

Knife to the gut. I'm literally gutted watching her. I'm fighting my own damn tears and I didn't even know the man.

"Okay. Now I feel like the biggest dope. I'm … I didn't mean to make you cry, Hope."

"It's fine. I'm fine. I just wasn't expecting that … question. The rings. This one is mine. My husband's is here." She points to her thumb. She spins the piece around before she looks back at me. "Um, the one Daire wears is fake. I mean, it's a real ring with diamonds and whatever other gemstone but it isn't linked to anyone. It's his way of keeping people at bay. He simply lifts his hand, and most people will back off."

"Oh wow. Okay. W … why would …?"

I try to get the question out, but I'm cut off. Hope looks at her watch then up at the large clock in the center of the wall. I can't help but look at the ornamental art piece that keeps Hope on schedule. It's beautiful. At first glance, it looks as if there are clear jewels that swoop up as well as down. From the jewels, there are peacock colored leaves following the pattern. If a person were to move closer, they could see the entire clock is made from metal and stones.

"That's a Jaxson addition. He said it felt like the right piece for me and this office. He was right. I mean, of course, he was right. He has an eye for these things. He's the reason this office is designed the way it is. All the décor is designed around that piece. I wish we could talk longer but I need to eat something then several interviews before I must get ready. If you want, we can talk after?"

She snags some papers off the printer then moves towards me. Giving me a brief hug, she moves towards the door.

"Sure. I mean. It'll probably be the day after tomorrow that we'll see each other but we can talk some more then."

"You're not coming tonight?"

"No. I don't think I should. Things are off between me and … Jaxson."

"I didn't know. Did something … nope. I can't get into that. I hope you stop in. The food is going to be spectacular and the deserts divine. Don't let whatever's going on keep you from that. Also, don't worry about them 'puzzle pieces' so much. They'll come together when you're ready for them."

She gives me a parting smile then she's out the door. Journee is going to be happy to know I have some answers to some of her questions. I even have a few of my own answered.

*Savannah, GA*                                      *May 5* - Friday evening
### The Anniversary Event
"Are you sure you don't want to come? I mean, we did all this shopping to get the perfect dresses. You're telling me, you're going to let it collect dust in your closet?"

Journee has asked me at least five times to change my mind. I'm just not up for another round with Daire. Plus, I want to take time to go through the contents of the box and my journal. Seeing my own handwriting seems to make things a lot realer than hearing details about my life from other people.

"For like the four billionth time, I'm going to stay home tonight."

"I'm sad for you. You've been looking forward to this just as much as I've been. I wish I could change your mind."

"Sorry, Girly. This chick's staying in and working. I've got things that need my attention. you go. Have enough fun for the both of us."

"Fine. I'll go. I will pretend to be miserable for the first thirty seconds. I'll then, shamelessly, send photos of all the gorgeous things we expect them to have at such an occasion."

"Please do that."

She rushes to me where I'm sitting in the library and gives me a huge hug.

"Love you, Blazing Beauty."

I laugh out loud then blow her a kiss.

"Love you, Journee Belle!" She blows a kiss right back to me. "Be safe."

"Will do, Party Pooper."

Laughing again, I flip the pages of my old journal as I listen for the car we ordered to drive off. The instant it drives off, I arm the alarm then begin my evening of reviewing "Life According to Me".

An hour later, I hear music and feel a vibration. I'm no longer in the library, I'm on one of the couches in the living room. I must've fallen asleep.

I'm dazed and confused as I feel around for my phone. I have to blink a few times before I can focus on the screen.

"Hello?"

"Get dressed. The car will be there to get you in fifteen minutes. Wait ... were you asleep? Wake the hell up and get over here, right now."

"Journee, we talked about this already. I told you ..."

"Nope. Get here. Trust me. Go get dressed. I'll meet you at the doorway, so you don't get lost." She's quiet for ten seconds then she's speaking again. "Fourteen minutes. Get. Dressed."

As much as I don't want to go, I don't have the energy to argue with her.

"It's going to take me longer than that to get dressed. I have to do my hair."

"I don't care. Just go get ready. The driver will wait. Damn!"

"I'm going, Bossy Pants. BTW, I don't like Bossy Journee."

"I love you too. Now, GO!"

Thirty minutes later, I'm meeting Journee at the front doors of a hotel I know far too well.

"Hi honey! you look absolutely gorgeous. I can't wait. let's go."

I laughed to myself as I try to keep up with journey who seems to be double timing it too an elevator.

"OK you're going to have to tell me why you're so excited."

"I'll tell you tomorrow. just know it'll be worth it."

"you're being weird."

She scarves then makes a face.

"what's new about that? you're going to lose it when you see how gorgeous it is. it's everything we thought it would be and more."

I'd expect nothing less given where we are and who is behind the event.

The moment you step off the elevator a large sign with the word "hope" in capital letters and the colors of the HFH enter is what greets guests. There is a wall of banners that showcase what the auction items are that are being donated by JD J on one wall. on the other wall is a large green television that has photos of different families that have then helped by Hope House. the lighting of the walkway from the elevator or stairwell to the entrance is low and shifts between the colors of Hope House. The doors that lead to the actual rooftop are decorated with lights and balloons that match the color scheme.

It's spectacular and I'm awestruck. I haven't even made it to the event space. Journee leads me out to the rooftop and an audible gasp escapes my lips. A rooftop that was already breathtakingly gorgeous has been transformed into this magnificent space with a white backdrop. That backdrop is created by lines and lines of light that have been strung up around the entirety of the roof. Everywhere a person looks, there are lights. Guests walk through a small hallway created by the lights then through a curtained area which prevents attendees from seeing anything until they walk through.

Once on the other side, absolutely, stupendously gorgeous. In keeping with the theme of Hope House colors, tables with clear vases have flowers that match perfectly. Round lanterns are hanging in the center "stage" area. The outer areas have rectangular lights that cast the colors on the guests walk by.

"I told you," Journee says. "Aren't you glad I made you come?"

"Yes! this is ..."

"So much more."

"I know right?"

"Alright. you're here. I'm here. let's do this."

for the next half an hour, Journee and I make our rounds. the entire time, I feel like I'm being watched. I know he's here. I can feel the familiar pole that says he's in the area. Unfortunately, I haven't been able to lay eyes on him.

Journee gets called away, which means I'm left alone to fend for myself until she can return to my side. While she's away, add decide to venture to one of the other areas. from far off, I could swear the woman standing add a reception area is my mother. She has her same dark hair. My mother colors her hair to keep the gray away. Her profile looks exactly like my mother's. I wonder why she's here. She's not one to usually come to things like this. mother considers herself a walking charity. She once said something about in the type to write the check but not get her hands dirty.

Gotta love a woman like that. Apparently, husband number four, I think it is, does. I'm making my way to where she is when I see a little girl. The little girl as huge, beautiful eyes, straight brown hair that's pulled up into two ponytails, and huge smile on her face as she runs back to the woman side. I freeze right where

I'm standing. it isn't the girls looks that get me. It's the laugh. It sounds exactly the same.

Just like hers. Just like my baby girls. I feel my legs give out as my hands began to shake. I feel like I'm in quicksand about to be taken under. His voice call to me and keeps me above the depth of darkness.

"Brooklynn? Brooklynn, are you okay?"

Tears stream down my face as I shake my head. He leads me away. I don't know where we're going but I walk with him. I can't stop crying. The tears keep coming. A woman who comes into my line of side. Just as quickly as she comes, she goes. He says something but I can't really hear him.

I'm still sobbing. I can't get the tears to stop. My breaths are coming too fast and so are the tears. I'm in a car, not the one I arrived in, but another one. I'm still crying. All I can see is the little girl. The more I see her the harder I cry.

I don't know where we end up. all I know is I feel cushion beneath my body before I feel the warmth of him surround me. that warmth is my comfort as I feel the tears and pain starts to subside. I curl into his chest and drift off to sleep dreaming of different life and a happy family.

Sometime in the night I get antsy. I have all this nervous energy bundled up inside of me. The scent of him surrounds me. Like I'm dreaming. I'm too warm, so I slip out of my dress. He must have felt the same because I feel his skin next to mine when I crawl back into him.

We're beneath some covers or a sheet is above us. I touch his chest then run my hand down his stomach until I can slip it beneath his boxers. When I come in contact with his semihard shaft, I moan. I missed this so much. Using my thumb, I rob slowly over the tip. He jumps in my hand. Stroke my hand up and down the length then run my nail over the vein that I know is sure to get his attention. His eyes popped open and focus on mine.

"You're entering dangerous territory there, Blaze."

[134]

I close my eyes, allowing that word to wash over me. I've always loved it when he called me that. I run my thumb over the head of his growing hard on.

"You giving me a choice when your erection is growing in my hand?"

He grabs hold to my wrist. My pulse kicks up a notch. I've not seen this side of him in a long time. I miss this version of him too. A growl rumbles deep and low causing the bed to vibrate when I tighten my grip on him.

"Not why I brought you here. Do I want you? Fuck yes, I do. Earlier ...?"

I shake my head and try to shift closer to him. Leaning in, I do something I've wanted to do for a very long time. I kiss him.

"Not now. Later.'

I close my eyes the immediately open them again when I feel wetness slip from one of them. Licking my lips, I silently plead with him.

"That tongue will be put to work if you don't let go. Final warning, Blaze. I'm not in the right mind to beat it back once this starts."

Light from outside shines from some window. His eyes turn that delectable shade of green that used to heat me from the inside out. They seem to still have the same effect on my libido.

"I need to feel something other than ...," I can't finish the thought. I just know I need to drown out that feeling. "Your choice. Mouth or cunny?"

That's all the invitation he needs. My wrist is released, and his mouth covers mine. I part my lips and he accepts the second invite. His tongue plunges into my mouth. He tastes warm and sweet. Like my one tasty treat as he takes charge of the kiss. One of his hands grips my breast through the strapless bra I'm wearing while the other teases along the skin of my side. His fingers trail over the lace of my panties.

"These? Did you like them?"

"Um?"

I hear the fabric rip and look down to find once side of my panties are gone. Before I have a chance to react, one of his long fingers is sliding over the slickness That's a waiting.

"Slick. Wet. Ripe for the picking. always ready. Just the way I like it."

His deep voice is the most scrumptious sound. A different type of warmth begins to stir as his mouth descends as he strips the remaining fabric away from my body. The chair from the cool air causes a shiver to run over my body. One he catches, causing the current to immediately shift back to heated.

My body doesn't know what to react to but I'm enjoying every moment of it. I wanted to feel something else he damn sure is keeping the failing stirred up inside of me. His mouth descends on my core while his hands hold tight to my hips, keeping me pressed into the mattress. as his tongue delves deep inside of me, I want to lift into his actions. He won't allow it.

His thumb presses down on my clit then slowly rubs over it while his tongue and fingers work together on my center. the rush of heat to that area is instantaneous. He groans as I feel myself tighten around his fingers. He begins to pump in and out of me as the orgasm begins to build. Suddenly he presses both of my legs up by the feet causing them to bend. My ass automatically lifts off the mattress as he voraciously continues to lick and pump through that orgasm and coaxes me into a second.

Daire allows my legs to fall to his side as he kisses up my body. He stops at my breast and finally releases down from their cage. The bra is tossed to the side before he leans down to take one of my breasts in his mouth. He licks slowly around each of my erect nipples just before I hear another growl.

"This is new. You didn't have these when we were together before. Male or female?" he questions.

Anyone else would be confused right now. Considering how well I know Daire, I know he wants to know who saw my breasts. We haven't been together in six years, but he needs to know who seen them well enough to have the ability to pierce them. I just orgasmed twice but possessiveness of his tone has me on the brink of a third.

"Wouldn't you like to know?" I tell him, knowing that's going to piss him off.

"Still full of sass, let's see how much you have when I'm finished.

He spends a little more time teasing me with his mouth on my breast while stroking the head of his engorged shaft over my slit. It feels so deliciously wonderful, but the taunting of his closeness is too much. Just as I'm on the verge of screaming for him to finish me off, he lifts up then drives deep in one long stroke. He doesn't give me any time to adjust or acknowledge what he's just done. His mouth is on mine and his tongue is mimicking the action that's happening between my legs.

If there is any other sound in the room, I can't hear it. All I hear is our bodies connecting and our combined moans as we race towards completion. He won't go over the edge into ecstasy until he knows I've already hit that precipice. My hands move all over asscheeks and squeeze as he repeatedly pumps into me. I feel that familiar tightening within just before my walls began to spasm around him. Once he feels me slipping, he ramps up his pace. I feel him pump once, twice, then a third time before he let's go.

He drives deeper inside of me as his release fills me.

His mouth descends to mine as he gives me a light kiss before dropping to the side. Side by side, we work to catch our breath. He slides out of the bed then walks around to the other side. I hear a door, water, then I see him come back to where I'm turned on my side. He presses my legs apart but keeps his focus on my face. I feel the warm cloth as he cleans me up.

When he walks away, he looks as if he's limping. He returns to what I'm guessing is his bathroom. By the time he returns, I must've drifted off to sleep again. I awaken to his hard on pressed against my bare ass. Wiggling closer, I am rewarded with his answering groan. His hand slips beneath my leg, opening me up to him. He slips inside me from behind. We find our rhythm as he kisses me while palming my breasts.

We continue until I climax. He shifts so he's on his back.

"Take me for a ride, Blaze. If I recall, you like it best when you're driving the beast."

Drive the beast, I do. I ride him until we are both sated.

Neither one of us moves when I slide off his body and into his side. I don't have the energy to do anything but sleep. This is the best way to fall asleep. I wish I could always fall asleep like this.

I know I can't. I have some explaining to do tomorrow. There are things I need to finally share. Right now, I nuzzle into his heat and allow myself to enjoy this moment of bliss.

# CHAPTER 17
## *BROOKLYNN*

What a night? I want to relish the beauty of what the two of us shared but I can't. As beautiful as the sky is when the dawn greets me this morning, I must tear myself away from staring out the window. I internally laugh because nothing has changed in the last twenty plus years I've lived. Actually, many things have changed but that's not the point.

For as long as I can remember, I've had a standard routine. Wake up from dreamland, stretch, greet the day with whatever I'm feeling that morning, then I must empty my bladder.

*That sounds awful.*

It's the reality I must contend with. It takes me a few minutes to find the bathroom. By the time I do, the urgency is the most important thing on my mind. Looking around the room, I see elements that I've always wanted for my own bathroom. I'm so busy mentally cataloging all that's in this massive place that I almost miss the pain-filled groan.

At first, I ignore it. I continue to take stock of the room when another moan reaches my ears. Rushing out of the room, I must exit the wrong way because I'm in what looks like an office. The

sound rings out once again. It echoes across the upper floors. The pain of it sends a chill up my spine.

I hear rushing footsteps. A male and female voice call out the name that was on my lips most of the night. When the sound comes again, their worried voices join in.

"Daire, wake up!"

"Mr. Shaw?"

"No. No, no, now. No. This isn't real," he cries out.

In my panic, I head out the open door instead of retracing my steps back through to the bathroom. When I slam into the doorway, I realize I don't have on any clothes. I rush back to the office and hope like hell there's something in there to toss on my body. I find a shirt hanging in a closet.

I hear my phone begin to ring. Once I cover my nakedness, I use the sounds to lead me back to the room. My phone rings again but I ignore it.

The sight before me stuns me. The room is darker but there's still enough light for me to see.

"Mr. Shaw?" A woman with straight, honey blonde hair is standing over Daire, trying to wake him. She looks over when I walk in. "I'm guessing you're the owner of the dress?"

I don't acknowledge her. My focus is on Daire. The man who is thrashing on his bed and reaching for his leg. His reaching, but his hands find no purchase. Below his left knee is nothing.

He screams again, then he opens his eyes. Daire's hands go immediately to his head. He runs his hands over his long hair then he reaches out. His hand pats the sheet next to him then rubs it before he sits up.

"Fuck me," he groans as he runs his hand over his face.

It's then that he notices he has an audience. I don't move. I don't say a word. I remain exactly where I am. He looks at each of us while I stand there watching him.

"Patrick. Kennedy. I'm good. The usual."

# Plunge

The man and the woman, Patrick and Kennedy, nod and take that as their cue to leave. I watch them go then I turn to look at him. He looks exactly like the same man I've always known, but he's not. Things have changed. Obviously. I didn't even notice. How had I not noticed?

Thunder crashes and lightening lights up the sky. Just like that, the day shifts.

## *JAXSON*

*Savannah, GA*                                                          *May 6* – Saturday dawn
*That damn dream again. Fucking hate it.*

Another morning has begun and with this morning doesn't come the morning sun. no, today, brings rain showers. Thunder crashes as I blink and wipe the sleep out of my eyes. I stretch and take in the feeling of gratefulness for last night and this morning. It's the first time in a long time that I'm not hungover or reaching for something to take the edge off.

When I reach over, I feel ... nothing. As a matter of fact, the sheets next to me are cool to the touch. The softness, comfort, along with the heat and warmth she once brought to them are gone now that she is no longer there. I pat the bed but nothing.

She's gone. No explanation this time. Just gone.

"Fuck me."

I can't believe I fucked her last night. Those eyes got me. She looked like she needed to get out of her head. I know that feeling well. I've been there plenty of times. I gave in. The feel of her tiny hand stroking me overruled anything else I had going on in my brain.

I'm sweaty and sticky. Doubly so, now that the sex compounded with that fucked up dream.

I finally look up to see that she didn't leave as I thought and we're not alone. I must've yelled out this time. It doesn't happen

[141]

often. When it does, Patrick and/or Kennedy usually must wake me. I thought I was getting a handle on this.

"Patrick. Kennedy. I'm good. The usual."

They each nod and begin to file out of my room. they've been here since before the accident. Unfortunately, each has learned once I'm awake I'm fine. I don't want to talk about it. Nor do I want to dwell on the fact that it happened. Those two are going to go about their normal day.

The one I'm worried about is still standing in the room, seemingly frozen in place. Given her line of work, I wouldn't think this would be too big of thing to wrap her head around. Although, it might be too much since I still don't know what caused her breakdown yesterday.

I open my mouth to call her name and she moves. She climbs onto the bed then wraps her arms around me.

"I'm sorry," she says. Tears track down her cheeks, off her chin then onto my shoulder. I release a breath as she clings to me. "I'm so, so sorry. I didn't know. How could you not tell me? When? When did this happen?"

Relief courses through my body. Not many people know the extent of the damage I had as a result of the accident. Most people know a car wreck happened and I was injured. I've gotten better watching people respond to seeing my amputated leg. Most do a double take. Others send a pitying look my way. The last group usually doesn't know how to react.

Having her hug me then apologize even though she had nothing to do with it is new. The questions don't surprise me since she's been getting over her own trauma. One day, we'll sit down and talk it out.

Today is not the day. I don't want to talk about it. I do want to know that she's okay.

"It was a while ago. I'm fine now. Fitted with a prosthetic and doing therapy. Your turn." I have to practically peel her off me, but I successfully extract her from my body. I'm hating the fact her warmth is gone, but it's necessary. "You were triggered yesterday. I don't know what did it, but something upset you."

She nods as she wipes at her eyes with her … my shirt. A phone rings and I watch as her brows knit together.

"You're right. I do have to talk to you. There's a lot I need to share. I was triggered. Last night, I wasn't prepared for what …"

A phone rings again and she turns, looking for it.

"Yours?" I ask as I point out the door.

"Yeah. I guess I never silenced it. It's a little early for someone to be blowing up my phone. I think that's the third time I've heard it ring. I'm sorry. It must be important."

I watch her slide off the bed. Her generous ass peeks out from beneath my shirt. I feel a stirring beneath the sheet and groan. There are a few reasons for the groan. First, I know we have shit we need to work through. Second, I'm guessing she's going to need to leave shortly which means we're not talking through anything. Lastly, now that I've had her again it's going to take me some time to get over knowing the fit of her.

Blaze … Brooklynn looks around the floor for her. As I open mouth to tell her it's on the table in the hall, it starts to ring again.

I hear her answer the call then her feet padding up the hall.

Kennedy appears in the doorway. I keep trying to tell her she doesn't have to make up the days she takes off, but she refuses to listen. She took Friday off so she's here working today.

"Did you want Chef to prepare breakfast for both you and …?" she inquires.

I laugh at her not-so-veiled attempt to figure out who the woman is.

"Not yet. I don't know if she's staying for breakfast or anything else," I add as an aside to myself. "Kennedy, that is Brooklynn Emory. I'll formally introduce you if this becomes more than what it was. I'll be down shortly. I'm going to take a shower. Please ask Patrick to pull the sheets."

She nods then walks towards the door. I snort because I know she wants to pick the clothes up from the floor. I take my time heading to the bathroom. One, to torture Kennedy. Two, waiting to see when Brooklynn will return. After five minutes, I head to the bathroom to wash the night off.

# CHAPTER 18
## BROOKLYNN

The phone call was important. I'm freaking out. I rush back to the room to let Daire know I need to leave. When I get back to his room, he's not there. The Kennedy woman is there.

"Um ... where's Mr. Shaw?" I ask her.

"He's in the shower. He wanted to get cleaned up. It usually doesn't take him long. I'm sure he'll be out any minute."

A pang of jealousy washes over me. I feel possessive of him, and I shouldn't.

*Even though the two of you had sex multiple times last night?*

I ignore that thought.

"I wish I could, but I can't. I'm going to leave him a note. Thank you."

I rush out of the room and back to the office I'd found earlier. Jotting down a quick note with my number included, I rush back to the room, toss on my discarded clothes then remember Daire shredded my panties.

"Guess I'm going ass out."

I toss Daire's button-down shirt back over my body and make my exit. I don't know where either of the people went so, I rush out

the first door I find. I'm happy to find, I guessed right, and it leads me out the front.

My feet can't carry me fast enough. I need to get to her. When I saw the name of a hospital crossing the screen on my phone, I knew I had to answer. As soon as I picked up, I realized I had to leave. I'm the emergency contact for exactly one person. I know it was about her. It was just a matter of finding out what exactly happened.

The person on the phone told me Journee was in hospital. He wouldn't give me any details; just told me I was on her emergency contact list. The hospital wasn't far from Daire's house. As my good fortune would have it, the person who drove us last night was standing near the car as I rushed out of the house.

I don't even care that I am wearing one of Daire's shirts and last night's outfit. All I care about is getting to the hospital. By the time I arrive, Journee's parents and Noelle are waiting for me.

"What happened?" I ask.

I don't bother with greetings or anything else. I know it has to be serious if we're all here.

"She was ... attacked," her mother shares.

That's all she can get out before she falls apart. Her brown eyes pool with tears. Mr. Forrester pulls he wife into the comfort of his arms. Mrs. Forrester and her husband, an older gentleman with graying brown hair, look like they were awakened out of their sleep to come to the hospital. Both are in what looked like their pajamas.

"Forrester family?" a young woman with blonde hair, green scrubs, and a white coat calls.

All four of us stand and move towards her.

"Hi. Do you mind following me?"

We all shake our heads then follow the doctor into a room right off the main hall.

"Mr. & Mrs. Forrester, I was advised that the two of you were made aware of what's going on. I was also advised that there will be two friends here what happened to be doctors."

"Psychology," Noelle clarifies.

At the same time, I say, "Physical Therapy," pointing to myself then pointing to Noelle, I say," Psychology."

"Yes. she listed the two of you as emergency contacts and stated it was fine to share with you what is going on."

"Okay. is she alright?"

"For the most part. Yeah, he went mind taking a seat, I'd like to prepare you for what you're going to see."

For the next fifteen minutes or so, the doctor lets us know what happened to our friend and their daughter. The good thing was she wasn't sexually assaulted. The bad thing was she was physically beaten. When she was called away at the party, the person on the phone said she was needed at work. She was at the gate of Hope House when she was attacked.

The doctor wanted us to also know the extent of the damage. She gave each of us a chance to leave the room. No one moved. The doctor told us that most of the damage happened below the neck. Journee has a broken rib and leg. She has facial bruising and a busted lip. There are also lacerations on her arms and legs from a broken glass. She also has a black eye.

By the end, each of us is wiping away tears.

"I wanted to speak with you first, so it isn't as much of a shock when you see her. This is a difficult situation, and we don't want to make it worse for her. She hasn't seen herself so she's possibly going to look to you to deduce the damage."

"So, we should lie?" Mrs. Forrester asks.

"No. That's not what she's saying. She wants us not to breakdown in front of Journee. That might make things worse."

"Do we know who did this?" Mr. Forrester asks.

"We do. I can't divulge that information, but he's back in the facility and under the care of his doctors."

Mr. Forrester nods but looks as if that isn't the response he wanted to hear.

"Can we see her?" I ask.

"Yes. Normally, we'd limit the number of people going in at once but. I'll allow you all to see her. Just remember what we talked about."

Hand in hand, Noelle and I follow Mr. and Mrs. Forrester along with the doctor to see our friend. Nothing ever prepares you for a situation like this. The entire time I'm walking towards the door, I try to find the words to say.

No words were necessary.

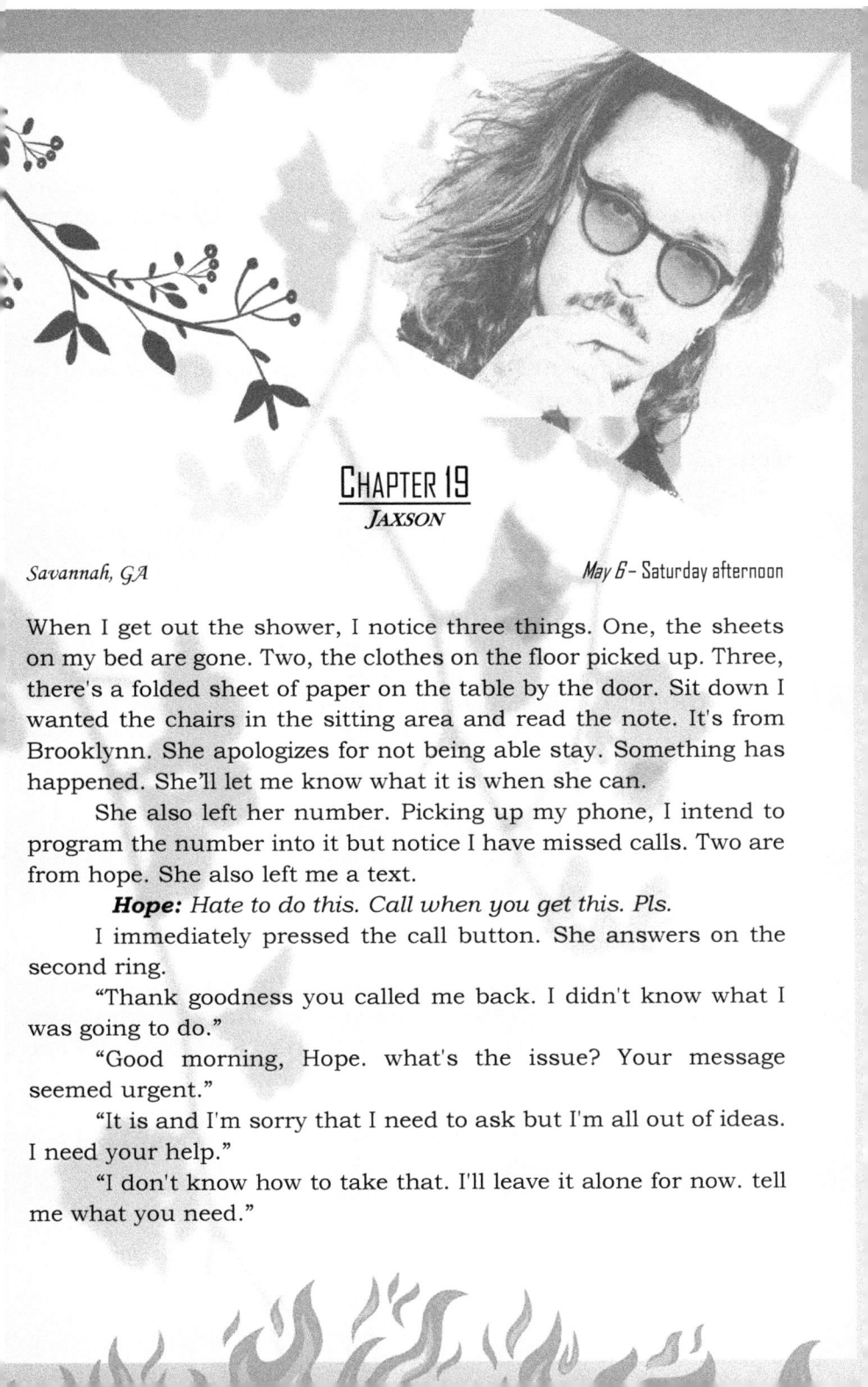

# CHAPTER 19
## JAXSON

When I get out the shower, I notice three things. One, the sheets on my bed are gone. Two, the clothes on the floor picked up. Three, there's a folded sheet of paper on the table by the door. Sit down I wanted the chairs in the sitting area and read the note. It's from Brooklynn. She apologizes for not being able stay. Something has happened. She'll let me know what it is when she can.

She also left her number. Picking up my phone, I intend to program the number into it but notice I have missed calls. Two are from hope. She also left me a text.

> **Hope:** *Hate to do this. Call when you get this. Pls.*

I immediately pressed the call button. She answers on the second ring.

"Thank goodness you called me back. I didn't know what I was going to do."

"Good morning, Hope. what's the issue? Your message seemed urgent."

"It is and I'm sorry that I need to ask but I'm all out of ideas. I need your help."

"I don't know how to take that. I'll leave it alone for now. tell me what you need."

"Jakob is over a friend's house. He spent the night over there last night with some friends. They're all supposed to go to another friend's birthday party this afternoon. I'm supposed to pick him up from that party at around 4:30pm."

"Alright. what do you need me to do?"

"Two things. The first, I need you to pick him up for me. The second, I need you to keep him until I'm done. The issue with the second is I don't know when I'll be done."

"Mmm, hmm. Fine. Fine. Do I need to get some clothes from your house? Wait, he has some stuff here already."

"You'll do it?"

"Yes. Why do you sound surprised?"

"I had just expected you to give me grief or make some smartass comment. I never would have believed you would be so amenable."

"I'm in a decent mood. enjoy it while it lasts."

she laughs.

"OK. I'll see you tonight."

"Sounds good. Oh, and Hope?"

"Yes Jackson."

"Have fun."

"I wish. I'll fill you in when I can."

"Okay."

That didn't sound ominous.


*May 6* – Saturday afternoon

The address of the little boy's party is to one of those places that have an insane number of games where kids can win tickets to exchange for prizes. I've never really been a fan of them. The one time I went as an adult, my niece got sick, another kid was having a meltdown because he didn't have enough tickets to win some prize, and the birthday boy was pissed because he didn't have two cakes like his little brother did.

When I walk in, I hope no one will recognize me. I just want to get my nephew and make it out without an incident. I'm not inside the building before I hear my name being called.

An older woman with dark brown hair, dark blue eyes, a set of green bifocals, and a book in her hand flags me down from a bench in the front. This is where kids have to take off their shoes. There are a hell of a lot of colorful cubbies with abandoned shoes in them. Children are running around kicking their shoes off, while their parents run behind them putting them back.

"Hey, I heard you were in town. I can't believe I haven't seen you before now."

When I really look at her, it's like I'm looking into an older version of Brooklyn's face. I had forgotten how much she looked like her mother. The older Emory... I don't even know if she's still Emory or if she married again. Either way she's dressed as if she's going to some important business meeting or event. She's wearing her signature color of cream or beige with a hint of rose in the accents that she's chosen to wear. I don't know much about her because she wasn't really in Brooklyn's life. When we were younger, Brooklyn spent the majority of her time with her grandmother. As far as I know Mrs. Emory was more interested in traveling the world than she was with spending time with her daughter.

As I look around, I wonder who she's here with. I'm here to pick up my nephew and I was told this was a 7-year old's birthday party. A little girl whizzes by me as she continues on her way to a table filled with treats and trinkets. She looks like she's completing ballerina turns. I catch a passing glimpse of her. It's enough to make me question what I'm seeing. The little girl looks like she's a younger version of Brooklyn. That can't be right.

"Do you have a moment?" Mrs. Emory asks me. "It's been so long since I've seen you. I would love to just have a moment to talk to another adult. It feels like it's been forever since I've had a chance to speak to someone outside of my family. My husband is away for another week or so. My daughter ... well, she doesn't really come around anymore. It's ... been a challenging time."

I look at my watch then around the room. It should be okay for me to take a minute. It doesn't look like anybody's preparing to leave so I can sit down for a few.

"Sure, I don't have to be anywhere right now. Jakob can keep playing for a little bit longer."

"Oh, you're here to pick up Jakob. Isn't that your...?"

"My nephew." I answer her question for her. "You would be correct. Jakob is my nephew and Macey is my niece."

"Oh, is Macey here as well?"

She grabs her things, then starts to move further into the thick of things. I follow behind her. When I get closer, I respond to her question.

"No. If I know my niece, she probably thought she was much too old to attend a children's party. Even if it was a party for her little brother, she'd find a way to get out of it."

As we make our way to a table, one of the few that doesn't have cupcake paper and plates or abandoned cups on it, I search the area for the little girl to see if I can get another glimpse of her. I'm not liable to find her before we take our seats. I'm not in the seat good before Mrs. Emory begins speaking again.

"Tell me how things are going. I had no idea you were in Savannah. It wasn't until I was sitting down, talking to a couple of my friends at the club, that one of them mentioned you were here. I know this isn't your hometown, but I heard you were a big fan of Savannah. Did you know the Brooklyn and I were here? Is that what brought you to town?"

I don't immediately have a response to that question. The honest answer is that I didn't come to Savannah in hopes of seeing Brooklyn. It was just a coincidence she ended up living here. I've been in love with Savannah, Georgia for many years. When GiGi, Graham, and I decided I needed a place to set up, I didn't even blink or hesitate. I knew where I wanted to be when I had downtime. I gave GiGi this spot when she stated she needed a city and state.

Georgia is my home. Now and forever.

"If I'm being honest..." I begin

What I'm about to say is cut off by the screech of a child who is being chased around not far from where we are sitting. When I look up at Mrs. Emory again, the look of complete disgust and annoyance brings a smile to my lips. This woman really hasn't changed. It makes me wonder once again who she's here with. Or even why she's here. She never struck me as the type to enjoy being around children. Like I said, she left her daughter with her mother so she could have the freedom to roam the earth however and whenever she wanted.

"Kids. Gotta love them," she tells me.

Her words are much too sunny to be genuine or even believable. Nothing in her demeanor tells me she is a willing party to having her presence here.

"Right." I nod while I wait for something to clue me in as to how she got here. Nothing happens. "Are you here with someone?"

Just as she opens her mouth to answer me that same little girl comes rushing over. She is a barrel of energy and love. The little girl's voice echoes around the area as she joyfully yells.

"Pippa! Pippa, look at what I got! I can't believe I won it!"

"What, my darling girl? What did you get? Show me, show me, show me!" Pippa or Mrs. Emory reflects the same energy that the little girl is giving her.

"Oh, my goodness, look at this gorgeous bear. Oh no. Wait a moment it's not a bear, is it?"

The little girls tinkling laughter fills the air. Something about it touches me. My heart warms as the girl smiles up at her Mrs. Emory. Of course, my brain is working overtime to connect the dots. Brooklyn is an only child. How could Mrs. Emory be a related to this little girl. Unless the man she married has a child who is the parent. The only problem with that theory is this little girl's features.

She has the shape of Brooklynn's face. Her eyes look like her, but other features look familiar for a different reason. I'm not about to scrutinize the little girl any longer because she's talking to me. I guess she figures I'm safe to speak to since the person she's with was talking to me.

"Hi! My name is Starlight. What's your name?"

"Um ... her great-grandmother gave her that nickname and, as you can tell, she loves it. I've had to have so many things created with that name plastered over it."

Mrs. Emory releases a breath as she looks at the little girl. Starlight doesn't seem the least bit fazed by her the older woman's obvious frustration.

"I'm five and a half years old. When I have my birthday party it's going to be so much fun. I'm going to be an extra big girl then and everybody will come. I want everyone to be there. I'll be six years old."

"Yes, you will be. You're going to have the best party any little girl ever wanted. Your Pippa will make sure of it. Now, go get all your things together and tell your friends you'll see them soon. We have to get home."

"Okay, Pippa."

Just as quick as she came is as quick as she runs off again. I'm remain quiet as I allow this new information to process. I need a moment, but Mrs. Emory isn't giving me that.

"Are you all right, Sweetheart? You don't look so good."

"No. I'm... Good. I'll be fine." I can't seem to get my thoughts off the little girl who has disappeared into the crowd of children and adults on the other side of the room. It doesn't stop me from staring after her. "Cute kid. She's your granddaughter, right?"

"Yes. That's right. I know I didn't do the best with being a mother. I didn't think I could be a grandmother because of it. Having that little Angel in my life has shifted a lot of things." She trails off, staring at the little girl. She's probably lost in her thoughts as I just was. "She's been through so much already in her short life. She was a twin but now she isn't. So much pain and loss. You couldn't tell it by the huge smile that just brightens up the room."

I'm stuck. My world feels like it's crashing again. Brick by brick, my chest receives the strikes. My breathing slows with the shock of this revelation.

*It can't be.*

It's not possible. There's no way. She wouldn't do that. That's not who she is or who she was. It's impossible.

Starlight comes back to the table with a little backpack and what I'm guessing is a gift bag full up candy. As she gets situated on her grandmother's lap, I see it. It's clear then. There's no denying it. She has the features of her mother. She also has the features of her... father.

The wide eyes, freckles on her cheeks and her nose are her mother's. Her little smile, her eyebrows, even the dimples are Shaw traits. Those are genetic markers that show up in every member of the family. Another little face joins our group as I'm working to put things together in my head. I'm trying to figure out what to say next but can't get anything to link up.

"Uncle Jax!"

My nephew's voice snaps me out of the inner swirl of questions happening in my head.

"Hey Speedy Junior."

That's all I can manage to get out before the truth hits me. I'm not just an uncle. I'm so much more than that.

Judging by the way Mrs. Emory is gaping at me, she's put things together as well.

"You're him? You're the one ... I can't believe she lied to me. Well, not directly to me. She left me a message via a video. Regardless, there you are. You're right here in Savannah. This is wonderful!"

She continues to babble on about something, but I can no longer hear her. I'm focused on the little girl who is sitting in her lap, sifting through the goody bag. She's completely unaware of what's happening or the connections that are being made. Suddenly, she looks up and those hazel green eyes lock onto me. She smiles then laughs. That's it.

I'm a goner. My heart squeezes then feels as if it's filling my chest. An overabundance of emotion explodes inside of me. A feeling I didn't know was still kicking around courses through me. A tear rolls down my cheek. She hops down from her grandmother's lap then walks over to me. Handing me a napkin, she pats the hand that's resting on my knee. She produces another one then wipes my cheek.

As if that action wasn't unexpected enough, she then reaches out with her little arms to give me a hug.

"It's okay. I hope you feel better."

I hear my nephew speak again.

"Yeah Mom, he's here. I don't know if he can drive me though. He seems sad or something. He's crying in FunCoVille. Can you come pick me up?"

I don't know what to say or even do. All I do know is I don't want to let her go. I know I have to do it because she doesn't know what's just happened. She probably wouldn't understand it.

"Jayla, Sweetheart, that was so nice of you. Let's get our ... belongings."

"Will he be, okay?"

This little girl ... my daughter ... doesn't seem to want to let me go any more than I do.

"Sure, my darling girl. He will, soon enough."

"He looks like my picture book man."

"What picture book man?"

"The one that has all the pictures of my daddy. He looks just like the man, Pippa. Is he?"

Mrs. Emory looks at me with concern and confusion written all over her face.

"Did … we should go." Mrs. Emory scoops up … Jayla … my daughter then places her on her hip. She turns to face me. "I don't know what to do."

"Me either."

I genuinely don't know. My arm is being tugged on. Noise, whispers and giggles along with music, float around us. A chill runs down my spine as the air conditioning kicks on again. None of it registers. I have a billion questions. No answers are coming. The tears are still slowly trickling down my face as I recall that night. The night I had my heart broken then destroyed.

"What's going on? What's the matter? Jake, are you alright?" I hear Hope ask. I am able to stand but can't respond. "Honey, go get in the car while I talk with your uncle. Will you do that for me please?"

I watch him go while I try to figure out my next move. The good thing is the crying has ceased. The bad thing is I'm pissed, and I'm annoyed because I couldn't follow through on the one task that was requested of me today.

"Jaxson? How're you doin'?"

I shake my head then move passed her, heading out the front door. Mrs. Emory and … my *daughter* are long gone.

"Brooklynn …"

"She's doing fine. I just left her and Journee at the hospital." My focus snaps to her face.

"Why are they at the hospital? Did something happen to …"

Hope pulls me away from the doorway so a group of people can enter.

"I'll tell you all the details later. They're both fine. Brooklynn is there with Journee. I'm worried about you. Jake said you were crying in public. He was worried you had some breakdown?"

I snort at the accuracy of that statement. That's what it feels like. I feel like the shit keeps piling on and I'm close to buckling under the weight of it.

"I got some unexpected news that I'll fill you in on when I have a chance to work it out for myself. I'm sorry I couldn't take Jake like I said I would."

"No, it's fine. I've got him. Are you okay to drive? Do you need me to go with you?"

I wave her off. Leaning in, I kiss her cheek before I turn to head to my car.

"I'm good. I'm fine now. I just need some time."

I toss a wave to my nephew who nods but still looks worried. As I climb in my car, I make a mental note to call him later to let him know I'm going to be fine, and I'll make it up to him.

Now, I have to determine how to make that thought a reality.

After an hour of vacillating from one choice to the other, I finally muster up the nerve to call the one number I never thought I'd dial again. I can't believe it's the same. It's been years since I reached out to Brooklynn's mother.

I'd only reached out then because I needed to know her daughter was all right. At that time, Brooklynn had been living with her mother and her then second or third stepfather.

Mrs. Emory has always been a fan of mine. When I was younger, I thought she wanted more than what I could offer her. I never found out if that were the case or not. She reigned in her flirtatious nature when she realized how serious Brooklyn and I were. I swear she was more upset about our breakup than Brooklynn ever seemed to be.

Either way, I've saved her number to every phone I've had over the years. When I dial her number, it sounds like there is an echo of a ringing phone near my house. She answers on the third ring.

"Great minds."

"Um, hello?"

"Hey there. You wouldn't happen to be home, would you?"

I pull the phone away from my ear. I'd planned on calling her to find out if she would have an issue with me stopping by. I'm hoping she has some answers to my questions.

"I am. How do you know where I live?"

I hear her laughter from the other side of my front door. When I open it, there she stands.

"I'm the wife of the mayor. Of course, I know where one of our most infamous faces lives. May I come in?"

Ending the call, I step to the side and allow Brooklynn's mother to enter my home.

"You're married to the mayor? I had no clue."

She nods as she strides through to the kitchen and takes a seat. I follow her but remain standing at the counter.

"That's not what you want to talk about, and we both know it. You want to know about your daughter. I'm just as shocked as you are. I was told you weren't available when that was the furthest from the truth. When I brought Brooklynn and Jayla to Savannah, I had no notion of your connection. As far as I knew, the two of you had broken up. Nowhere in the time of dealing with everything, did I do the math." She pulls out a tablet from her large bag. "You have to forgive me. When I first received this information, I was a little … distraught. I received paperwork and files in the event of something happening to my mother and daughter. No one could've predicted what would happen. They had me dead to rights as being the least logical choice."

"Neither of them named me?" I ask as I try to remain calm.

"That's what I'm telling you. My mother's video mentioned Brooklynn being afraid of 'the father's' reaction. At the time, I took that to mean Jayla was safer with me. Seeing how you reacted to her today, I realized my assumption was wrong. It hit me then that you didn't know about her." She stands then taps the tablet. "I had a copy of everything I was given put on this file. I'm off to pick up your bundle of energy from ballet class. When you're ready to talk more, set some things up to spend time with her, or whatever, you know how to reach me."

She gets up and starts to leave the kitchen as if everything is worked out.

"That's it? That's all you have to say?"

"What else is there?"

She looks genuinely confused.

"A lot. I've seen a lot of Brooklynn over the last couple of months. Not once have I seen that little girl. Why?"

Mrs. Emory dons the shades she was wearing when she arrived at my door all of thirty minutes ago. Straightening her shoulders, she takes on a haughty posture.

I snicker because I've been around people who believe themselves to be more than they are all my life. Her acting as if I don't have the right to question her is laughable. I don't give a damn what she's married into, I'm not letting her leave until I have answers.

"I don't know why you haven't seen Brooklynn with ..."

She can't even get the lie out without her face screwing up. Her eyes are fixed the floor the entire time.

"Lying isn't a good thing. It ages people. Did you know that?"

Her face is hilarious. The question in her eyes makes me want to frame this moment. She looks at me as if she's trying to verify if there's truth in my words. I keep a stony look on my face.

"The fire. Brooklynn didn't handle things well. The last thing she remembers is trying to get her daughter out. When she woke, she was screaming for Jayla. This is second-hand information. She was hysterical. No one got the chance to tell her what happened that day. She was catatonic. Slowly, she came back but the damage had been done. If anyone tries to speak of that day, she has ... episodes."

Mrs. Emory runs off the information like she's listing the items of clothing in her drawer and not talking about her daughter's condition.

"Why not just tell her the truth about her ... our daughter?" I need to get used to say that. "What does she think happened to her?"

Mrs. Emory looks at her watch. Given how she was at the birthday party, I don't believe she's trying to get to her granddaughter. If I were still a betting man, I'd expect her to have a spa or nail appointment.

"Different things have been tried. The doctors say her mind isn't ready to accept what happened that day. She used to live with me but would go into hysterics when she saw Jayla."

Initially, I don't understand. When it hits me, it hits me hard.

"Fucking hell! She thinks she's dead."

"Now, you're all caught up. I need to go. Let me give you the card to the caretaker. She ... um ... can coordinate things with you."

This time, I don't stop her. My mind is spinning. All this information is tumbling around in my head. It's hit too fast and I'm not processing it well.

"Man, what I wouldn't give for a drink right now."

I drop to the floor of my kitchen and sit in silence as I try to work through it all. No part of me knows what my next step is to take.

# CHAPTER 20
## JAXSON

*Hampton, GA*                                    *May 10* – Wednesday

I'm slowly losing my mind. I'm sure no one would blame me for doing so. As much as I want this to be the truth, I don't want to believe Brooklyn would do this. I don't wanna believe she would keep me away from my child. I've gone back and forth on this. I've been debating the issue, trying to recall every single moment leading up to that last conversation. I've even replayed what happened from the moment I arrived at the hospital, all those years ago, to the moment she changed both of our lives. None of it makes sense.

If I insert the fact there was a possible second child, I still can't make it right out. Her words still break me. She told me to go. She said we lost the baby. I mourned for that child all by myself. That's one of the reasons my first year away was so difficult. I said goodbye to her, my child, and our future.

On the rooftop of the *Thompson Savannah*, we'd talked about our dreams and the life we would have together. At the hospital in Hampton GA, she snatched all of that away and left me to figure out what my next steps were. Needless to say, I didn't handle things well.

I've wanted to confront her, but I don't know how. She's got a "mental block" in her brain. On top of that, her friend was hurt in the worst way. Brooklynn has been there with her, for her. I've heard charges are being brought against the guy. I'm told Journee is having a hard time with everything. She has a lot on her plate. Brooklynn has been the friend and roommate she needs this entire time. I don't want to call her while they are in the thick of this.

I've seen Jayla, my daughter, a couple times. From a distance. I'm not sure the best approach. The picture book thing threw me. It made me wonder where it came from. Since I seem to have more questions than answers, I've decided to find them on my own.

Mrs. Emory is worthless. She's called a few times. Her reason for calling is always to see if I want to spend time with Jayla. Judging from the short time I spent with my daughter, I've gauged she's very intelligent. If she's anything like Brooklynn or I were at that age, then she's going to have some questions. I need to have answers.

I've been playing investigator. The last three days have been spent looking for all the information I can find on Brooklynn and Jayla. I've been working my way through this last year and a half. I've spoken to Hope and the Noelle and the doctors who have been treating Brooklynn. I argued with some of them about not telling Brooklynn the true. All have spouted the same thing.

Brooklynn will come to terms with everything in her own time.

The more I did, the more I feel guilty for not being with her when all of this was going on. I shake those thoughts off and press on. I've got to have it all which means I need to go back home. All my notes lead me back to Hampton.

Ryder, Graham, and I arrived in Hampton two hours ago. They went to visit some friends because they don't know why we're in town. All I told them was I needed to go to the Hampton house. Up until about twenty minutes ago, they had no clue I was at the hospital. Both come barreling in the emergency doors.

The worry on their faces is nice to see. I know it's a messed-up thought. I probably should've told them they were just meeting me here. If this were any other situation, I'd probably laugh. It's good to know they care.

"What the hell?! Daire, you're a fucking asshole," Ryder tells me the instant he sees I'm perfectly fine.

Graham chooses to take it a little further. He grabs my face and gives me a good once over before pulling me into a hug. After he slaps my back twice, he steps back then punches me.

"FUCK! Are you kidding me? What the hell was that for?"

"I've dealt with some crazy shit dealing with you over the years. Don't you ever do that to me again! We thought something happened to your dumb ass."

Ryder's in the background laughing it up.

"Didn't think you had it in you, Big Guy," Ryder tells Graham. He then looks at me, "You want to tell us why we're here?"

"Yeah. I'm hoping you're still friends with one of the clerks here. I need access to a file that's not mine."

"Obviously. What file?"

I look at Graham then at Ryder before taking a deep breath.

"I need access to Brooklyn's file from the day before I left to for California six years ago." I'm watching their faces to gauge their reactions before I continue. "I also need her file from a year and a half ago."

The two share a look before Ryder nods and heads towards the nurses' station.

"You going to clue us in to what's going on?"

"Yep. As soon as I see the file. I need answers before I share."

"Good enough. How's the nose?"

[164]

"It's felt worse. Hurts like a bitch. You didn't pull that punch."

"Like I said, I've seen a lot of shit and had some whoppers come my way being friends with you."

I snort and have a seat as an older black woman with a full face of makeup and curly hair walks up to the counter. Ryder leans down to give the woman a hug. Not what I expected but hopefully that works in our favor.

Twenty minutes later, Ryder and the woman signal for us to follow them. The woman leads us around the corner to an empty office space. She closes the door behind us.

"Hi. Nurse Aretha Tillman or Auntie Angel. Ryder tells me the two of you are friends of his. What he didn't tell me was you were connected to Grandma Elle."

That surprises me. Not many people know I was close with Brooklyn's grandmother. This woman must've been really good friends with her too.

"Yes. How did you know that?"

"Grandma Elle spent a lot of time here at the hospital. Very few many people were aware of the extent of her illness."

"Wait ... Brooklyn's grandmother was sick? When was this?"

Nurse Aretha or Auntie Angel, as Ryder calls her, silently signals for us to have a seat. Once we're all seated, she explains.

"Grandma Elle had cancer. She'd been diagnosed about six years ago."

*Well. Fuck. Me.*

I catch bits and pieces of the rest of what Nurse Aretha tells us about Brooklynn's grandmother's illness and the care she received. My thoughts center around one question and one question only.

"I'm sorry. Do you mind if I ask you a question?" I ask as the words thump around in my head. Nurse Aretha nods. "Do you know when her granddaughter found out about her grandmother's illness?"

"Brook was there the day Elle got the news. I stayed with them until they were ready to go home."

"Damn," I hear Graham mutter.

I second that.

"I'll leave you to your search. Rye, have one of the nurses call for me when you're ready to return the files. Okay?"

"Yes ma'am."

Ryder walks her to the door then turns to face Graham and me.

"Dial me in. What am I missing? Something about that timeframe is significant."

I forget Ryder wasn't always with us during that last year. He doesn't know everything that went down.

"I think we just found out the real reason Brooklynn told me we no longer had a future together."

"That's what she told you that day?" Ryder asks. "Damn. Nee told me something was up with the two of you, but she never said what. The next thing I heard was you two weren't together any longer."

"Yeah. That's not the half of it," I add.

Ryder and Graham have a silent conversation as I reach for the files that are left on the table.

"What's up? I have a feeling something more is going on that you haven't shared."

In response to Graham's statement, I nod.

"There is. If what I've learned is true, I have a daughter. A daughter I wasn't told about. I have a sinking suspension as to why that was. I'm going to go to the source for that one."

"Shit. Are you serious?" Graham runs a hand over his bald head before he snaps his fingers. He does a rhythmic snap when he has an idea, or he figures something out. "That's why you want to see the file. You want to find out if she lied to you that day."

[166]

"Fuck Man, that's heavy. She lied to you about the kid. She knew she couldn't go. Knowing Blaze, she wasn't going anywhere if she knew her grandmother was sick," Ryder adds.

"No way in hell would she have let you stay with her when she knew everything you ever wanted was right there," Graham finishes.

"Yep." I sniff then blink a few times, trying to fight the wave of emotions coursing through me. "Dammit."

"That girl fucking loved you."

"I fucking know, Man. Shit."

I turn to face the wall as close my eyes. It takes me a few minutes to collect myself. The guys don't say anything until I turn back to face them.

"You good?" Graham asks.

"One down. One to go. I need to know what the hell happened the day of the fire and in the days that followed. Brooklynn has been in dark for a reason. I need to know why."

Ryder and Graham pull up a chair and pour through to files with me. They also make phone calls. We don't leave Hampton until we have a clear understanding of what the hell went down a year and a half ago.

*Savannah, GA*                                   *May 11* – Thursday afternoon

Answers. I have them. I have a lot of answers. My brain is full of them. Still, I sit alone in my house. I told Ryder and Graham I needed time to digest everything. I gave everyone the day off so it's just me and all the answers floating around in my head. Of course, I didn't take the time to think of what to do after I chose to go digging.

I did check on Brooklynn's business. Met the assistant in Hampton and here in Savannah. It was good to see what she'd built. I could see how Moonbeam and Rehab Center an, Hope

Foundation, and JDJ could work together. It's good to have a new vision but I don't know if it's a possibility.

The previous feelings I had towards Brooklynn have flip flopped a lot over the last week. Now there's guilt that dances beneath everything else.

I've tried keeping busy. Lose myself in work. Answered phone calls with short and concise responses. Didn't work.

Now, my favorite movies are streaming on the big screen in my living room. It's as I'm doing this that Hope joins me.

"I should've known you and *Jack Sparrow* would be hanging out," she says.

"What do you know about my love of *Pirates of the Caribbean*?"

She makes this kind of snickering sound then gives me an incredulous look.

"You really don't know, do you?"

Settling back into my previous position of permanent couch potato, I work to balance the bowl of chips on one thigh and a container of trail mix on the other. I do an inner cheer when I'm triumphant. My outer smirk triggers an eye roll from the woman I'd all but forgotten was still here.

"Congratulations! Was that the goal for the day? Let me get a picture of this. I'm sure you'll want it for your wall or something."

She's being sarcastic. I know she is. There's nothing about her tone that says she's serious. Regardless, I carefully extract my phone from between the pillows where I'd stuffed it earlier then hand it to her.

"Thanks. That'd be great."

The look of absolute annoyance is priceless. Still, she takes the phone from me.

"That explains why you didn't answer the phone when I called or texted. Jackass."

"Thank you."

She freezes then cuts her eyes at me. For a second, I think she's going to chuck the thing back at me. She doesn't. Nope. Hope snaps a photo or two of me looking like the greatest form of slug ever. I'm loving the vibe. I should. I plan for it to be my standard state for as long as possible. When she turns the screen to face me, I wonder what she's about to do.

Hope doesn't make me wait for long. She tilts her head like she's going to take one of those standard selfies then sticks her tongue out. Once her middle finger is lifted and touching her lip, she snaps the photo. She takes a couple more before returning my phone to me.

"You know I'm going to make that my screensaver."

"Great."

"I'm also making that your contact photo."

"Even better. Still a jackass."

I chuckle.

"You can continue calling me that and I'm just going to thank you for it. It's like you're tickling me with your words when you say it."

She turns to face me. Her blonde hair has more of the lighter highlights she told once she likes to have when she's feeling good. It's also a lot longer than she usually keeps it. The curls are tumbling close to her ass. It reminds me of when we first met. That seems so long ago. Yet another thing I can't believe. I've been good friends with a female for well over ten years and we've never slept together.

Hope gives me a quizzical look when I smile in her direction.

"What? Why do you have that weird look on your face?"

I shake my head then reach in the bowl to toss a pretzel in the air. I'm lining up to catch it when she reaches out and snags it out of the air.

"Killjoy. That would've been perfect."

She turns away from me. Hope tries to use the curtain of her hair as a veil to keep me from seeing what she does, but I notice her wiping under her eyes. She feels me sit up.

"It's fine. I'm good. Just give me a sec."

Shifting the snacks off my legs, I set them on the table in front of me. I turn to face her.

"Bet you didn't think you'd be the one who needed a 'check in' when you came over here to rescue me from myself, did you?"

I hear her snort laugh before she turns to me. She slaps my leg but there's no real power behind it. Her head lands on my shoulders seconds later as she allows herself to cry. It doesn't happen often. When it does, it's beyond time. I hold her as she lets herself feel whatever it is she's feeling right now.

"Some days are harder than others. I still can't believe it's been a year. I have these moments when I think he's going to pull up, gun the engine, and ..."

"Hit the horn three times. Yeah. It was our signal when we were younger. It was our way of telling the other the coast was clear."

"Really? He never told me where it came from. It was just his way of letting us know he was home. Jake would go racing out the door the instant he heard the first blare of the horn. He always knew when it was his dad. Your mother tried it once a few months ago and Jakob just burst into tears. I couldn't even console him. I was a sobbing mess myself."

"Yep. I asked Jake if he wanted to go to the track with me a few months ago. He told me he didn't want to go yet. 'It's too soon'."

"I pretty much got the same response when all of his race car stuff suddenly disappeared from the shelves." She's quiet for a long moment. "He shocked the hell out of me the other day though."

"Oh yeah? How?"

"He came and sat down next to me on our front porch. He'd poured us both a drink of lemonade and tea with freshly sliced strawberries." She smiles a little and I'm a little confused. "It was

[170]

something Jeremy used to regularly declare he hated but he secretly loved. I didn't know anyone else knew until Jake handed me the glass."

"Wow. I didn't know that. He always told me he hated the taste of strawberries."

"Learn something new every day. That wasn't what shocked me though. Jake looked at me then said he would be ready to put all his racing stuff back up when his Uncle Jax was ready to be Daire again."

*Well. Fuck. Me. Running.*

"Wow. That's low. Even for you."

Hope nuzzles close to me then kisses my cheek.

"Yeah, I pretty much had the same response when he said it. Practically gutted me with one statement." She leans away then looks at me. "The two of you, the Shaw brothers, have so many similarities it's frightening. I think that's been the most difficult and best thing about this."

I shake my head. My reasoning for my funk all but forgotten as I take in her words.

"He was so much better. The man perfected everything he tried. He was my idol."

I watch as she swipes away a lone tear. She smiles again then takes my hand.

"He would say the same thing about you. The man was so stubborn and solely devoted to his little brother. You could do no wrong. He would always say …"

"There's a reason for everything. Yeah, I remember. For the life of me, I'm trying to make this make sense. I want this to have a reason because I'm not seeing it."

She rubs my hand then lifts it to her cheek. We share a watery look as we both fight back tears. Hope takes a deep breath then stands.

"There is a reason for it all. We may never know all of them, but they are there. I wish he could be here to see you through this next part."

Hope walks towards the door, grabbing her shoes and slipping them on before she turns back to face me. When she takes in the confusion written on my face, she chuckles.

"You'll be fine. I know you will. Oh, and the earlier thing was about *Pirates* and boats. Jeremy loved both because it was something he could share with you. It was your thing. I was surprised I didn't find you there. It was always where he went to think."

I nod because I usually would go to the docks where the boat Jeremy and I own still sits. I didn't because I couldn't find my keys.

"Like we said, 'There's a reason for everything'."

She nods. As she pads to the door, she has more to say.

"Go see her. She's lived without you long enough. You never know. It might do both of you some good. Dad."

That last word is tossed over her shoulder as she exits my front door. As usual, she's right. I probably need to see Jayla as much as she needs to see me. Probably more.

# CHAPTER 21
## *BROOKLYNN*

*Savannah, GA*                                    *May 12* - Friday evening

The last few days have been some of the most challenging for Journee. She's practically moved into my room with me. I don't mind. Whatever she needs. Journee has been here for me the entire time I've tried to work through whatever happened to me after the incident. Nothing has been all that clear from that time. She's been the friend I needed when I cried out my frustration. Her shoulder was the one I leaned on when my mind was so foggy, I could barely recall my own face.

Now, it's my turn to be what she needs. Paislynn has been amazing. She has been here, providing whatever I needed. It doesn't matter if it was business related or personal. Old me did an excellent job choosing an assistant. Noelle has spent just about every night with us. Mr. and Mrs. Forrester have practically moved into the guest room. If Journee isn't with me then she's with them. Yesterday, she was willing to talk about some details about the attack.

Hope House sent over gifts, cards, money, and get-well items. Seeing all the items, made me think of Daire. Not that he's far from

my thoughts. I have so much to tell him. One of the main things I want to talk to him about is what happened the night of the anniversary dinner. I haven't heard from him. It's been all hands-on deck here at our house. I haven't wanted to be far away from my friend.

She has waking nightmares. It's a scary time.

Still, a part of me yearns to hear from him.

"You should go for a walk or something. you've been cooped up in here with me for almost a week. Go out and see the world," Journee tells me as she joins me in the sunroom.

"I'm completely fine being right here with you. In yelling distance."

A small smile plays at Journee's lips. She touches her cheeks. That small action brings tears to my eyes.

"You have been the best and I am so grateful to know I have someone like you in my life. I don't want to be the reason you don't live. You've been working so hard to regain some semblance of self. I refuse to be the excuse for why you don't that damn puzzle still going in your head."

I'm shaking my head well before she even finishes her statement.

"I'm not … "

"Hiding out? Avoiding?"

"Right. I'm not doing either of those things. I'm here, caring for my friend."

"That friend loves you more than you know. She also knows you very well. I've seen you checking your phone. I've watch you pacing the floor and looking at the journals you don't think I know about. I also know you never called your mother. Do I know why you can't bring yourself to live with your mother? No. You have your reasons. I do know what it feels like to have a curious mind and not have access to any of the answers." She pulls me into a hug. The first one she's initiated. "Start with a small thing. Leave your friend with her parents, your other friend, and her boss. Go for a walk. Make one of your lists and commit to completing it."

Ten minutes later, all those people she mentioned are practically pushing me out the front door. I'm glad I was dressed.

I decide to walk towards the shopping center not far from where we live. As I walk, my mind drifts to the last time I saw Daire. I've been checking in with Hope who checks in with Graham on a daily basis. Daire and his friends went out of town. Apparently, Daire has some business to take care of and Ryder and Graham wen with him.

Journee was right. I have been repeatedly checking my phone. I was hoping he'd send me a text or call. He hasn't. That's been disappointing. I don't know what I expected to happen afterwards. I didn't exactly explain myself nor did I tell him what I should've told him a long time ago.

Fear makes people do crazy things. Back then, I was fearful of him remaining at my side, caring for our daughter and my ailing … I didn't want him to eventually hate me or us because he was unhappy with his subpar life. Things were expected of him and loved him too much to have him settle.

That day was the worst day of my like. I'd been so happy for him. I couldn't tell him just how thrilled I was knowing what I to say to him. Once I gave him the news about one of our children, I paused, and it hit me. I knew what I had to do. Just like that, I changed the course of the "us" we knew. No one knew what I'd told Daire that night. It was easier that way.

*He should know.* I was afraid he wouldn't understand. The more time that passed, the more I feared he would be too angry to understand why I did what I did.

The cruelest thing I did that night still haunts me.

*"What's wrong? Blaze, tell me. why are you crying?"*

*He'd looked so happy when he came in. His short hair, freshly cut. The balloons, bear, and flowers all bunch together in his big arms. Arms that would wrap around me so tight if I asked him to hold me. I wish I could, but I can't.*

*I'm crying for so many reasons. He'll stay if he knows. He won't go and I know it.*

*I've hidden so much from him already. What's one more thing?*

*The huge smile that crept all the way to his dangerously gorgeous green eyes is gone. He's worried for me. He doesn't know what's happening, but he can tell something's wrong.*

*"The baby ... is gone. The baby didn't make it."*

*I feel like my entire body is in pain. Everything hurts. I feel it twice over because I'm causing him pain.*

*"You should go. I need to stay here and heal."*

*"No," he says. I hear the catch in his voice, and I have to fight back a sob. "I'll be right here. I don't ..."*

*"NO! Jaxson, you need to go. I can't go with you. We don't have the same dreams. Everything is different now."*

*He recoils as if I've struck him. I never call him by his first name. Tears flow freely down my face, soaking the pillow beneath me.*

*"What ... what do you mean?"*

*His tears, they are like knives to my chest. I'm wounded because I'm wounding him.*

*Taking both hands, I wipe my face to clear away some of the tears then I look directly at him.*

*"I dare you to go and be a famous NASCAR driver."*

*Death. Blow.*

*He stumbles back. Leaning against the wall, he shakes his head before squaring his shoulders, and walking out my hospital room door.*

*I feel the moment he's gone. The wail that leaves me is even more devastating than any sound I've ever emitted.*

It was easier to tell myself that he'd left me. If that's the story, then I can blame someone else. Otherwise, I have to accept my part in it. I didn't want to do that. This way, he's the bad guy and I can direct my anger at him. Not that he ever deserved it.

I'm tearing up and not paying attention to where I'm going when I walk into someone.

"I'm so sorry," I tell the person.

When I right myself and look up, I see green eyes. Green eyes that look happy to see me. I turn slightly to see if there's someone behind me. when I turn back, the smile is hidden.

"Are you all right? I wasn't paying attention," Daire tells me.

"Neither was I. I'm so sorry. I think I got some of my …"

"What? What is it? Is something wrong?"

I'm distracted by the item on his necklace. I don't think I noticed this before. Around his neck is a silver chain. On that chain is a black ring with pink jewels.

*It can't be.*

I know this ring. I lean in to get a closer look at it.

"Where did you get this? How do you have it?"

He looks at me as if I've lost my mind.

"I bought it."

The look of incredulity on his face pisses me off.

"What do you mean? How could you have purchased one that looks almost identical to mine? My grandmother gave me that ring."

Unbidden, tears begin to form. I'm angry that he has something even remotely close to an item I've treasured for so long.

"Right. She …"

I can't fight them, and I refuse to cry in front of him again. I do the only thing I can. Run. I get away from him. I keep running.

*When you're ready, I'll tell you the whole story.*

My mother gave me the ring. She told me it was meant for me. My grandmother wanted me to have it. That was what she said. I almost called my grandmother to ask her why she didn't give it to me herself. It took me a moment to remember why I couldn't call her.

"Why can't you call her?" Noelle asks me.

I ran all the way to Hope House. My safe space. Noelle's office is where I finally stopped running. I scared her when I burst through her office doors. She's one of the only ones who has two French doors to enter her office.

*You were asked a question. Answer.*

That's right. I note that Noelle's voice sounded different when she asked me the question.

"I don't know if she's forgiven me. I couldn't bear knowing she's still angry with me." Noelle settles back in her seat. A look of disappointment shows on her face for the briefest moment before she nods then smiles. "I know what you're thinking. You don't have to pretend with me. I'm avoiding a difficult situation by choosing not to call her. You're right. Of course, you're right. Baby steps. I'm back at the company I created. Baby steps."

She offers me a smile, but it doesn't reach her eyes.

"Right. Baby steps."

She scribbles something on her notepad then pulls the sheet from it before looking up at me again.

"Are you alright? You seem upset, frustrated even. I don't think I've ever seen that look on you."

Noelle waves her hand then stands.

"I'm fine. Did you want to talk about what brought a very sweaty you to my office today?"

She smiles again. This time her usual serene and calm look is in place. Whatever it was, she's put it away. I wish mine were that easy. If it were then maybe my life wouldn't be the drama fest it's become.

*You would think.*

I don't know why a trinket has such an effect on me.

"That's a good question. Did your mother say anything else about it when she gave it to you?"

*When you're ready, I'll tell you the whole story. You're not ready yet.*

[178]

"No, not really, but I guess I could ask her."

Noelle nods then returns to where she was when I first arrived. She takes a seat at her table then looks at me expectantly.

"Well?"

"Oh. I should do it now?"

"No time like the present." She writes something on her notepad as I head to the door. "Brooklynn, if you're going in person, I'd stop home and shower first."

I look down at my clothes which are still drenched in sweat.

"That would probably be a good idea."

First home, shower, then head to my mother's for some answers.

# Chapter 22
## *Brooklynn*

It's a new morning. the start of a new day. My plan was to hit all the things that were on my list yesterday. When I got home, I looked at the time and knew there was no way my mother was going to let me into her house at that hour. It doesn't matter that I'm her daughter. If it's after 7:00 pm and I haven't called first, then she's not letting anyone including me inside.

If I were being chased by an axed murderer, she'd leave med out there, wishing me bon chance or something. In the morning, she'd shed a tear, one, step over my corpse then have someone take care of "the mess". My mother missed the empathy gene when they were handing them out. Hell, she missed the sympathy and caring gene as well.

Step one. Get dressed and come here. Step two. Knock on the door or ring the bell. Either one. I've been out here, for at least 15 minutes, debating which one I'm going to do. I'm still out here.

"Come on, Brooklynn. Just do it. Ring the bell or knock on the door. Stop making this more than what it is. Just ring the damn..."

The door suddenly opens. On the other side of it, isn't my mother. It's a very perturbed looking older man.

"Dr. Emory, Your mother says she can't take you dilly dallying at the door any longer. Please do come in," the older gentleman requests.

I don't come here often enough to know the staff who works here. My mother has been married to the mayor for the last year and a half. Maybe two years. Hold on. She might have been married to him three years now.

It's not important. Either way, I don't know who the man is that opened the door and he doesn't bother to introduce himself to me. I guess it doesn't matter that I'm her daughter. I don't live here so I'm unimportant.

"Hello Brookie dear. Thank you for finally coming inside. I couldn't take you being out there any longer. It was driving me crazy."

"My apologies. Mom."

My mother doesn't care to acknowledge the sarcastic tone to my voice.

"Not a problem. Are you here to pick up some more of your things?"

"No. I'm here because I wanted to ask you some questions."

"Sure. What do you want to ask?"

She looks like she might be open to sharing.

"I have questions about some things I saw in the box and the note you wrote."

My mom begins to busy herself with things that are on the table where she's sitting. I'm still standing next to one of the extra chairs in the room. She's folding napkins. I don't remember the last time I've ever seen her folding a thing, less more, a napkin.

"What about the letter?"

"You said something about me not being ready. Ready for what?"

"Nothing. I don't even recall why I put that in there. Um, I probably had too much wine that night."

"Really? Mom, just tell me." I'm not getting it. I know there's something. "I keep hearing voices. Before you go thinking I'm going crazy or something, let me explain."

She puts her hands up in mock surrender but doesn't say anything.

"The voice I'm hearing is yours. When I read the words, it felt like they weren't so much as me narrating but more a memory. My friend said something to me yesterday that got me to thinking. I don't know why I don't live with you. I know why I left before but I don't know why I'm not here now. Actually, I don't know what brought me to Savannah other than you saying I came to live with you. Why did I come to live with you?"

"Fine. I'll tell you this much. You came to live here with me because you didn't have a home back in Hampton. It was decided that this was the best thing for you."

That tidbit is new.

"Who decided? Why was it the best thing for me? What happened"

She waves her hands and shakes her head before replying.

"Brooklynn honey, I don't know if this is a good idea."

"Yeah. What's not a good idea? The two of us talking? I feel like people in my life are keeping something from me as a way of protecting me. The issue with that is it's having the opposite effect. I'm getting more and more frustrated because I can't figure out the pieces and how it all fits together. Something happened. I know something happened. My friend looks like she's just waiting for me to figure it out so she can finally say 'YES' then congratulate me for finally clueing in. It's so aggravating. I'm being told that maybe I should talk to you, but you don't want to talk. What am I missing?"

My mother groans. I don't think I've ever heard her groan before,

"Brooklynn, look at me. Look at my face and understand my words. If I could tell you what you want to hear, then I would. I

[182]

can't. Everything that has happened is already in your head. You know it. These 'pieces' you keep going on about, they're missing because you want them to be missing. You were the one who shut it off. Your brain closed that down. I don't know if it's to protect you or to keep you clueless or what. I just know it's there." My mother stands then walks towards the opposite doorway before she looks back at me. "There is nothing I can do about it. I can't keep doing this. I stopped ... I'm trying. That's all I'm saying. I'm trying to do right by you, but I can't keep having you attack me the way you have been. This is not my fault. I'm sorry. It's just not. It's not only me. Not this time. As I said in my letter, when you're ready to talk, I'm here. There are some meetings I need to get ready for so you can let yourself out."

Her orang sundress billows behind her. I don't immediately move. I stand there shocked by what she just said. I watch as she walks to the room she calls her "receiving area". After a few minutes, I do as she asks. I let myself out. The hope that this confusion would be over has been destroyed. I replay the conversation in my head the entire way home. I try to make it make sense, but it doesn't.

When I get home, I check on Journee and some things at M.R.C. then I head to my room. I study some things in my journal before calling it a night.

That night, I go to bed one version of Brooklynn and wake up another.

# Chapter 23
## Jaxson

Sometimes things just happen. You can't predict them. They are just there, and you must roll with the punches.

Over the last month, I've been playing the avoidance game with my mother. It turns out, she's been doing the same with me. Unbeknownst to me, she has been travelling for the last five weeks. She and my stepfather have been all around the world. I had no inkling that she wasn't in town. I'm a total slug for not picking up on the fact that she isn't the type to wait for me to take initiative to fix things. She's a fixer, a doer. Jeanine Shaw is the type to make things happen.

My father used to tell us all the time. "Your mother could run the entire Shaw empire and not break a sweat if she chose. Instead, she prefers to remain in the background and allow others to shine."

I miss watching the two of them together. They were the best.

My front door opens, and she walks in just as I'm coming down from the shower. She looks like she just stepped off a runway after spending some quality time catching some sun. This time away did wonders for her. She looks good.

"Congratulations, you have on actual clothes this time!"

# Plunge

I'm initially startled because I don't expect it to be her. When I see who it is I immediately pull her into a hug.

"Look who finally decided to rejoin the common folk. Welcome back, World Traveler. How're you doing?"

She pulls back and her baby blues take me in. Tears begin to pool in her eyes.

"Welcome back yourself, Daire." She pulls me into another hug. "I've missed you."

"I've been right here."

"No. No, you haven't," she sniffles and rubs my back.

"I'm sorry, Mom," I tell her. "For everything I did. I'm really sorry."

I've been wanting to say those words but didn't feel right not saying them face-to face. In this case, face to shoulder.

"You, my sweet boy, are more than forgiven." She hugs me even tighter. I love a good "momma" squeeze. "Goodness, this feels good. Now, you have to catch me up on everything that has been going on. I've spoken to Kennedy, Graham, Hope, and even Patrick on occasion but I want to talk to you. After. I have gifts and items to add to your walls and shelves. That library of yours has been screaming for some much-needed attention for too long."

We both laugh as I nod my agreement. For the next hour or so, we go through her bags, boxes, and other packages that she had delivered. Another thing I didn't know was happening this entire time. She, Kennedy, and Patrick have been coordinating things.

As she unpacks things, instructing me where she thinks should go, we talk about everything. We talk until the breakfast she requested is complete. We eat and talk some more. After breakfast, she kisses my cheek then tells me she'll see me later.

One would think, after spending all that time talking to my mother, I would be all talked out.

I'm not.

"Hello Mr. Shaw. So, to what do I owe the pleasure of this visit?" the good doctor says as her usual greeting.

I smile as I take my regular seat. This time is different. I feel it.

"Good afternoon, Dr. Embers. The pleasure is all mine."

The doctor squints her eyes, takes her glasses off, and stares at me for a moment.

"Mr. Shaw, for about a month now, roughly a month and a half, you've come into my office, just about every single day that Hope House is open. Every day, we do this little dance with words. You say something then I say something or vice versa. During your weekly sessions with Dr. Price, I'm told you are quite verbal. You share a lot about your past, but he tells me it seems like you're holding something back. Do you feel like you're getting something out of therapy?"

I sit back in my seat and take in the room for a minute or so before I speak.

"Did you know my mother used to bake?"

Dr. Embers smiles before flipping a sheet on her notepad and beginning to write. I smile to myself at the familiar action.

"No, you've never mentioned that before."

"Right. She used to bake all the time. When we were younger, she would tell us she baked when she was sad. The older we got, the more she baked. One year, when I was about twelve or thirteen, she stopped baking. It would be years before she even baked a pie again. You know why she baked so much?"

"She was sad?"

"No. She baked to keep herself busy. She baked to keep herself alive. Her children needed her. She didn't want to leave them. Her way of staying sane what's the focus on making something sweet. My mother said she was depressed. Frustrated with her life but didn't know how to ask for help. It wasn't until she got the help, that she found true happiness. Her life was truly saved and so was her marriage."

[186]

I hear Dr. Ember's pen scratching across the notepad.

"Why did you share that with me?"

"Five years ago, I nearly lost everything. I was doing all types of crazy things. My heart was broken when I was nineteen years old. I didn't handle the ending of that relationship well. As a matter of fact, I spent the better part of a year testing my limits and seeing how far I could go with things." I pause to take a breath. "When I was younger, someone dared me to do something like jump across a Creek and I did. I enjoyed the rush I got from it and being able to declare myself victorious. Every time someone would ask me to do something that might be deemed a little crazy or dangerous, if they attached the word 'dare' to it I would immediately do it. I had to do it. I needed to be successful. I took the middle name that was given to me, handed down to me by my parents, as a way of living my life."

"Did that make you happy?"

"I don't think so. It was more about the rush than anything else. Anyway. I found other ways to get a similar rush. I was racing in the big time. I finally made it. That did make me happy despite not having the person who I thought wanted to share that life with me. I started betting on horses. It was another race. The thrill of watching took away some of the pain I'd been living with since I left Hampton. I would go if I had money to bet and even when I didn't."

Again, I hear the scratching of the pen against the paper. I don't know why that sound is so calming.

"You said you almost lost everything. What happened that kept you from losing it?"

"My mother and my two siblings happened. I don't know how my mother did it. I don't know exactly what she said to the bank representatives, but she froze my accounts. They sat me down and staged a mini-intervention. They basically told me I needed to get my life together and find another way to deal. So, I did. I focused on doing things for my niece and nephew. When I wasn't busy doing that, then I was working on my brand and trying to maintain a reputation that my future children that be proud of."

"That's a good thing."

"Right. It is. Should have been." I pause again to take a deep breath. This next part might be a little harder. "Last year, someone mentioned this app. It's an app that shows you information about thoroughbreds. I almost downloaded it, just to check it out. Instead, I went to visit family. I don't know how he knew but he did. He knew something was wrong and he called me. That call saved me from doing something I know I would've regretted."

"Sometimes it happens like that. It shows you have someone in your life who cares."

I sit forward, placing my head in my hands. I'm feeling the tears that have started to form.

"Don't you get it doc. It's the domino effect that led to the worst night of my life. That phone call …" I have to stop because this is the thing that I've told no one. "It's my fault."

My shoulders begin to shake as I give in to the pain. I quietly cry. Doc let's me. She places a comforting hand on my back and allows me to let it out.

A blue light flashes on then off.

"Shit," she mutters, and I snort. That's the first time I've ever heard her curse. "Sorry."

I run a hand over my face then use the bottom of my shirt to wipe away the rest of the tears.

"It's all right. I'm going to slip out through the room over here."

"You don't have to …"

I hold up my hand, cutting her off.

"Yes, I do. I didn't even have an appointment, but thanks for listening."

She nods as the light flashes again.

"You're welcome anytime."

"Right. Thanks. I'll go so you can see your actual patient."

# *Plunge*

I look at the time as I make my exit. It looks like it's time for my date anyway.

*Savannah, GA*                    *May 19*- Friday afternoon

My "date" yesterday went better than I ever could've expected. I spent the day with my daughter. We went to Tybee Island. I told her stories and she shared her "picture book" with me. She said it was a gift from her great grandma Elle to her Starlight.

"*I'm Starlight. I was her bright star. Mommy is ...*"

"*Moonbeam. You're right. She's mine as well.*"

She is. I've been slowly spending more time with Jayla or J.B., the name I prefer calling her. She said it's what her mother would call her. I'm good with using the name. It's a challenge going to spend time with J.B. when her mother doesn't live far from where Mrs. Emory lives. Knowing what I know about Brooklynn and seeing how much my little girl misses her mother makes it worse.

I have to fight my inner urge to make this better for both of them. Keeping them apart isn't my choice. That's what the doctors say is best and I'm not the expert on these things.

I'm still dealing with my own shit, and I don't have a "block" to blame it on. Not one I'll admit to having.

I'm home with my family today. Not my entire family because some things still need to be ironed out. Most of them are here. The sharing and "reveals" continue.

"It was a ripple effect. As you well know. You were there when most of it happened," I tell Graham.

"Don't rewrite history, Shaw. I was there only in the sense of being at your side when you recovered."

I don't know why his words affect me, but they do.

*You know why. You know it as well as he does.*

"Because he ...," I quickly catch myself as I look around at the faces before me. All the faces that are here and the one that isn't. "You weren't the one with me, sitting next to me."

"No. He wasn't, but who was, My Love? Who was right next to you?"

Hearing the words, the endearment from my mother, is almost too much. I want to retreat from the edge, the place where they all want me to go. It's been so long since she's uttered the "My Love" phrase. I didn't think she even knew how to frame her mouth to speak them. Or maybe I haven't heard them because I didn't believe I deserved to hear them any longer.

I take my eyes off my mother and focus on the one woman who has been right here with me this entire time. Hope shifts her gaze from mine, but I can still see her profile. I watch as a tear trickles down her face.

"Jeremy," I choke out. "Fuck! I should've been the one driving. It should've been me."

I collapse into my mother's awaiting arms.

"No. No, my darling son. No. It shouldn't have been either of you. You didn't deserve the double loss. His wife didn't deserve to lose the love of her life. His children …" My mother's voice hitches, and I hear a slight sob. I reach up and pull her into me. "Those babies don't deserve to live without one of the best men we've ever known."

I hear another pain-filled sob. When I look up, I see Hope frantically wiping away her tears.

"Shit," she whispers as she uses her sleeve to catch them. "Sorry."

"No. I'm... so sorry. I didn't think... I've been selfish in refusing to deal with my pain. It was easier to ignore it than to deal with it head on, but I've been hurting you in the process. I'm sorry. I'm so so sorry."

"You did what you needed to in order to cope. My coping mechanism has been taking care of his little brother. He wouldn't have had it any other way. As a matter of fact, he would have my head if I left you to fend for yourself."

We share a laugh but it's a tear-filled one. I then snort because she's right. We both know it. He's always been the one to take care of everyone. If he were still here, he'd be pissed to know I don't have any idea what's going on with our sister. He'd be disappointed in me for not making sure Macey and Jakob were doing okay.

"I've been a really shitty uncle and brother-in-law. Hell, son and friend. This ... guilt has been a weight I've been carrying around like it's my best friend."

I take in every face in the room. Each of us looks as if we can finally breathe. I didn't realize I'd had this hold on all our lives by not dealing with the pain.

"You've helped them in ways you don't know. You're here. Mace thinks you're amazing for that alone." She releases a small laugh. "You're her idol. She brags to her friends about you all the time."

Some part of me cannot be prouder in this moment. I want to puff my chest out but know my mother would slap my chest if I did.

"Really?" I ask.

My mother's hand connects with my chest, and I realize I've failed at trying to hide my pride. Graham snickers. I glare around my mother at my friend. He gives me a look that says he's unrepentant as he wipes his eyes, trying to hide his own emotional reaction to all this.

"Oh yeah. You're Uncle Daire. You had this horrendous thing happen, but it was something she could relate to. So, you're on a whole other level with her."

"I can't imagine how she sees me that way."

"You're also the one who is the hardest on yourself. All the guilt you feel came from within. None of us blamed you for anything that happened that day. Jer would kick your ass for carrying this the way you have, Man, and you know it."

Graham's words are truth. Jeremy would be pounding on my arm for being such a major pain all this time.

"You're right. If he were here, he'd tell me I stole his thunder. Here he was. This great hero. All I can seem do is dwell on the loss of his life."

"That settles it!" We all look up at my mother who is the only one of us standing. "Tomorrow, we get together and have the celebration I should've had for my sixty fifth birthday. I'll even get Jovi on one of those video apps. I got to spend some much-needed time with my sweet girl while I was away. I think we've mourned and cried enough. Let's have some fun. Invite your closest loved ones and I'll invite mine."

She then looks directly at me and winks. I turn to look at Hope and Graham who just shrug their shoulders. What is my mother up to?

I guess we'll find out tomorrow.

# CHAPTER 24
## *BROOKLYNN*

### Jeanine Shaw's Second Birthday Affair

Strange. Strange things are happening. That's the best way for me to describe what has been going on. Last week, I went to bed feeling completely lost. It seemed as if I wouldn't find the answers I'd been looking to find. The next morning, it was like someone drew back the shade. The lights were on, and everybody was home. All the messages and notes and the voices, good gracious, were clear.

I'm aware of the fire and the loss of the house. I now know exactly why I can't call my grandmother. Had I ever called, I wouldn't gotten a prerecorded message on her voicemail. It would be my voice letting all the well-wishers know what happened and where they can send cards, gifts, or well wishes.

Being at Journee's was an active choice. I could've gotten my own place. I can afford it. I inherited money from my father, my mother's first husband. The Emory name is well-known for its fabrics. I didn't want to take the helm of the company. I wasn't ready. I wanted to start something that was mine. That's how M.R.C. came about. Turns out, Paislynn is an executive assistant who has been pulling double duty being the office manager at MRC and the liaison for Emory Holdings.

So many strange things happening. Journee is feeling a lot better and more comfortable in her own skin. She's taking self defense classes. The consummate passivist is learning to protect herself. A guy might have everything to do with that. She told me his name is Hudson Stone. That's all she'll tell me and nothing more.

The last strange thing happened not too long ago. As I walk back inside the house, Journee handed me an envelope.

"Package came for you while you were out. You going to be good here by yourself? I can call Noelle and tell her to head back before she turns in her keys."

"I still can't believe you convinced her to let go of her place to move in here with us."

"I'm being proactive. She practically lives here anyway. Plus, we live closer to where she works."

"True. Hold it. Rewind. What do you mean you're being proactive?"

"Sorry. Gotta go. Mom's taking me shopping before my appointment."

"I hope you purged your closet. Not another thing is going in mine unless I can claim it as my own," I yell after her.

"Love you," she responds just before sliding into the car with her mother.

"Love you too."

I close and lock the door before flopping down to the couch. When I pull out the card from within the package, I see it's a formal invitation to a birthday party for Daire's mother. I'm shocked to discover it's in a few hours. Talk about a last-minute affair.

Pulling out my phone, I send a text to the number on the card.

**Me:** *RSVP for two*
**Unknown:** *May I have a name to go with the response?*
**Me:** *Brooklynn Emory*

**Unknown:** *Don't you mean, Dr. Brooklynn Emory*
**Me**. *My turn. Your name?*
**Unknown:** *wouldn't you like to know?*

Somehow, I know exactly who it is. I know it's him.

**Me:** *a famous race car driver?*
**Unknown:** *correct*
**Me.** *Chance "the Trailblazer" Devereaux*
**Unknown:** *nope. He's happily married*

I giggle as I type my next response.

**Me:** *I don't know anyone else*
**Unknown:** *officially uninvited*
**Me:** *was Daire Deville's pride hurt?*
**Unknown:** *no comment*
**Me:** *see you tonight?*
**Unknown:** *it is a party for my mother*

A few hours later, I'm ready to go and saying goodbye to Journee. Her parents are stopping by shortly. They've been coming by instead of staying with her all day. She asked the to dial it back, so she doesn't cling to them being around. Journee says she'll be fine and to tell Noelle to enjoy herself.

Noelle is my plus one tonight. We might be each other's plus one. She received an invitation as well.

The car ride to the location is a quiet one until we pick up Noelle. I literally can't shut up. She listens to me blather on about everything and nothing. It's as if I didn't see her two hours ago, she isn't moving in with us, and she doesn't know most of the crap I'm telling her already. The stunner in her signature color of red quietly excepts all my words. Tonight, I'm rocking a multicolor ensemble that has major green accents. My jewelry and purse are green as well.

One guess as to who I thought about all day. If Daire and his transfixing green eyes were the guess, then absolutely correct.

I hear raucous laughter as the car pulls up to the house, I fled a few short weeks ago. The inside is lit up. Navy blue and silver are everywhere. It's a spectacle that only a Shaw could pull off in twenty-four hours. Hope told me Jeanine Shaw announced yesterday afternoon that they were having a party in her honor. From what she said, they scrambled but they pulled it off. It looks just as dazzling as Hope promised it would.

The front door is open, and a sheer curtain hangs from it. We walk inside and I get to take in Daire's home. I look around the open living room and try to take it in but am immediately accosted by two little people. Hope's children rush me.

They drag me around, showing off their uncle's house and their favorite places within. I'm then passed on to their mother who introduces me to some people I don't know. Graham and Ryder find me next. I'm introduced to Gemma, who is Daire's manager. I also get to reconnect with two people I haven't seen in years. Cynt, my high school friend, and Nee, Ryder's other half, and I sit down on the deck, catching up for a good hour. Ryder's brother is here. I watch the birthday woman talk to her daughter on one of the large screens. Daire's voice can be heard but I don't get to see him. Someone pulls him away. He seems to be as popular as his mother tonight. I've literally seen everyone else but just missed him. His house is too damn big. That's another thing that's strange. The number of rooms and the astronomical amount of space he has just to himself. I've even seen the man's garage.

Yet, I haven't seen him.

I feel it. The familiar tingle then his hand grazes mine. Just before our fingers lock together and I'm being pulled into the kitchen. The heart of the home and very few people are here. I am in love with everything here. This room is one of my favorites. The kitchen opens to the deck. There is a glass wall so whoever is in the room isn't staring at a wall as they prepare the food. It's beautiful.

"Hey, let me see 'em."

I smile at the familiar request before I face him.

"Hey, let me see yours."

He smiles as he looks at me.

"I've been sending you texts all night. You haven't answered one."

"You have. I must've put on silent instead of vibrate."

I look down to my purse, where my phone is, but he taps my chin.

"It doesn't matter. They weren't important. We're here now."

He's sitting there, looking at me the way I've always wanted him to look at me. It's the greatest and worst feeling all at the same time because I have no right to enjoy it. I'm in the know and he's not.

*No time like the present.*

I hear Noelle's voice as those words play in my head. Steadying myself, I look up over at him.

"Do you remember that last night? The night ... well morning when we were here?" I ask him.

Daire smiles then leans in. He takes my hand and I feel the play of his fingers as he glides the tips of them back and forth over my skin. He nods.

"I do. I recall wanting to talk to you and you having to run out."

I nod in agreement.

"Yes. You're right. I did have to leave that day, but I did want to talk to you. I'd wanted to talk to you about something I'd liked about. A thing I've kept a secret."

He suddenly stops moving. His eyes widen. The look on his face makes me even more nervous. Still, I want to press on.

"Blaze ... look ... "

I physically react to him using that name again. He'd used the last time we were here together, but I thought nothing of it. I chalked it up to him being caught up in the moment. This time, it's different. It means something more, but I can't get lost in that right now. I need to tell him or I'm not going to feel right about anything if we possibly move forward. The look he's giving me tells me there is a chance of that. I can't have that if I don't set the record straight.

"The night you came to my room, I started telling you what was going on. I paused to put the words together then something hit me." I take a deep breath then blow it out through my teeth. "People used to joke and say I looked like I had more than one baby growing inside of me. Turns out, they were right. I was pregnant with two babies that day. Only one ... passed away. I never told you about the other one. There's a reason for that."

He grabs both of my hands and I feel him shake his head. I hear a door close that I didn't hear open.

"Okay. We should ..." he tries to speak but I cut him off.

"This is probably the worst time for me to tell you this. I'm so sorry. It's just, you were giving me this look and it gives me hope. It makes me feel like there could be a second chance for us. I don't want this to be the thing looming over us."

"I know. I understand."

His eyes dart over my shoulder. Turning, I see that people I care about are trying to appear as if they are talking to one another. It's evident they are watching us, watching me. I'm the one who doesn't know what's really going on. Without turn back to Daire, I begin to speak.

"Can I let you in on another secret?" I ask him.

When I turn to face him again, his concerned face is... interesting. To say the least.

"They don't think I know, but I do. I know everything. I remember."

His posture is off. It's as if he's trying for one position but didn't quite get it right. Tension rolls off him.

"You do?"

"I know all about the losses I've suffered in the last eighteen months. I'm not 'over it', per se, but I believe I'm ready to deal with it."

Daire deflates right before my eyes. His response isn't exactly what I was expecting. It reminds me of Noelle and how she reacted the last time I was in her office. I'm preparing to ask him what's wrong when I hear the group join us again.

"We have a surprise and it's here. I'm so excited. Come on. I know you want to see it, Little Brother."

We both stand. Daire's hand slips from mine as he moves to join the group. I remain where I am until he turns to me. he beckons me with a gesture.

"Little Brother? That one's new."

"You don't like it," Hope asks him.

"I do. I like it a lot. Thanks, Big Sis."

I follow behind them. No longer part of the festivities. I'm replaying what just happened. The entire time, he seemed to be waiting for me to get to the point. It's strange. It's as if he didn't need me to tell him anything. Like he already knew.

*How?*

That's the million-dollar question, isn't it?

# CHAPTER 25
### *JAXSON*

**Day before the Annual Hope House Family Fair**

Life sometimes throws you a curve that you don't expect. It's those unexpected moments that begin to change how you see your life and world.

My curve came when I received a phone call asking if I would be interested in driving for a charity event. All drivers are donating to a children's hospital or facility of their choice.

I've been working out, getting back in shape, and this feels like the right time. Mace and Jake haven't stopped talking about it since they found out I was going to do it. Hope told me Jake has started to return his posters to the walls and things have slowly begun to appear back on the shelf.

One curve that hit me square in the chest came from Mrs. Coleman, Emory's mother. Never could've called that one even if someone would've lined it up for me. I've been spending a lot more time with J.B. Hearing that little girl call me "Daddy" is the greatest feeling in the world. I've also been stepping in to help so I get to spend more time with her. I'm picking her up and dropping her off every day.

# Plunge

Not having Brooklynn with us is killing me, but I can't tell her. She seems to be making some headway. Hope said she went with her to visit her grandmother's gravesite yesterday. She and I have been sending messages daily. I haven't been able to see her because of the training, interviews, and meetings.

We both have meetings. Being the boss carries a heavy burden.

*Curve ball?*

The mother, not the daughter. I picked up J.B. today and she wasn't her usual happy self. I asked her what was wrong, but she wouldn't tell me. It took me a second to connect the dots. On Fridays, I've been picking J.B. up from school then taking her to karate practice. Today, she said she didn't want to go to school or practice. I got her to go to school but practice was still a "no go".

As soon as I dropped J.B. off at school, I turned around and headed back to Mrs. Coleman's. No one answered the bell, and she didn't pick up when I called. I had to reschedule one of the interviews that was first thing this morning. My next call was to the mayor's office. The snotty secretary informed me the mayor would be unavailable for the next week.

I'd made plans for J.B. to be with me for the weekend not a week. That was just the tip of this particular iceberg. I received a call from the school. One of the teachers wants to speak with me when I come to pick up J.B. from school this afternoon. When I started picking J.B. up, I thought it would be a good idea if they had my contact information on file. Little did I know, they already had me listed as a parent.

Interesting tidbit of information.

The school called me again thirty minutes later. I started receiving emails from the school about functions and assemblies. Messages from the PTA and the schedule for upcoming practices, games, and meets. When an email about the following week's meal request came through, I had to stop the phone interview I was doing.

What the hell was going on? My next call was to the school.

"Hello. Hi. This is Mr. Shaw. May I speak with the principal?"

"Hello, Mr. Shaw. This is Ms. Abigail. I work in the office. Mr. Tanner isn't in right now. Is there something I can help you with?"

"I don't know who I should speak with about the number of emails and messages that I'm being flooded with today. Is there a glitch in the system over there?"

"No Sir. No glitches. I was under the impression this was a special request. We were told you needed to be informed of everything that happens at the school, so you were well aware. Also, all things related to and having to deal with Jayla Shaw would go through you. Were you calling about next week's breakfast and lunch choices?"

I believe my brain imploded just then.

"No. I'll have to call you back with those. Um … just out of curiosity. Who advised the office to do all of this?"

"Mrs. Coleman left specific instructions last Friday. She stated she'd be out of town for a while, and you would be handling things being her father and all."

Fuck. A. Duck.

That got my morning started and running in a different direction. Between interviews and meetings, I made phone calls to Kennedy and Patrick. I'd already started converting the closest room into a space for J.B., but now I had to have as much completed as possible. My little girl was now my responsibility, and I wasn't ready for that.

I had to figure out a way to rearrange meetings and interviews as quickly as possible. There are three more hours in the school day, and I was running out of time.

Forty minutes later, I have all, but one interview rescheduled. It's for one of the major publications so GiGi is chomping at the bit to make sure we get this one done. It's the only reason I don't cancel it all together. The only problem is it's directly after J.B.'s pick up time.

"I can do this. It'll work itself out."

Graham and GiGi have been holed up in my office. I ask them to get a variety of toys and games together. They have a different job title. Today, they get to be babysitters.

I arrive on time to get J.B. but I forgot about the teacher who wanted to speak to me.

Thirty-eight minutes. She talked to me for thirty-eight minutes about the class expectations. The last three minutes were her expressing her concerns about change and how it could affect a child. I wanted to tell her it isn't exactly a picnic for the adults. I refrained.

"Daddy, will you go away too?"

That question, that one question tabled all plans I had for the day. I wished I could call Brooklynn and tell her to come see her baby. Our daughter needed to know she hadn't gone anywhere. I can't. That's not a fucking option because we might lose her forever.

"Baby Girl, Daddy is going to do everything in his power to make sure he's here with you for as long as he can be. Is that good?" Her big, beautiful eyes looked up and caught my gaze in the rearview mirror before she nodded. I had a question of my own. "Did your gran ... Pippa tell you she was leaving?"

J.B. nodded.

"Julie told me today that Pippa wasn't coming back, and I would go live with you. I hear the sniffles and immediately start looking for a place to pull over. "What if mommy can't find me because I'm with you? I want to be with you, but I want mommy too."

I pull over just as she finishes her statement. I'm parked, out of the car, and holding my sobbing baby girl in my arms before the first tear hits her cheek.

"We'll make sure Mommy knows where to find us, okay Baby?"

She hiccups and sniffles.

"You promise, Daddy?"

"I promise."

I end up calling for a car because my little girl is tightly wrapped around me and she's not letting go. We talk the entire ride to Hope House. I let her know I have to do something really quick for work. I remind her where my office is then show her how far away I'm going to be before I leave her with Graham and GiGi.

How my parents handled this with three of us is next to amazing. Each one of us had our own version of demands and our parents fielded every one of them.

I cross the hallway to the room where I expect to find the interviewer only to find it empty. I hear conversation closer to the conference room near Hope's office. Shooting Graham and GiGi a text, I let them know I'm in another area.

**Graham:** *All good. Building with* Legos.

Instead of immediately entering the conference room to interrupt the women, I take a minute to gather my thoughts. I straighten my clothes then turn the corner. I'm frozen in place as I take in the room and faces inside it. My eyes dart up the hall to where a certain little girl is currently playing.

Gray eyes focus on me when I look back in the room. I don't know what my next step is. All I know is I don't think my daughter can handle her mother melting down in front of her today.

I pull out my phone to send a text when Hope turns to face me.

"Finally. I though you were going to be a 'no show'. Daire Deville meet ..."

"Paris Isabel Kelley. We've met."

P.I.K. has always been one hell of a storyteller. She does that almost as well as she takes photos. The two come so easily to her. She has a nose for knowing what her audience wants. I'm not surprised Graham convinced her to come down from New York to do this photo shoot and interview. GiGi told me she wants it featured on the website.

"Not only have we met. We know each other quite well. Don't we, Mr. Shaw?"

"Yes." I usually don't mince my words, but I don't want to shred Hope's brother in front of her. "Glad to know you're no longer working with L.A. or this interview would be over before it begins," he tells her.

"We are going to take that as our cue to leave. Ladies, let's leave them to it. Brook, you can follow me. We can talk in my office."

I breathe an audible sigh of relief when I hear those words. That means they could be there for hours, especially if Hope closes her door. I watch, like a stalker, as the two women walk to the door. Brooklynn turns to look behind her. I step out of the doorway then lean into Paris giving her a hug. She says something about being ready to get started. I nod as I step back. The door closes and the light above it turns on.

*Success!*

Bullet dodged for the moment. I spend the next thirty minutes counting the seconds until we are finished. Once we are down and Paris is leaving, I practically sprint to my office. We are packed and exiting the building five minutes later.

This isn't going to work. I'm going to cause myself to have some major issues if I keep this up. A message from Hope later that evening changes the game and makes me believe in something I didn't think I'd ever have again:

A future.

# CHAPTER 26
## *BROOKLYNN*

**Day before the Annual Hope House Family Fair**

This morning, my mother called me. If that weren't strange enough, Then the fact that she hung up when I answered would be. She doesn't really call me too often. Actually, our calls are pretty non-existent. When I try to call her back, it goes straight to voicemail. another thing that was odd. her voicemail was no longer set-up. it just repeated back the phone number that I called. A few minutes later, I hear Journee on the phone. Deciding to just try my mother again later, I jump in the shower. when I come out, I have another missed call from my mother in a note from Journee.

The note from journey said my mother called her but didn't give a reason why she called, nor did she leave a message. She just asked if I was at home. Strange. I get dressed then I leave for work. This has become my routine. today just feels weird. Yesterday, I went to my grandmother's grave site. I left with one major question. I've already reached out to Hope because I need to talk it through. Normally, add talk to Noelle but she's busy with movers today. Hope said she wouldn't be in the office for another couple hours. That meant I had time to kill.

# Plunge

After about an hour, I checked my phone and realized I have a voicemail. My mother is message wasn't what I was expecting.

*Hello there Brooklyn, I'm calling to let you know that I'm leaving. I'm going out of town indefinitely. I know I said you will be able to talk to me when you were ready. I have to apologize because that's not going to be the case. my hope is things will work themselves out. My promise was I would try. I did and quickly realized that's just not who I am. I know you and your grandmother once argued about me. Sorry to disappoint you, Sweetheart. As much as I hate to admit this, she was right. this doesn't suit me. take care of yourself. hopefully you'll find the answers you're looking for. Love you, Girlie. Your Mother.*

I couldn't even bring myself to react to that message. Nothing in it surprised me. It does hurt to know my grandmother was right for protecting me from her all those years ago. Grandma Elle knew her daughter well. She told me once that she hoped my mother would change. Beatrix never did. She was selfish when she was younger and acted spoiled. It was nothing that her parents had done. Beatrix took on a persona and remained in that character.

No matter what they said or did, their daughter wouldn't change her ways.

It was one of Grandma Elle's greatest heartaches. It broke her heart even further to learn my mother didn't contest my father's decision to leave me in the care of my grandmother after he passed away. The only reason Beatrix returned was to collect her check.

That is the woman who was my mother. Her leaving is just another situation. I'm not even shocked by the way she left.

My phone rang as soon as I finished listening to the message. It's Noelle.

"Hey there, how's the move going?"

"Good. I'm almost done already. Were you expecting some boxes today?"

"No. Did some arrive?"

"Yes. quite a few. So many that I don't know where you want me to put them."

"Did they deliver them to the porch or is everything at least in the house?"

"I haven't put everything in the house. What could fit in your room, I had them put it in there. If it didn't fit in there, I had them put it in the guest room. You know how I am. I got all my stuff sorted and situated so I started unboxing your stuff."

I couldn't contain my laughter. Again, this doesn't surprise me at all.

"I understand. Don't worry about it. I have a feeling I know where it came from. I'll see you later."

An alarm on my phone buzzes. When I look down, I see a reminder to head over to Hope House.

As I'm heading to Hope's office, I notice her and another blonde woman in a colorful pantsuit heading towards the conference room. Journee sees me and rushes over.

"Hey Honey, did you tell me you were coming here today?"

Smiling, I shake my head.

"No. What's going on?"

"Interviews for the upcoming charity race that Mr. Shaw is participating in."

"Who's with Hope?"

Journee shakes her head then pats my hand. I didn't even feel her grab it.

"I forget you don't follow the fashion world or magazines or anything really." She sucks their teeth. "Her name is Paris Isabel Kelley. She used to work with Hope's brother, Logan Alexander. They went their separate ways. I think there was a domestic dispute or whatever. Either way, Paris is this really amazing photographer. We have her book on our coffee table at home. I also follow her blog. the stories she tells some of the most entertaining I've ever read." Journee tugs my hand. "Come with me. Hope asked me to sit with her while she waits on Mr. Shaw."

I'm so happy to see Journee smile and practically all her wounds healed. I allow her to lead me towards the room.

"I apologize. Do you mind sitting with Journee and Ms. Kelley for a little bit? I'm sure Jaxson is running just a little bit behind. I have some paperwork to clear up for tomorrow's fair. It's something that slipped through the cracks even though Jaxson and I have been double and triple checking things." When I nod, she squeezes my hand. "Thank you for understanding."

"It's fine. I probably should be in there anyway. Journee is floating right now. She's a fan."

Hope laughs then heads towards her office. I, in turn, join my friend and her idle in the conference room. My arrival time is perfect. Journee is about to drench the pour woman in water. I tap Journee's shoulder just in time. I take the seat next to Journee and tune in to the woman's story.

"I was recently the photographer for a wedding where the bride walked down the aisle to the theme music of *Thor: Love and Thunder*," Ms. Kelley tells us.

I watch as Journee's mouths drop open. I'm thinking this must have been an amazing sight. I do recognize the movie.

"Tell me you have pics. There has to be evidence since you witnessed this thing," Journee says.

"Hell yes! This shit was epic. The bodice of the bride's wedding dress was pure, starch white. From the waist down were the most stunning arrangements of colors I've ever seen. From the bottom up was black then blues through to a vibrant red. The colors kept going through, from a yellow to a pale beige to finally a staunch, perfect white that matched the bodice. The train followed the same pattern. I'd never seen a dress like hers before."

"It sounds like it was unbelievably stunning," I state.

"It was." Ms. Kelley nods then continues. "The bride's bouquet matched the colors of her skirt and train. It was breathtaking. The guests didn't get to initially enjoy how beautiful it was. The bride is a theatre major with dreams of being on Broadway. Which means ..."

"This wedding was a full-on production and spectacle," Hope adds as she walks in.

"You can say that again." Paris turns to face Hope then quickly adds. "Don't. It's not necessary."

"I forgot how well we know each other. Continue for the uninitiated."

Journee snickers before Paris continues with her retelling of the events of this wedding. She's just finished telling how the bride had someone toss her "the hammer" and her new husband caught it when I feel the tingle. Daire appears in the doorway. He doesn't look like his normal self. He's tightly wound, but it seems I'm the only one who can see it.

"Finally. I thought you were going to be a 'no show'. Daire Deville meet ...," Hope begins when she sees him.

"Paris Isabel Kelley. We've met," he says.

"Not only have we met. We know each other quite well. Don't we, Mr. Shaw?" Ms. Kelley asks.

"Yes. Glad to know you're no longer working with L.A. or this interview would be over before it begins," he tells her.

"We are going to take that as our cue to leave. Ladies, let's leave them to it. Brook, you can follow me. We can talk in my office," Hope instructs.

I follow her to her office but feel like eyes are on me. When I turn, I see no one. I close the door behind us.

"Sorry about that. Thank you for being flexible."

"I completely understand. I'm on your timetable."

"You said you needed to talk to me."

"I do." Taking a seat and one of her chairs, I begin. "What I'm about to tell you, no one knows. I know it's confidential, but I felt like I needed to say that. Yesterday, I went to my grandmother's grave site. It was ... well it wasn't what I expected."

"What were you expecting?"

"I was expecting to go there and see two gravestones. That's not what I saw. I've spent the better part the day doing research. I've called around places but I'm still not getting response I need."

"Need for what? What response are you looking for?"

"I know this is going to sound ... for lack of a better word ... crazy but I'm looking for my daughter. "

"Your what?"

"That's right. you don't know about her."

Tears pricked my eyes. I'd expected to find them lying there side by side. I was ready for that. Seeing only one gravestone had me wondering where was the other one?

"Brooklynn, tell me what you're thinking or what you're asking."

"I'm asking if this is a sign that I'm losing my mind. Am I hoping for a different outcome because some part of me doesn't want to accept the truth? I'm afraid of slipping back behind that block. I don't wanna lose myself again."

"Does that mean you remember?"

Hearing the hope in her voice makes me look up. Hope's eyes are full of tears that match my own.

"Everything. Mostly. It's just this. I need to know. My grandmother was trying to tell me something before she died. We argued about telling Daire the truth. She wanted him to know, and I was afraid to tell him. It was my fault. I'm the reason for that fire. Grandma Elle was upset and probably wasn't paying attention. She wasn't paying attention because she was unhappy with me. She was disappointed."

Hope moves to sit next to me. We spend a couple hours talking. By the end, I felt a lot better than I did and I arrived. We even talked about my mother leaving. She tried to convince me to go to the fair tomorrow, but I can't. I think that would be too hard since I don't know the outcome of my inquiries.

My afternoon is spent with Journee and Noelle. I was right about the packages and boxes. My mother had all of it shipped to me from her house. She really wasn't coming back. I can't dwell on it. I've done enough of that in my life.

Picking up my phone, I do something I never expected. I begin a message. In it, I ask the one man I've always wanted out to dinner. I don't send it.

I join my friends in the living room. Journee and Noelle talk about the fair and all the fun they've had at the previous year's event. For the rest of the night, all I hear from them centers on the fair and how much they're going to miss me if I don't go with them. They try and try but failed to wear me down.

I can't do it. My puzzle still isn't complete.

# CHAPTER 27
## JAXSON

### Annual Hope House Family Fair

My "date" for the night isn't the one I thought it would be considering how hard the Blaze Fanclub pushed for her to here. The one who I have on my "arm" is no one to snub. In a way I have Blaze with me. having JB holding my hand is almost better.

*The best would be if all three of us were here together.*

Agreed.

I'm glad Hope agreed to change the design of "A Gambler's Delight" to a more kid friendly venue. At first, she fought me on it. When Hope found out she had a niece, she nearly lost it. Her entire demeanor changed. Suddenly, she was more amenable to everything I wanted to do. Given who I was doing it for, she couldn't help but agree to it all. We've converted a portion of Forsythe Park to our own "Vegas Strip". Every game has an adult and a kid-friendly version. There are so many different attractions including a bounce house that J.B. has said we have to go in before we do anything else.

Right now, she just wants to walk around to sketch out a game plan for the evening. That is definitely a quality she picked

up from her mother. She's making notes on a notepad she had in her purse. If the purse hadn't thrown me for a loop already, the damn notebook would've blown my mind. She giggles causing me to look down. I want to know what caused her to laugh. I want to know everything about her. Six years is a long time and I have a lot of catching up to do.

"I knew it!" She starts to skip while pulling me through a small crowd. "Come on, Daddy. Come on!"

I don't know what she sees but whatever it is has her excited enough to drag me. Her grip tightens as the crowd parts, and I get a glimpse of what she sees. Correction. I should say who.

The look on Brooklynn's face worries me. Maybe those doctors were right all along, and she can't handle the truth. Her face initially registers shock as she stands frozen in place. Confusion is the next thing that moves across her features as she looks from me to J.B. then back to me. I don't know what to think. I'm in unknown territory here. I don't know how to proceed. Our daughter has no such problem. She's bounding forward without a care in the world.

Mrs. Coleman has been busting her ass for the last year to keep this from happening. It's not something I set out to do. Even though, it is something I said we should. As fear begins to be the predominant look on Brooklynn's face, I'm feeling I was totally fucking wrong about my belief that we should let her see her daughter.

J.B.'s let's go of my hand and leaps. Every part of my being is freaking the fuck out. I'm scared Brooklynn isn't going to catch our little girl. I'm afraid this perfect, little bundle of joy is about to be devastated and I'm not ready witness that heartbreak.

I do the only think I can. I'm hoping it's the right thing to do, but who the hell knows.

[214]

# Plunge

*Savannah, GA*                                    *June 10* – A Gambler's Delight Event

My arms wrap around her. Two little arms reach up and hug my neck.

*Please let this be real. Please don't let it be a dream.*

I know I'm not going to be able to handle it if she's not real. She must be real, right? Her hand was in Daire's. If this is a dream, the fear I saw on his face right before I caught her wouldn't have been there. It was never there before.

*"It's his right to know, Moonbeam. This isn't right. Why would you keep this from him?"*

*I stand from the kitchen table and walk to the sink. Quickly washing my dish, I try to calm myself. This isn't something I want to hear.*

*"Now that you've shared your secret, I guess everyone should share theirs!"*

*It's the first time I've ever raised my voice at my grandmother. She gasps and I turn on my heel, making my exit.*

Not ten minutes later, the house was on fire. Tears stream down my face.

"Oh God."

Daire steps closer as I begin to break down. His arms wrap around the two of us as the last of the puzzle begins to slide into place.

"I knew you'd be here, Mommy."

Her little voice. That little voice has changed. How did this happen? She sounded the same but also so different. It's too much. I want to take a moment to make it all make sense, but I don't want to let her go. I'm afraid if I let her go then she's going to slip away again. She's here. She's with me. She's real. I'm not imagining her. I'm not looking at some memory. If I were then Daire wouldn't be here. He didn't know about her. He didn't know she existed. Him being here changes things. I want to know how this happened. So many questions.

[215]

A sob breaks free from me. I hear a sniffle then feel wetness on my shoulder.

"It's okay, Baby Girl. I'm right here."

I feel her shake her head before she pulls away. It's then that I realize she was on my other shoulder. His hold on me tightens and I step closer to him. Jayla wraps her arms around the both of us. The familiar feel of a pressure takes over.

*"He's your familia, family, Nieta. Moonbeam, tell him. No mas secretos. No more secrets."*

It was the last thing she said before she told me she loved me. My legs give out as I recall the last time I heard her voice. I also remember why all of this hit so hard. Pain. I feel a sharp pain.

Daire is right there. He has me. He has both of us. I feel him lift me into his arms.

"I've got you, Blaze. I've got you both."

That's all I hear before I give in to the darkness. This time, I hope I remember everything. I don't want to lose ...

# CHAPTER 28
## JAXSON

Panic. I'm fucking losing it. She fainted. It was too much. I'm an asshole. I should've known.

"Jaxson? Jaxson?"

I hear my name, but I'm too wrapped up in my thoughts to respond. She fainted. My little girl is wrapped around me as we wait. We're waiting to see if this was too much, and her mother reverts or some other thing the doctors rambled off when I brought her in.

"Mr. Shaw? I can take her," Dr. Embers offers but I can't.

I'm not letting her go. No fucking way. She's the only reason I'm still standing. The thing I feared happened. J.B. was afraid she did something wrong. She started to blame herself for what happened. She asked me if she'd held her mother too tightly. I had to reassure her and let her know that nothing she did made her mommy sick. Still, she cried. She told me she missed her mommy all this time.

"I don't want her to go away again, Daddy. Please tell her to stay. Make her stay, Daddy."

*Fucking. Gutted.*

I haven't cried this much since they told me the news of what I thought was the worst thing that could ever happen to me. This is worse. This is a hell of a lot worse than that. No one could've prepared me for how protective I am of this little person. No one could've told how much I would open myself up to this little person with my eyes and her mother's smile.

"Jaxson, have you heard anything yet?" Hope asks me.

Graham, GiGi, and Brooklynn's friend, Journee, come rushing into the waiting area. I don't know who called them. I made one phone call and one phone call only. Graham is my emergency contact person. He's been there with me this entire time. I didn't think to call anyone else. Hell, I didn't even call my ...

"Mom?"

She walks in with Ryder close on her heels. I didn't expect this. I know all of them care but I didn't expect all of them to be here just because I made one call.

"You naughty boy. Why didn't you tell me?" Tears spring to her eyes as she looks at me then to my daughter. Her granddaughter. "I'm so mad at you."

She can barely get it out before she's wrapping me up in her arms. I didn't know what I needed until all of this happened. I didn't know I needed her to be here until she was. Just like I didn't know I wanted this little girl until she was here, in my life.

"How ...?" I ask but I already know.

Graham made a phone call. It's what he does.

"Not now, my darling boy. It's okay. Everything's going to be okay."

As I hold tight to my mother and my little girl, I take in the faces surrounding us and somehow, I know. I know we're going to be all right. I don't know what's coming but I know we're going to figure it out.

Someone clears their throat. A male. We all turn to face an older male in scrubs with a stethoscope around his neck. My hand immediately goes to J.B.'s back. The doctor looks around.

"Is a Jackson Shaw here?" he asks.

I guess I'm being blocked by the people in the room. Everyone turns so the doctor can see me. It's then that I realize he's about half a foot shorter than I am and that's the reason he probably couldn't see me. He looks up at me and scrutinizes my face for a moment.

"Hey Doc. I'm Jackson Shaw."

He gives me a onceover once more before he snaps his fingers.

"You're Daire Deville. Boy, have I missed you on the track?"

*I will not punch this guy. I will not lose my shit on the doctor man. I cannot hit a fan. He has news about Brooklynn. Plus, they will probably fine me.*

"Apologies. She ... Miss ... Dr. Shaw ... no, Dr. Emory is awake. She asked for you. Is this ...," he fumbles around in his pocket and it's taking everything in me not to hit this guy. "Jayla Shaw? If so, she was asking for her as well."

I don't know why, but I look at my mother. I'm suddenly unsure of my next move. I don't know if I want to take the chance of this going "ass over elbows" as Jeremy would've said. My mother nods her head but it's Hope's voice I hear.

"I dare you to go in there and have everything you've ever truly wanted happen."

Facing my sister-in-law, I pull her into a hug then kiss her cheek. I follow the doctor around the corner then through a corridor. The doctor immediately goes in, but I stop. Adjusting my precious cargo, I kiss the top of her head before taking a deep breath.

"Here goes nothing."

Opening the door to Brooklynn's tear-streaked face is not what I was expecting. The instant she sees me everything changes.

"It was real. I was right. It was real. This is real, right? Please don't let me get my hopes up and this is some horrible nightmare. It would be a nightmare ..."

As quickly as I can, I move to the bed and grab her hand. She reaches out with her other hand and pinches me.

"Ouch. You've got that wrong, Doc. You're supposed to pinch yourself."

She laughs then covers her mouth.

"Is this, okay? I mean, are you alright? I feel weird asking you. The doctor said you asked for us."

She nods her head then winces. I move to check it but she waves me off.

"I did. I needed to see both of you. Seeing you with her makes this real. All this time, I didn't want to believe it was. I didn't think I had any right to ... this."

I understand that feeling. I know it well. It's what I've felt all this time.

"We've got a lot to talk about. So, fucking much. I should be pissed at you, but I can't be right now. Not right now."

The doctor clears his throat. I forgot he was in the room until just then.

"I'm going to leave you to it. Just wanted to say we're going to keep you overnight for observation, Dr. Emory, then you're free to go as soon as tomorrow. Keep an eye on the bump on her head though."

We both nod our heads. I listen for the door to close behind the doctor.

"First stop ...?" she begins.

"Hope House."

# EPILOGUE
## *BROOKLYNN*

*Savannah, GA*                                    *April* - Monday morning
### Ten Months Later

We sit on a park bench waiting. It's a beautiful day in Savannah. I love these days. Yesterday, it rained all day. As much as I love how quiet the city is when it rains, it makes me miss the hustle and bustle of Savannah streets. Taking a deep breath, I inhale the scent of fresh flowers, newly mowed grass, and the exquisite flavors only downtown Savannah could produce.

Jayla suddenly hops off the bench and takes off running. I move to follow her but instantly stop because I see exactly where she's headed. Her father spreads his arms wide and catches her when she launches herself from the ground. This little bundle of energy is being enrolled in gymnastics today. We've also talked about possibly getting her into a rock-climbing class. If she's not leaping, flipping, or tumbling, she's climbing on something. mainly, her father or her Uncle Ryder or Uncle Graham. She even has her cousin climbing things with her. Those two instantaneously hit it off. They're inseparable. Seeing them together makes me feel bad for not telling Daire about Jayla sooner.

I shake myself. Repeating Dr. Broughton's and Noelle's reiterated words, I tell myself I need to let go of the guilt of that. Daire has forgiven me. for the most part. Every so often, he taunts me with it. The instant he sees how I react to it. He changes his tune.

Seeing Daire with Jayla is one of my favorite things to see. I love how much he loves her, how he dotes on her, how much he cares for her. It's the best thing. It's better than anything I ever dreamed up. We've talked a lot. So much has been shared. The good, the bad, and the ugly has all been laid out.

We both have had more than enough of holding on to the mess. All our baggage is out there for the both of us to claim. The both of us see personal therapists. We also see a couples' therapist.

It's official. We are a couple and I'm loving every moment of it. Daire is even returning to racing. He's been training and is finally able to get himself in and out of the car with no trouble. I didn't know they had to get out of the cars in seconds with all the racing gear and his helmet. He is like a kid in a candy store because his new vehicle is equipped with CD Enterprises neck protection device. Knowing my guy is thrilled to have his idol's equipment in his ride makes me one happy chick.

"What are you thinking about?" Daire asks me. I smile up at him as he holds our daughter on his back. "You can't think of that for a number of reasons."

I laugh out loud.

"What's funny, Mommy?"

I shake my head preparing to respond but Daire beats me to it.

"Mommy's being a bad girl."

I swat Daire's leg but he's not paying me any attention.

"My turn. What are you thinking about?' I ask him.

He turns then puts Jayla on the bench before taking a seat himself. Jayla leans in and kisses his cheek.

"Now, Daddy?"

[222]

He nods his head, and she smiles a toothy grin. Minus one tooth that she recently lost.

"Brooklynn Nicolette Emory, my Blaze, mother of my child, owner of my heart and so much more. I know we've been through our share of pain and heartache. Some we caused each other. I always said I wouldn't screw up what I had with you if I ever got a second chance with you. Here we are. Will you make me the happiest man in Savannah? Or sitting on this bench in our park? Will you marry me?"

Jayla pulls the band that Daire gave to my mother who then gave it to my grandmother who gave it to me. at the same time, Daire opens a ring box with a gorgeous pink and white diamond ring with a black band that matches perfectly with the band. I'm momentarily speechless as I look at both of them.

Daire looks over at Jayla who nods her head. For a second, I wonder what else they cooked up. I don't have to wait long to know.

Jayla clears her throat, then says, "I dare you, Mommy."

Who could say no to that?

Of course, I say, "Yes". Leave it to Daire to one up himself.

"I dare you to marry me right here and right now."

Suddenly, people hop out from behind trees. Journee is there, holding a garment bag. Noelle has her makeup case and a rollaway cart.

"I haven't even said I would. Why do y'all have all this stuff?"

"Are you really going to turn this man down?" Journee asks.

"No. Wait. are you backing down from a dare?" Noelle adds.

I laugh at them both.

"I'm not the one with the issue of not backing down from a dare."

Several people call my name, including Mrs. Shaw, a woman I've grown very close to over the last few months. It took her a little bit longer to forgive me for keeping her grandchild from the family, but now she loves me. Obviously.

On April 13th, a gorgeous day in Savannah Georgia, I agreed to marry the man of my dreams. I also agreed to never keep another secret from him. As a result of that agreement, I made an announcement at our impromptu reception on the rooftop of the Thompson Savannah.

"Jaxson Shaw, I dare you to be the best father ...," I whispered in his ear as we watched our family and friends laugh and dance the night away. He smiled then moved in to kiss me, but I stop him with my finger over his lips. "To both of our children."

He looks confused for a second. I see the moment he understands.

"You're ... we're pregnant?!"

I nod and he kisses me.

"I'm going to be a grandmother again!" his mother screams and the room erupts in cheers.

Congratulations go around. A twinge of sadness overtakes me as I think about my mother. Looking at Daire's mother, seeing how thrilled she is, makes me wish my mother could be like her. Sadly, Beatrix Coleman wasn't created to be that person. When I found out how quickly she handed Jayla off to Daire, I was so mad I called her to tell her what I thought of her. That's when I found out the numbers we had for her were no longer in service. During one of our chats at Hope House, Noelle told me I should write her a letter, mail it, but don't put a return address on it. She said if my mother received it then fine. If she didn't then I'd never know and that would be fine too. The point of the letter is to write it all down, get it off my chest, then let it go.

So, I did. It isn't until moments like this that I have a lapse. I look around, take in all I have and choose to dwell on what it is I still have. When I do, I feel one thousand percent better. I chose to take the plunge, gambled  with my heart, and I've come out a winner.

# Plunge

I'm going to make sure to hold on to this happily ever after. Leaning over, I kiss my husband while our little girl dances and eats wedding cake in the chair next to us.

*The End*

Want to keep up with all the other books in K. Bromberg's Driven World? You can visit us anytime at www.kbworlds.com and the best way to stay up to date on all of our latest releases and sales, is to sign up for our official KB Worlds newsletter HERE.

Are you interested in reading the bestselling books that inspired the Driven World? You can find them HERE.

*Myrtle Beach, SC*                                    *May 5*- Thursday

Finally. We're finally able to get away from everything. It's been nonstop motion getting our lives to become one. Moonbeam wouldn't agree to leaving Savannah until we were all settled. She couldn't leave our daughter until she was comfortably surrounded by all things Blaze and Daire. I beam from ear to ear every day I get to say those words.

Our daughter. Our home. Our lives.

It feels good to think that. Almost as good as it feels to tell people "I'm going somewhere with my family" or "I'm going to speak to my wife about that". It's good to see the light back in my wife's eyes.

*My wife.*

I have a wife. I didn't think I'd ever get to say that. That's a great feeling as well. I'm riding my bike around town today. I'm restless. My pregnant wife is back at home resting. I kept her up last night. Being able to have my wicked way with her is the icing on top of the cake.

My phone rings causing me to break away from thoughts of my wife riding her "own version of Woody" this morning. I'll never look at that damn toy the same way.

"Hey, you've got Shaw."

"Hey Man, where are you?" Ryder asks.

Judging by his tone, some shit has gone down.

"I'm in South Carolina. What's up?"

"It's 'The Judge'. Nee is ..."

Signaling, I switch lanes then pull over.

"Did something happen to her?"

"Don't know. All I know is she's gone and the bastards who took her are making fucking demands."

Not what I was expecting him to say. I'm sending texts to a couple of my contacts.

"What do you need?"

"I'm probably going to need you to toss money at the situation."

"Done. Where are you?"

He chuckles.

"South Carolina. Meeting with an associate."

"Give me the address and I'll be there as soon as I can."

"Daire, thanks, Man."

"Not necessary. You're family."

I'm on my bike and racing back to my wife. She's going to want to know what I'm about to do. I wasn't always on the right side of things. It looks like I have to kicks some old rocks. I'm more than willing to do it. Like I said, this is family.

# THE RING

*BROOKLYNN*

Daire shared with me the story of our rings. He was out with his brother one day and his brother asked him to go somewhere with him. It turned out it was to a jewelry store. Nothing there matched what his brother wanted. Seven stores later, one of the owners told them of a unique ring designer.

He and his brother set up a meeting. Daire had just been along for the support. After observing the process, he got an idea for something for his future wife. The more they spoke, the more he thought of me. Hence, the pink and white diamonds with a black gold band. There are two interconnecting rows of white and pink diamonds on the ring that interlocks with the band. at its center is a square shaped pink diamond. It is nod to the ring my grandmother once wore.

Once he had it, he knew he couldn't keep the band. In his heart, he said he knew who it belonged to. Daire sent the ring with a note to my grandmother. In his note was an apology to her and a message to give me the ring when I needed to know I was truly loved.

My grandmother did exactly that. Three years ago, I was questioning everything. I didn't know if anyone really ever wanted me. To my mother, I was a means to an end. A way for her to capitalize on some money. To my grandmother, I felt like her

burden. The one she was sacked with because of her failure with my mother.

We all have our burdens to bear. My grandmother and I cleared all of that up later. Still, that is what I felt. Grandma Elle sent my mother the ring and told her to deliver the message. My grandmother added that I was loved much more than I will possibly ever know. I didn't know just how true those words were until Daire shared the story with myself and our daughter.

Greatest gift I could ever receive: Hope.

I'm so glad I took the plunge.

# The Playlist

- "Mirror" by Madison Ryann Ward
- "Mmm" by Laura Izibor
- "Is This Love" by Corinne Bailey Rae
- "Feels Like" by Gracie Abrams
- "Fire in the Sky" by Anderson Paak
- "Shortie Like Mine" by Bow Wow, Chris Brown, Johnta Austin
- "So Sick" by Ne-Yo
- "Trip" by Ella Mai
- "U Move, I Move" by John Legend, Jhene Aiko
- "Falling in Love at a Coffee Shop" by Landon Pigg
- "Loved by You" by Kirby
- "Say So" by PJ Morton, JoJo
- "Anything for You" by Ledisi
- "Best Part" by Citizen Queen
- "I Can't Make You Love Me" by Tank
- "Healing" by Fletcher

# ABOUT THE AUTHOR

Kelsey Elise Sparrow is an author and lover of romance novels. She writes in various genres: rom-com, MC, PNR, and historical to name a few. As a lover of great movies, music, and books, her characters express interests in each as well as so much more. The worlds she creates are based upon dreams and imaginings that will take the reader on a journey unlike any other.

Kelsey calls Georgia her home. She is mother to a wonderful son, loves playing games, Marvel, and exploring. Her most notable series is The Norton Sisters. Watch for what's to come with The Whiskey Sweet and Inked to the Max novel series. Stories with Heart. Sass. Shock.

**Website**: http://kelseyelisesparrow.com
**Facebook & Twitter**: @kelseyesparrow
**TikTok & all other social media:** @kelseyelisesparrow

# AUTHOR'S NOTE

Yay for you! You made it to the end! Congrats! I'm so glad you did. My characters and I are riding on a dancing cloud knowing you made it this far.

Thank you. From the bottom of my heart, I say thank you for taking the time to read my work to its completion. I'm so thrilled you did. My hope is that this wasn't a lesson in "How to labor through a novel". It is my goal that every work devoured by readers is enjoyable. If it isn't, then what's the point? I also hope that an emotion or two was sparked, all good emotions, of course.

If you *did* enjoy this book, there are several ways you can support it and its author:

First, you can message a friend and tell them about it. If you *really* want them to read it, then gift them a copy.

Second, please "like" my author page. When you post statuses, be sure to click the smiley face button at the bottom of your post entry, and select "Reading," then type in the title of the book. This will help your friends easily find the purchase links and information on it.

Third, please consider leaving a review for this book. It is always appreciated, and I read every review posted.

Fourth, you could also use the "Recommend" feature of Goodreads to spread the word.

Once again, thank you for taking the time to read my novel. Be sure to check back soon, there are more to come.

Remember to "Live life out loud!", "let your imagination take flight through a good book" and HAPPY READING!

~Kelsey

# *Join Reader/Fan Group*

Hey there,

Kelsey here. If you are a fan of my work, then you have to be here. I'll share details of what's to come, do giveaways, and give you exclusive access to ARC copies of my works. Join this world of fantasy, fun, and fanaticism (Yes, I typed that!) Would you like first chance at exclusive access to prizes and swag?

Know what's coming next by joining my reader group: Kelsey's Sparrows.

*Kelsey Elise Sparrow*

Join here:
https://www.facebook.com/groups/kelseyssparrows/

Feel free to sign up for my newsletter here:
www.kelseyelisesparrow.com

## Acknowledgments

It's always a difficult task to recall all the names of those who had a hand in the development of a work. I never want to forget anyone, so I make it easier on myself and say thank you to each set of eyes who read this work then gave me feedback. I'm grateful for the Sparrows who keep me entertained and remain supportive throughout this journey. To each and every reader, you are the reason I write. If it weren't for you, I wouldn't have a purpose beyond penning novels for myself. Thank you to all of you. I hope you enjoyed what you read and will come back to see what's next.

☺Kelsey

Milton Keynes UK
Ingram Content Group UK Ltd.
UKHW021043020824
446373UK00014B/594